FRANKENSTEIN'S DÆMON

A Sequel to *Frankenstein*

MICHAEL MEESKE

USHER BOOKS

AUTHOR'S NOTE

The narrative components of *Frankenstein's Dæmon* were reportedly found in 1846 in a leather trunk in London, England. The trunk was embossed with the initials M. S., Margaret Saville, who was the sister of Robert Walton, the captain of the ship upon which Victor Frankenstein died. How the material was transported to the United States from the inventory of a London dealer in antiquities is unknown; however, many rumors abound. There are tales of its transport on a slave ship traveling to America before the Civil War. A small clipping from an 1892 New York City newspaper told of a "rare and nightmarish" manuscript purchased by financier J. P. Morgan. The newspaper connected the tale to a gruesome time in London history that had been obliterated from public records. Others have said the documents were found in 1939 "glowing with an unearthly fire," "corrupted by the devil's eyes," in a church graveyard in Baltimore. We may never know the true story. How the narrative arrived at my door must remain a secret. I will leave that speculation to readers.

ROBERT WALTON'S JOURNAL

September _, 17—

The most unimaginable horrors have occurred since I last wrote. If you by chance read this journal, my dear Margaret, know that my survival is a miracle of God's good graces; yet, presently, I am left only with the strength to tell this story. Even as I endeavor to put pen to paper, I am racked with tremors so great I must steady my shaking hand. But my fear is not solely my own; it is for the whole of humanity.

I pray, my sister, you are safe in England; as the opposite is true for the scribe of this journal, your loving brother. My ship rocks with each icy crest in the northern seas and my body quakes in terror. How long I will live I know not, for I have resolved to honor Victor Frankenstein's request to destroy the filthy monster and with it his malicious evil. How kind and dear Victor was to me – a true comrade and friend – his death will be avenged! I thirsted so long for so noble a companion – only to have his genius and body taken away by the vile creature. My sole consolation is that Victor's soul now rests with the angels, so unlike his hideous progeny. My conscience dictates that any unintended reader know that my actions in pursuit of the dæmon were not taken without due consideration. The choice was mine – what I have wrought falls squarely upon my head. But how often during this excruciating captivity has my thirst for adventure weighed heavily upon my heart, as I recalled those joyous, blissful days with you and your family on the Emerald Isle. Such happiness could have been mine had I forsworn my own desires. How I delighted in the sciences! My love of exploration was my sole and fair companion.

But my thoughts now turn to my affection for Victor and my thirst for revenge. Once the creature sprung from the cabin-window and was borne away in the darkness on his Arctic ice-raft, I knelt on the floor and cried bitterly over the corpse of my dear friend. With tremulous fingers, I touched his face: It was cold, lifeless and his closed eyes were directed toward heaven. My mournful reverie was shattered by a sharp blast against the ship, like the splitting of timbers. I thought perhaps the ice had rent my vessel in half. I rushed to the window of the cuddy where we had taken the body, and looking into the darkness and white foam breaking over the icy landscape, I saw the dæmon wield a wooden mast in his gigantic hands. He had smashed it against our starboard, but the hull had stood firm. The frantic heads of my crew peered with bewildered and astonished eyes over the top deck. They hurled invectives and fusillades at the monster as he pushed his ice-raft away from the ship with fantastic force, sending us rocking in our narrow channel. As he shrank in the distance, he unleashed a shrieking cry I can only describe as emanating from the bowels of hell. I and my horrified crew stood frozen, our blood curdled by the monster's vengeful remonstrations.

In that instant, I realized that despite his promise to wreak no more havoc and his stated intention to end his pathetic life; the will to survive ran deeply in him. Displaying his true nature, the dæmon was intent upon the obliteration of my vessel and crew. I knew I must follow him to the northernmost extremity of the globe to make certain he carried out his funeral-pile; for he who had sought my sympathy with his question, "Polluted by crimes and torn by the bitterest remorse, where can I find rest but in death?" must die. I had no doubt of his previous suicidal intention; he had already gathered upon his ice-raft fuel for the fire, but I distrusted his sincerity. Victor himself knew the creature twisted the truth, as well as the necks of those who stood in his way.

There was no time to tarry. I called for the ship's master, Mr. Foster, a man of remarkable disposition and dauntless courage, to arrange a small search party. With each minute, the creature drew farther away from the ship and, in time's passing, the possibility of his escape and murderous retribution upon other innocents multiplied. Before his death, Victor had relayed this message, "The task of destruction was mine, but I have failed . . . I asked you to undertake my unfinished work and I renew this request now . . . ." These words rang in my head as I gathered my gear and then waited at my vessel's bow for Foster and his crew. In short order, the ship's master, looking as stern and forbidding as a silent Turk, appeared with Mr. Sparrow, my lieutenant, a man always desirous of glory, at least in word. Also accompanying him were Mr. Chumley, the ice master; two Marines and the lone surviving dog from Victor's sledge. Our party looked ill equipped to pursue a preternatural fiend across the ice, but fate dictated otherwise. The men had hurriedly dressed in winter slops and carried a day or two's worth of provisions. The Marines shouldered their muskets, and the dog, an Inuit breed of black and silver fur, yipped excitedly on deck.

"Captain Walton," said Mr. Foster, "the men are wary of the monster upon the ice and restless for their return to England. They will not hold the ship for long, particularly if the channel opens yet wider." Through the darkening gloom I could discern the fiery intensity of his steely-gray eyes. He patted a long knife with his gloved hands.

"I understand, Mr. Foster," said I with as much calm as I could muster. "I have given my word – I will lead them from danger, but the fiend must be stopped. If not, we have abandoned our duty to mankind and my pledge to Victor Frankenstein." This speech assuaged the men enough to outline my plan. "Tell the crew we will be on the ice for twenty-four hours at most. If we have not returned by then, instruct them they are free to sail under the command of the topsc'le lieutenant, Mr. Chase. God willing, we will have safely returned from our mission, and our good news will herald a return to our beautiful England. If not, they must make all haste before the channel closes."

The ship's master left with an abrupt "aye." While we awaited his return, I put on my fur cap and cast my gaze upon the frozen wonderland that stretched to a horizon broken only by iridescent ridges of ice. The frozen mountains stretched their

7

peaks toward the cold sky; the clouds parted now and then to reveal sparkling pinwheels of stars and the disc of a luminous moon. The hour was early, yet the heavens were dark and forbidding. I shuddered and wondered how I could have ever regarded the northern regions with delight. My heart was filled with dread that I might fail in my quest and my ship and crew be destroyed by the malevolent beast created and cursed by Frankenstein.

Mr. Foster returned and I could not judge his mood for his countenance lay concealed in the shadow of his fur hood. He nodded and I understood we were ready to begin our task. The ship lurched in a sudden gust of wind and I called out orders: "Mr. Sparrow, leash the Inuit dog and have him lead our way. I'm certain he remembers the scent of the creature we seek. Mr. Chumley: We are in your good hands. We will rely upon you to navigate us safely over the ice." Mr. Chumley replied affirmatively and I concluded with one more command: "You Marines: Be ready at my order to load and fire. The beast should fall against your onslaught."

"Captain," Mr. Chumley said, as he surveyed the low plateau of a gigantic ice mountain locked beside us, "we should make our departure now. We can travel down the slope and reach the sea ice beneath."

With the ledge a yard away, I hoisted myself by line over the bow to the flat surface. My boots crunched in the packed snow with barely an impression and my footing was firm. Soon, the remainder of my party followed, Mr. Sparrow being the last to hoist the dog to one of the Marines before he swung agilely from the ship to the frozen landscape. As we stood upon our perch watching the sails of my vessel shiver against the black horizon, I felt as though we were about to embark upon a great journey into the unknown.

Then, the race across the ice was on.

We carried no lamps or candles so we depended upon the ambient light of the heavens to guide us over the terrain. We fairly tumbled down the slope, slipping and sliding our way to a broad sheet of level ice awash with the sea.

Mr. Chumley studied the black channels of water which wound around our floating ark and flowed toward the distant pressure ridges, seracs and frozen mountains ahead of us. "Keep to the center and watch your step," Mr. Chumley cautioned, "or risk being swept into the Arctic seas. No man can survive a plunge into the brine."

Mr. Sparrow led the way with the dog, which turned barking and snarling toward the north-west. I was certain the animal had picked up a scent on the stiffening breeze, for the creature was surely less than an hour ahead of us. As we proceeded across the shelf, the slanting moon beams shone like dappled rays of sun through the scudding clouds. My eyes, struggling to pick out any light or form in the distance, were shocked by sudden electric blazes of blue and green that wove like writhing snakes above us. Providence had showered its blessings upon us! The aurora would be our savior, of that I was certain. It lit the landscape harshly, its light reflecting like torches against the glittering ice. And, as if my thoughts were made manifest, on the distant horizon, wedged between two frozen mountains, a flame appeared. In its flicker, I distinguished the hulking figure of the dæmon I sought to destroy.

"There he is boys," I said, assured my pact with Victor would be fulfilled. "Make haste, so he cannot secure his escape and live another day."

I must put my pen aside for a moment, Margaret, and rest. My heart quakes at what I must now relate to you (and history). Know that blood is spilled, but the truth of my tale must be told. I am sorry that my letters from the ship have not reached you – when you take possession of my writings, as is my plan, all will be made clear. Then, if you desire to read no further, my dear sister, I would not chide you. I have no riches to give, no treasures to offer from my explorations other than this narrative – and it may be the last told by me. I have always fostered a restless spirit, Margaret, first inspired as a child by the science books of our dear Uncle Thomas, and then by you, who so kindly took a firm hand with my education. This propensity for exploration has taken me to the far corners of the world, introduced me to the natives of many cultures, but it has taken me far from home and left me without a wife and children, and, thus, my writings are my only legacy. Now I regret I have nothing more to offer. Search the ship, scour my possessions, for if my journal and letters are not delivered to you they may be concealed among other papers much more mundane than these written for the survival of our race.

My brief respite has revived my spirits and I shall continue my fantastic story: I prodded my group forward like horses whipped by the lash. Mr. Chumley led the way on the floes, expertly guiding us past the spears of ice, directing our jumps over small channels of dark water that reflected the garish blue-green of the aurora. Never did I let the creature, once spotted, out of my sight. I was alternately elated or despondent as I watched his torch weave near us and then, maddeningly, fade to a greater distance. Mr. Sparrow spurred on the Inuit dog until, in the general excitement of the chase, the poor animal slipped from the ice into the swirling sea. The lieutenant pulled heartily on the leash and the dog, shaking the water from his fur, plopped back onto the floe with no apparent harm. As an hour passed and we pressed on, I wondered how far we had traveled from our vessel and if Mr. Foster and Mr. Chumley's navigational abilities would be enough to guide us safely back once we accomplished our task. Despite my determination, a knot of fear settled in my stomach; however, I would not be held back by morbid thoughts of my party's destruction. My comfort lay in knowing my crew and ship would sail south toward England should we fail to return.

After another half-hour passed on the frozen wastes, the aurora suddenly blazed and the heavens shone with the brightest display I had ever witnessed. Swaths of red, blue, green and pale orange checkered the ice like a fantastical vision of hell. A sudden hush fell over us and even the dog halted his panting and clawing.

I stopped our party in the ghostly silence.

A strangled moan, not unlike the death throes of a wounded animal, arose behind the ridge to our north. I motioned to my crew to remain still as I crept toward the jagged ice that blocked our view. A second wail arose, which melted into a pathetic and hideous sob. The sound froze my blood and I shivered as I peered around the ridge. My eyes were little prepared for what I saw.

The dæmon sat atop a jumbled pile of wood, his single torch and the borealis illuminating his grotesque form. From whence he had collected his funeral-pile I could not say, but the timbers reminded me of the shattered hulls of ships such as my own. All the possessions he had conveyed to the north surrounded the pile: stores of food, a cache of pistols, cloaks and other garments. Horrifically, the six dogs that had carried him were lined end-to-end around the pyre. The blood from their throats streamed across the ice and sparkled obscenely from the flickering lights that danced overhead. The creature sobbed pitifully and then removed his hands from his face as if aware of my presence – a startling chill ran over me. Could the fiend have detected me and my men? My body shook as I contemplated the horror who had killed so many innocents in his quest for revenge. How do I describe the wretch who appeared to teeter upon the final moments of his malevolent life? He was no more than ten yards beyond the ridge, his hideous face quivering in the torchlight. The flames revealed the yellow skin that scarcely covered the muscles and arteries beneath. His flowing black hair was tangled and unkempt and matched the color of his thin, straight lips; his watery eyes, deeply set in their sockets, were made more so by his tears. He was gigantic in stature, his shoulders, arms and legs nearly bursting through his slovenly garments which were stained with blood and encrusted with ice. He put an enormous finger to his nose and sat upright, perfectly still.

After a moment, he said, "Walton, fear not, thou shalt meet your doom. I smell your miserable carcass. I have harnessed my impulse to destroy – sworn to you my insatiable passion has ended – yet you test me with your pathetic attempt at revenge. Thou art no better than the others of your traitorous race. Your destruction is assured."

Although I carried neither musket nor pistol, I sprang round the ice revealing myself to the monster. "Wretch," cried I, "I have come to make sure you honor your pledge. You have silenced the heart of the most gracious soul on this earth, and, thus, in honoring my promise, my death is of no consequence, although yours must be fulfilled."

He rose from the pile like a phoenix emerging from the flames. His black lips and white teeth formed a twisted smile. "I will die and my miseries become extinct. But before the flames torture me, and the winds sweep my ashes to the sea, I will extinguish your pitiful life."

11

Before I could shout an answer, Mr. Foster and the two Marines jumped from their hiding places behind the ridge. In the blink of an eye, the ship's master withdrew the long knife he carried from its scabbard and hurled it at the creature. But the monster, with even faster reflexes, wrenched a timber from the pile and held it in front of his heart. The flashing knife buried itself to the hilt in the wood. The fiend clutched the timber, and breaking it in half, hurled it at the ship's master. With a sickening thud, it pierced Mr. Foster's chest. The man fell forward, impaled upon the stake; blood gushed from his wound and spread in a dark pool across the snow. Mr. Foster screamed in agony and wriggled like a speared eel before he fell silent. My valiant Marines were also doomed by the quickness of the dæmon. As they knelt to load (unprepared as they must have been for such hasty maneuvers without my command), the fiend pulled the knife from the remaining half-timber and hurled it between the eyes of one. He crumpled on his left side with nary a sound. The other died with a resounding crack to the head from another hurled timber. Blood ran profusely over the ice and not a shot was fired. I knew Mr. Chumley and Mr. Sparrow were not armed and must be in hiding, or if self-preservation and sanity had overtaken them, had turned and fled to the ship.

With dazzling speed, the monster opened a small box, took out a pistol, packed it with powder and loaded a ball into the muzzle. I had no time to retrieve the Marines' muskets and load them. The creature pointed his weapon directly between my eyes and then lowered it to his side as if reconsidering his murderous retribution. I froze in my position, fearing some sudden action by me or my remaining crew might hasten my demise. "Dost thou know the agonies of Death as I?" he asked and wiped a rough hand over his eyes. He lumbered toward me, the torch throwing a yellow aura around his massive bulk, but leaving his demonic features in shadow. "Dost thou know what it is to suffer the pains of hell each day of your miserable existence? My creator and those that lived among his company are fortunate. Their earthly bodies no longer suffer the world's injustices and are fodder for the worms." With that, the monster stopped a hair's breadth in front of me. He placed a heavy hand on my shoulder and brushed it upward against my cheek. The odious stench of rotting victuals emanated from his contorted mouth. He placed his hand on my neck as if gauging the frantic heartbeat pulsing through my veins. "If only my creator had fulfilled his promise of a mate, it might not have been thus." He tightened his fingers around my neck. I had little time to contemplate my next action: I had relied too heavily upon my Marines for protection and not armed myself; the fiend was suffused with greater strength and agility than I could purvey; what course had I but to save myself in order to assure his annihilation? As the seconds ticked away, I knew I must concoct a plan.

A violent snap echoed behind the dæmon and he released his grip upon my throat. The monster spun with hellish quickness and when he turned, I saw Mr. Chumley, his eyes wide with terror, illuminated by the torch. He held the remains of a jagged icy spear, half of it glistening in his right hand, the other half implanted in the right shoulder of the dæmon. The creature howled and tore the icy weapon from his back, nary a splotch of blood upon it. The tissue had split like a slab of meat under the butcher's knife and then rejoined itself with miraculous precision. The monster grabbed Mr. Chumley by the neck, lifted him from the snow-covered ground, put the pistol to his head, cocked the hammer and fired. The ball entered the ice master's forehead and exited from behind leaving a fountain of blood and tissue upon the white ground. The fiend dropped the dangling man, eyes gaping, at my feet.

"Mr. Sparrow, flee . . . !" I was able to shout before the creature placed his hand over my mouth. My lieutenant must have heard my command because I heard steps crunch behind the nearby ridge; the sailor who had boasted so much of his own bravery had fled. Within seconds, the Inuit dog skulked toward us, his shoulders and withers hunched forward in supplication. The creature threw me to the ice and, planting a huge foot on my leg, pinned me to the snow.

"Unfortunate animal," the fiend said to the dog, whose vocal manifestations had shifted from a salivating snarl to a low whine, as if under a spell cast by the creature. "Of all those aboard the damned vessel, you especially have partaken of the kindnesses and perversities of the human race." The dog crept forward, keeping his glittering eyes on the towering creature before him.

13

"Thus, I will allow you to live, gathering what you can from the ice. It pained me to kill your brothers – they did no harm – but I wished to spare them a slow agonizing death from starvation. But you will have our bodies. Use your instincts, fine friend, after we have perished. Enjoy a feast upon our corpses." The creature turned to me as the dog cowered at his feet.

"And to you, Walton, breathe your last. Even now, my blood boils at the injustices I have suffered. Are you prepared to sleep with those who considered me an abhorrence to be spurned, kicked and trampled, while I sought only the pleasures of man: the warm spring breezes, the play of sunlight upon my skin? I received them not. You are finished."

The burning cold cut through my coat and cap, the blowing snow slashed across my face. The creature knelt by my side and held onto my arm with crushing force as his fingers inched toward my throat. "A final revelation, Walton. Because my creator is dead I shall take the name of Frankenstein in honor of my father. I will carry his memory to my funeral-pile."

My mind reeled in horror as my chance for survival diminished, induced by the terror beside me. As I lay shivering on the gritty snow, I held no fear of death; rather, I trembled in shame at my unfulfilled vow. If I died, who would assure the monster's destruction? Call him Frankenstein? Never would I take my dearest friend's name in vain! The fiend's fingers spread like a rope around my neck. A last thought occurred to me as he tightened his grip: What of his desire for life – a creature who had been so eager to learn the ways of man – and his desire for a mate? What of his power to create a child of his making? I knew from Victor's story that the fiend had studied his creator's journals and then returned them to him in the ice caves near Chamounix, in the valley of the Arveiron. Victor had sunk his medical equipment in the channel off the Orkney Islands, but made no mention of destroying his writings. Perhaps I could allay the creature's murderous intent long enough to carry out my vengeance. Mr. Foster's knife, sunk into the head of the Marine, rested only a fingertip's grasp outside my reach.

"Fiend," I half-yelled, half-gasped.

The creature dug deeper into my neck, nearly crushing my windpipe. My lungs heaved for air, and stars swam before my eyes.

"Frankenstein . . ." My voice cracked in terror. The name burned on my lips – I had broken my vow in order to save my life. The monster relented, leaned back and stared at me with his watery eyes. "I know the secrets of your birth and eternal life. Victor Frankenstein revealed them to me before he died. The knowledge you desire is in the journals he left in my trust. You can have your mate!"

A wide smile creased his sallow skin and he eased his deathly grip. "Oh, Walton, you lie to save your hide. What demonic spirit has tempted you with false dreams of eternal life? My father destroyed his work . . . and his promise of my mate."

"No," I said, lifting onto my elbows and shifting toward the dead Marine at my side. "I know where he secured his writings. He bade me keep their location a secret until my death."

The monster rocked on his haunches and howled with devilish laughter. The dog shivered near his feet. "Your death is assured, Walton, but let me ask . . . are his journals complete – from the first exuberant writings at Ingolstadt to his abominable ruminations in the Orkney Islands?"

"Yes," I said and stared into the horrible visage. The thin black lips opened to show slivers of pearly teeth. I waited for his reply as my fingers crept imperceptibly toward the dead Marine. The knife was nearly in my clutches. In order to extract the weapon and plunge it into the monster's brain – the only plan I could devise for his extinction – I would have to act with sudden ferocity. The horror of my situation shook my body and the monster detected my movement. His eyes burned with a demonic intensity – hellish fires blazing within his terrible gaze.

I struck while I could – to delay would only prolong my agony. I thrust my hand toward the knife with a rapidity that astonished even my agitated brain, but my gloved fingers slipped from the hilt.

The monster, in his agility, captured my arm as I vainly reached for the weapon a second time. The fiend glared at me and, with a laugh, ripped off my glove. "Fool," he said, "I mock your pathetic attempt at revenge. Victor Frankenstein was *my* father!"

His gigantic hand twisted my wrist until I writhed in agony on the snow. Then he paused as if to consider what further tortures he might inflict. He held me in his crushing grip, studied my fingers and then in measured tone said, "One digit will do." He took my left thumb and bent it backwards until it cracked with a sickening snap.

I howled in pain and screamed to be released from his devilish clutches. He relinquished my hand and let it fall to the icy ground where the cold, at first, burned my flesh like fire but then quickly numbed my broken thumb. His hands hovered over my throat in preparation for his evil deed, and, while I lay panting, I prayed for a quick and merciful death. I closed my eyes – my final vision being the dæmon hovering over me – and awaited his crushing grip. My appeal to the creature's sense of self-preservation, his desire for a mate had failed. An almost imperceptible moan issued from the monster. A stream of low curses then flowed from his mouth, their sound similar to prayers of atonement. I opened my eyes and saw his massive head, illuminated by the torch's yellow halo, lifted toward the heavens. His demeanor I can only describe as tortured, the mouth turned down in a hideous scowl; however, in my nervous agony I could not judge his true intention.

Slowly, he lowered his head and in a mournful whisper, said, "I led my creator across the Arctic wastes, bent on his demise. Yet, on his death bed I bid him farewell with the words, 'If thou wert yet alive, and yet cherished a desire of revenge against me, it would be better satiated in my life than in my destruction.' But 'twas not so. Now, by my creator's hand, you swear you have claimed his secrets to eternal life – the resurrection of the body from death. But what of the body, if one loses the soul? Frankenstein's soul looks down upon us from its heights and urges me to confess my transgressions. If I live, my father will exact his revenge in my earthly tortures, and I will suffer for my sins. But, with an easy death upon the funeral-pile my life will have been in vain." The creature lifted my head from the snow and placing his hands around my neck, said, "I swear upon my father's corpse, I will draw and quarter you like a beast of the field if you deceive me, Walton. You *will* deliver the journals and their secrets to me; so, for now, you live."

16

"Never," I blurted out. It was the last word I uttered before I saw his hand rise above my head and come crashing toward my face in a terrifying arc. As his hand struck, my eyes filled with a million stars and the black night settled over me like an impenetrable fog.

ROBERT WALTON'S JOURNAL

September _, 17—

I am sailing on a ship of horrors. What day it is, I know not. A strange silence has fallen over my vessel and I fear the worst.

I suspect, my dear sister, you may be deprived of the truth, if my letters and journals never reach their intended destination – your door in our emerald England. Soothe your heart, Margaret, and understand what herculean efforts were made to record these missives so you would, if I perished, know the outcome of my perilous journey. When I left Archangel in March last, little could I have imagined the terrors to the north. Recall the words I wrote: "I will not rashly encounter danger. I will be cool, persevering and prudent." That prescription was written for your sake as well as mine. However, by September's dawn I was uncertain whether any of my communications would ever see your eyes. Now, on my stricken vessel, I put pen to paper in the hopes I may secure this journal in a safe place away from the monster's hands. I write, huddled in my cabin, by the light of a single candle as the ship rocks on the foamy waves.

Chilling horrors overtook me when I awoke from the creature's blow. The licks of Victor's half-starved dog startled me from my lethargy; the monster had transported us to the ship. I can only surmise the creature has a heart for the lower animals and correlates their beatings, cruelties and punishments to those he likewise received from mankind. I rolled onto my side and an

18

intense, stinging pain coursed through my left hand. I shook the grog from my head and remembered the monster had broken my thumb. My first attention, however, was to my crew.

Margaret, how can I describe what I observed in the dim Arctic light? How can I count the tears that fell as I gazed on the horrible scene before my eyes? Was it chance or fate that drew my vessel into these horrific straits or was it the unintentional curse of knowing Victor Frankenstein, my beloved friend?

I judged the hour to be somewhat around eleven in the morning from the gray, trembling rays that filtered into my cabin. Sunlight, even on the clearest northern days, was sparse as fall marched toward winter. I crawled from my bed, opened my cabin door (for this day, *he* left it unguarded for his terrible reasons), and with the dog at my heels, ascended the staircase to the top deck's entry. The ship was ghostly in its silence and only the creaking rise and fall of its frame bore witness to its motion. How my hand trembled as I lifted the latch and opened the door. I gasped and fell to my knees. I could scarcely believe my eyes – a phantasmagorical sight danced before me – only the most fiendish devil could have conceived of such a nightmare. Five of my men – one being Mr. Chase, the topsc'le lieutenant – hung like pendulums, their bodies swaying with the rocking ship. They were strung across the bowlines like doves after the hunt, hung by their feet, their bloated faces staring into mine, their fingers, distended and dark with congealed blood, seeming to grasp at the air. As I gazed in horror, I wondered how I could have slumbered through the screams and agonies of these loyal sailors. But what of the rest of my crew? I caught the ravenous dog by the scruff of his neck and secured him behind the door so he would not be tempted to feast upon the gore that coated the deck. With great effort, I pulled myself to my feet and stepped forward, only to slide on an icy coating of blood. I managed to avoid a tumble; yet, my body was racked with tremors as I surveyed the scene before me. Frozen into the blood were the footprints of a gigantic being – the trail left by the murderous villain – Frankenstein's dæmon. I was either alone on the ship with the vicious monster, or set adrift with my dead crew until I perished on the open sea. The latter, I concluded, was preferable to any contact with the creature. My thoughts of a peaceful death were short-lived, however, as a chilling voice drifted toward me, from whence I could not say. Its deep gloom overpowered me, and the words, while seeming to emanate from the ocean depths, could just as well have fallen from the heavens. I steadied myself against a railing and turned slowly, my agitated brain searching for any sign of the monster. There was none: only the endless waves slapping against the ship, made even more abominable by an encroaching fog and the ghostly sway of the dead men.

"Walton, thou art witness to my revenge against man's treachery," the voice boomed from the mist. "They that hang dared attack me. Fools – they were a warning to the rest. The remainder of your crew fled the ship on rafts or escaped on foot across the ice, terrified as they were of my visage." Here, the monster stopped and a heavy sigh emerged from his throat. "Misery and loneliness fuel the devil; my vengeful fires scorch the soul. If only my father had honored his promise of a mate, such base emotions wouldst be banished. Could he not have extended the comfort of companionship to his only son? Thus, I would have dwelt in peace with all God's creations."

His voice covered me like a pall, exciting my thirst for his blood, yet extinguishing my hope of ever seeing you, my beloved sister, and your family, alive. I was bound now, by all that was Holy, to avenge the deaths of Victor Frankenstein and my crew. Yet, the dæmon's desire for companionship, in some minute degree, touched my heart. I felt no overwhelming compassion for the disgusting creature, but I understood how the years of human degradation, mistreatment and broken promises – in large part due to Victor's denials – could have fed his murderous retribution. I knew I must uphold my promise to Victor and shun any compassion until my own quest for revenge had been satisfied.

"Heartless monster," I whispered to the air, "I shall see you dead before I breathe my last." I despaired as the words left my lips, for I knew that in battle the fiend was superior.

"I hear your pitiful threats of retribution," the creature said and his hideous laughter echoed over the deck and across the boundless ocean.

I turned to the foremast and a cruel wind slashed my cheeks. Only the mainmast was under sail. The creature had disengaged the rest and commandeered the ship! I shivered and then squinted into the murk, attempting to spy my adversary in the faltering day – but my hopes were dashed by the shifting fog and salty mist that flowed over the deck. The mountains of ice that threatened my vessel had disappeared by some miracle of heaven. I judged my ship had broken free of the entrapping ice and been borne down the open channel. Through a momentary break in the clouds, I spotted the sun's red disk slipping below the horizon and was roughly able to gauge our direction of travel without the aid of a compass – south by south-east. I was cheered! My ship was headed toward the northern whaling land of Greenland and then perhaps to England; alas however, as the creature controlled the ship, our final destination was in his hands.

The dæmon's laughter died and a terrible silence fell over the vessel. I looked toward the bow. As the ship rose and fell with the waves, a lamp, as if held by spectral hands, bobbed near the bowsprit. The hulking figure of the monster followed in its hazy glow. I dashed past the mainmast, nearly falling on the hellish ice, in search of my target; but he, anticipating my actions, extinguished the light.

His laughter once again filled my ears; then his words drifted over the obliterating fog. "Come no closer, Walton, unless thou dost covet an early death. Test not my compassion, for thou hast seen my wrath with your own eyes. If not for my father's legacy, you would be hanging from the lines as well." He paused and then chuckled with delight. "Or perhaps hung as a figurehead for your vessel – a feast for the albatross until your bones fell into the sea."

"We are at an impasse, fiend," I shouted into the murk. No attack I could perpetrate could kill the monster: His strength knew no bounds; his capacity for vengeance was unlimited. I had seen Mr. Foster's weapon slice into the creature's flesh with little effect; such a blow was but a fly bite to him. Retribution, revenge, death were mere words against the monster's strength. He was too fast, too intelligent for any man to destroy. My overwrought brain readily sought a solution for his demise; yet, all my efforts came to naught whilst standing amidst the horrors on deck. I also considered that no affliction, physical or mental, would dissuade him in his search for the prize I had fabricated – Victor's journals.

We were indeed locked in a battle to the death – he in the quest for a mate and eternal life and I bent upon his destruction. Time, however, was my ally. "I value my life and you value yours," I said, hoping again to appeal to his self-preservation.

"Perhaps, but what are we to the world?" asked he. "Thou hast no mourners to weep at your tomb. Have you a family or is your only love for my father, your departed friend? Walton, your death would be meaningless. Who would shed tears for you? What is your legacy – a worthless ship and a dead crew?"

His question about my family disconcerted me; however, fortunate indeed am I that the creature knows nothing of you, my sister; your devoted Husband, John; and my young niece, Lila; and nephew, David. How I have treasured the years together with you– even though we are often apart – and the blessings time has bestowed: the love you have showered upon me, your affection for your dear husband and the birth and growth of your children.

"I, likewise," the monster continued, "am your ignored compatriot on this vessel. Mankind wishes to usher in my destruction; my death would be equally ignoble. Who would weep at the loss of a monstrous killer? Why do I kill other than for revenge and injustice? What did my creator impart to me through the mind and body I carry? Was I born for murder? My wish is to curse Frankenstein, and his name be forever shunned. I am lost for eternity with no marker for my tomb. Who would mourn for the 'monster, devil or fiend'? But, upon your oath, armed with my father's knowledge and my superior power . . . ."

He paused, stretched his massive frame and a thrill shivered across the ship: An aura arched across the bow toward me; the release of this supernatural force shook my body like an explosive charge. He lit his lamp, and his sallow face, made even more liquescent by the candle, floated in the yellow light. Transfixed, I become aware of the hypnotic power of the creature; I was sucked into the depths of his infernal maelstrom, much as the Inuit dog had been before me, and it took all my reserves to wrest myself from his control. Could he capture the will of man not only through his physical strength, but through his connection with the metaphysical? I hoped, for humanity's sake, that my senses were tempered by my circumstances and that his spiritual powers were limited.

He leered at me and proclaimed, "Mark my words, Walton; I could father a race that wouldst conquer heaven and hell." As he spoke, the lamp bobbed across the deck and I drew back in terror at its approach. The monster sensed my fear and lumbered toward me. I scrambled to the door, knowing any provocation or mockery would amplify his desire for blood. Despite my weakened state, I turned and said as calmly as my constitution would allow: "You will never set eyes upon his journals." The preposterous lie I had created was my solitary hope for survival.

His watery eyes gleamed in the light. "I searched the ship after your crew fled. My father's writings are not on board."

"No they are not, and for as long as I hold the secret, I will live."

The creature laughed and said, "I trust the truth will reveal itself. Perhaps the answer lies with you and Ernest Frankenstein, Victor's brother. I should have considered such an arrangement – the family has a thirst for power beyond measure." An eager anticipation flashed in his eyes. "However, you will succumb to my demands as the days proceed. In the meantime, retire to your cabin and show not your face until the next meager dawn. I will provide sustenance for you and the animal. And, take heed, make no attempt to search me out. There are terrors as yet unleashed aboard this vessel."

How the horror of his words opened before me – as wide as a chasm! The monster had searched my ship for Victor's journals. Had my strategy hastened the deaths of my crew aboard ship and on the ice, or would the creature have killed mercilessly despite any false bargain I might have made? I struck the terrible thought, my failing as an officer, from my mind. In order to exact my revenge I would have need of my full faculties; otherwise, I would drown in a morass of despair.

"Be warned," said he, as I reached for the door, "there is one other on this ship."

"Who?" I asked.

"He calls himself Sparrow. He went mad after your crew fled, but he is harmless and scurries about like the rats below deck."

I closed the door and secured the latch. A keg of lamp oil rested near the stairwell. With all my might, I shoved the fuel toward the entry with my right arm and shoulder (taking care not to strain my injured left hand). The keg was only half-full or it would have taken the efforts of two men to move its bulk. After great labor, I succeeded in positioning it in front of the door. Of its pitiful use as a blockade against the monster's strength I was certain, but the effort ameliorated my despondency over my diminished capacities. Stunned, I stood by the door calculating my next tactic. An eager sniff at my leg alerted me to the Inuit dog, which stood on shivering legs and watched me with downcast eyes. I patted the miserable animal and pondered our plights. He followed me obediently down the stairs and through the narrow passageway to my cabin. A horrifying thought overcame me as I stepped into my room – what of Victor's body? My men had moved him, after his death, from my cabin to the cuddy, the officers' quarters above. In my haste to capture his creation, I had left the corpse behind attended only by the crew. Now, with a madman for my sole human companion, I feared for the proper burial of my best friend. I bestowed a pat on the animal and then secured him in the cabin while I conducted my search. I ascended the stairs near my quarters, arrived at the cuddy and paced for a time until I gathered enough courage to step, with faltering legs, into the room. The wind howled through the smashed window where the monster had leapt to his ice-raft; the splintered frames rocked in unison with the ship, producing an eerie creak. A sepulchral light filtered through the breech – an overpowering gloom filled the chamber and chilled me to the core. I gazed at the bed where Victor had died – the draped sheet and blanket still covered the outline of his form; yet, I was uncertain whether he reposed in deathly slumbers under their protection. I spoke his name in the hope he would stir beneath the coverings and rise with a sleepy smile on his luminescent face. I crept to the bed, extended my hand to the gray woolen blanket and fully expected to touch the stiffened corpse; instead, my fingers melted into the cloth and I recoiled. A chilling blast of wind rocked me on my feet. Summoning my strength yet again, I reached down and yanked the blanket away from the form.

Victor Frankenstein appeared before me, his gentle face composed in a serene smile. His hands, clasping a rosary between his fingers, lay folded across his chest; yet, this scene gave me pause – I could not recall Victor ever having been in possession of any Holy symbol. A halo of yellow light, angelic in its composition, surrounded the body of my dear friend. Tears fell from my eyes as I beheld his slumbering figure, and I cannot describe the sense of overpowering loss, yet everlasting faith, that washed over me. I knelt near him, afraid to disturb his peaceful repose. As I prayed for Victor – God to care for his soul – a howl from the bowels of the ship arose like a banshee's cry on the northern wind. The blanket shivered as if alive and the body was suffused with lightning, like that generated by a summer storm. The monster had warned me – there were terrors yet unleashed on my ship. Or was I going mad? I ventured to touch Victor's face one last time to affirm my sanity before committing his body to the sea. To my shock, my finger sunk through the form as if it existed on some ghostly plane far removed from the hideous plight of my vessel. An electric charge coursed through the cuddy, and Victor, before me, transmuted from a soul coveted by the angels to a centurion guarding the gates of hell. The skin shrunk and melted before my gaze: His eyes, the nose and the perfect mouth, liquefied into putrefaction. The fingers dissolved to bones and the crucifix dropped through the rib cage of the gelatinous skeleton. I screamed and stumbled backwards toward the door. Before I could make my escape, the terrible skull turned its hollow eyes toward me and grinned in macabre delight. Below me, the dog, who sensed the terror on board, yelped, and its cries rose from the depths and sliced through my brain like a scalpel. The monster echoed the dog's howl and the ship resounded with unholy noise. The skull dropped from the bed and rolled toward me, its empty sockets infused with a demonic light. As quickly as the nightmare had begun, it dissipated – the ship lurched on the waves, the skull vanished into nothingness and the wind dropped to a soft murmur. I looked upon the bed once more before I retreated from the room – the body of Victor Frankenstein had vanished, leaving no trace of the man I had so cherished a few short days ago. My brain reeled at the fantastical occurrence I had witnessed. Was I to suffer from such scenes the remainder of my days? It occurred to me that I had witnessed the strange metaphysical power wielded by the monster. The thought fell upon me like a great weight and I raced down the stairs to my quarters and the company of the shivering dog, my only friend.

We, like two abandoned animals, huddled in the corner until we heard the scrape of footsteps outside the door. I watched the dog's eyes as he observed the entry intently, his brown orbs shifting between terror and pity for the monster who walked the passageways. He whined softly as the steps drifted away.

I could not recall the next several hours, which passed in a fitful sleep drenched with dreams of hellish creatures and torturous pain. I had somehow traversed the cabin and collapsed on my bed. The slavish dog, his tongue lolling in dehydration and starvation, hunkered at my side, as much in need of food and water as I. My knees crumpled when my feet touched the floor – exhaustion and lack of nourishment claimed me – but my first action was to attend to my injury. The monster had snapped the flexor of my left thumb; in my agitated state I paid scant attention to the throbbing pain until those fleeting moments of lucidity brought forth the extent of my impairment. I half-crawled, half-walked to the captain's desk across from my bed and lit a lamp; the soft yellow light filled the cabin with a warm glow. Then, I took my rule and broke it into quarter pieces to act as a splint. Having no gauze or bandage for wrapping, I tore a portion of my bed sheet, much to the consternation of the surprised animal, who jumped down in fear of some imagined retribution. He bounded to the cabin entrance and discharged a low, soft whine. I wrapped the cloth around my splinted thumb and set forth, candle in hand, for the door. I opened it cautiously and peered into the dark passageway. The ever-present rats, attracted by an object outside, scuttled away; otherwise, the hall was quiet and dark. I set the lamp on a stand and drew in a wooden box, which had been placed outside the door; I was fearful, however, it might have the same effect as that perpetrated upon Pandora. By slow measure, I unsecured the latch and lifted the lid. Inside, the creature, true to his word, had placed a meal of hard biscuits, pickled tern eggs and a flagon of water, and, for the animal, a bone dripping with red, meaty flesh. Hunger consumed me and I devoured the eggs and biscuits while the dog gnawed on the bone. We slaked our hunger and thirst and then settled in to cleanse our bodies – he, his paws and chops and I my face. Utter revulsion struck me as I realized what I surely had witnessed – perhaps the feeding of one of my crew to the Inuit dog. I clutched my stomach to keep from retching and looked upon the animal with disgust; but, I could not in good conscious blame the poor dog – he was but a player in the dæmon's drama, the same as I – and neither of us were assured of our continuing roles. The hopelessness of my forced imprisonment turned to anger as the hours passed and with it the determination to disobey the monster's command and seek him out with an intention to kill.

After the animal and I attended to ourselves, I conceived a plan. As I racked my brain in the tomb-like stillness of my cabin, I cringed at the dæmon's devious ways; my efforts to combat his evil were tantamount to those carried out by Sisyphus as he struggled in his monumental task. Having witnessed the effects of Mr. Chumley's ice dagger upon the creature, I regarded attacks with pistol and knife as futile. I knew from Victor's tale that the creature had survived a previous shot from a firearm. His death, I surmised, could only be achieved by two methods: by an ice ax, or some similarly formed and wicked instrument, plunged into the brain; or by fire. Fire, the sailor's curse, would of course consume the ship and end my life as well – I considered it as a last resort after all else had failed, when I could with felicity heed heaven's welcome call.

Where was the monster? Because the ship appeared to be sailing on a course determined by the creature rather than drifting in the northern seas, I was certain the fiend had stationed himself at the tiller in the gun room, two decks below my quarters. During his times up top, the monster had, by some method, secured the tiller so the vessel would continue its journey under one sail while he roamed about. But my astonishing meeting with Victor's apparition convinced me the fiend's hands were upon the rudder in the gun room when I heard his unearthly cries.

My first task would be to find a suitable weapon. I possessed no knives and none were within proximity of my quarters. However, I judged no knife would dispatch the monster – a sentiment I professed to my animal companion – several muskets and bayonets lay in the ward room, where my Marines had stored supplies, and the latter weapon offered a more likely choice. Revolting images ran through my mind as I contemplated my attack. The choice was clear: search out the fiend and ram a

27

bayonet through his malignant brain. Only then could I be reasonably assured of his death.

After a farewell to the dog, I departed with a single candle The ship's dim passageways swallowed the meager light like a coin tossed into a well. The decks, once so bustling with activity and now so devoid of life, closed around me with ghostly creaks and moans. Every footstep mocked me – every nook in the passage filled me with dread. The dæmon's hideous sallow face and monstrous hands loomed in my mind, and with trepidation I pressed forward, expecting, at any moment, the creature to burst forth from the shadows and end my miserable existence. As fate would decree, the fiend was nowhere to be found and I continued my quest, my heart throbbing in my chest.

I passed the bulkhead and descended to the ward room where several muskets, their bayonets reflecting the candlelight, lay stacked against the wall. I secured one from the cache and continued my journey to the gun room. With each step, my agitation and sense of foreboding increased. Could I accomplish the terrible plan? If I failed and the monster carried out his murderous retribution against me, so my life would end in ignominy, and, despite my efforts, the dæmon would be unleashed upon the world. Such failure was unthinkable.

With measured step, I descended the staircase to the gun room. At the landing, I blew out the candle and was plunged into a fearful yet exquisite darkness. My senses sharpened and for the first time since I had begun my pursuit of the creature, calm descended upon me. In that nether region within the ship, no sound came to my ears save that of the waves breaking as they swept past the stern; my eye detected a thin yellow streak in the dreary depths; the odor of a burning oil lamp crept into my nostrils. My eyes took several minutes to adjust to the overpowering gloom. I gathered my courage and pressed forward: past the mizzen mast and the bulkhead of the room, all the time gripping the bayonet tightly with both hands. Had the monster surprised me, I would have thrust the weapon between his eyes.

A hand fell upon my shoulder and I uttered a curse. The flare of a candle showed the ragged and unkempt face of Mr. Sparrow, the young officer so desirous of glory. He leered at me with the thoughtless grin of a lunatic.

"Mr. Sparrow!" cried I, and then dropped my voice to a whisper. "I am happy to see the face of another survivor. Where have you been?"

"Down 'ere, among the bowels of the ship. I been livin' on rats and things." He reached into his pocket a pulled out the carcasses of several robust vermin.

The sight made my stomach turn and I knew he was mad, but I sought his help despite his physical and mental condition. "You must aid me in my quest to destroy the creature," I implored.

"I tried to warn 'em," he said. "There's no stopping 'im. You'd best get off the ship, Captain, if you want to live." He thrust a bony finger into my chest and tears formed around the edges of his dark eyes. "I told 'em about the killin' on the ice – at the funeral-pile – and then they learnt first-hand what happens in a fight. That left five of us and Mr. Chase. Mr. Chase and the others tried, but . . . ."

"Help me, Mr. Sparrow," I said. "He must be stopped."

"I cannot fight 'im. I am finished; I have no strength."

With that, the candle flashed out and he scurried away in the bleak passageway. I had no choice but to continue my quest – alone. A murmur that sounded like a prayer entered my ears as I continued toward the gun room door. I endeavored to peer beyond the slight opening where I was convinced my prey had secured his sanctuary. Inside, a lamp burned and I spotted the shadowy creature I sought. Any description I attempt, dear Margaret, is feeble, compared to the scene my eyes beheld. As my hand writes these words, I still cannot make sense of what I witnessed on my own vessel. There, on a makeshift gurney, lay the body of Victor Frankenstein – my dear friend prostrate before the fiend he created. The monster hung over the corpse, much as he had done when I recorded our first astonishing meeting. The fiend's face, except for the tearful eyes, was concealed by long locks of ragged hair; his two gigantic hands grasped a small book from which he read exclamations in a mournful fashion. I was now convinced of my own madness – my encounter with Victor's apparition confirmed my instability – *here* lay the body of my friend. As if sensing my presence, the creature brushed his hair aside and cast his watery gaze toward the door. The wretched hideousness of his face shook me again into terror: I could not view the yellow skin, the black lips, the hands, so similar in texture and color to those of a mummy, without revulsion.

Rising like a slumbering giant, the monster threw the book upon the corpse, and after a series of wild and incoherent self-reproaches, said with unrestrained rage: "How dare you, Walton, interrupt the rites of the dead! I smell your miserable skin! Did I not say to keep to your quarters – dost thou have so little regard for your life?" Here, he paused, and thrust his hand toward Victor. "Thou hast seen the sting of death – it comes to all who have lived. I understand your bequest, my powerful and lasting inheritance – the power to abolish its deadly wound. How shall I proceed, father? How shall I fulfill your dream of death vanquished? How I sought your love and how I loved you. Frankenstein."

I could withhold my anger no longer, incensed as I was by his vile profession of affection. I burst past the door with the bayonet held high, charging directly for my target. He raised his hands in defense and they caught the brunt of my attack. The steel blade sliced through the air, past his upturned palms, with nary a drop of blood spilt. The blow was deflected into his left shoulder and he screamed in anguish, a cry not unlike that of a tortured animal. A thrust from his powerful elbows sent me clattering to the floor, blackness filling my eyes before they reopened with the stench of death and the revolting face inches above my own.

"I should kill you now and end your misery," he said with idyllic regret, "if not for my search for the truth of your tale. The day will come, Walton, when you lead me to my father's journals." With that, he stood over me and with supernatural effort grasped his hands around the blade and pulled it from his shoulder. This time, there was no exclamation of pain, only a leering smile as he stood over me and bent the blade in half until it was rendered useless.

How sad that my days had come to this, in the clutches of a monster so much greater in physical and (I reluctantly conceded) mental agility than I. As I lay sprawled upon the cold deck, an overwhelming despair filled my mind. The prospect of a reunion with you, my dear sister, faded as I contemplated my dire situation. The hope I would ever see England again vanished like fog under the rising sun; the brave fellows who accompanied me on my expedition, who looked to me for aid when I had none to bestow, had paid for their loyalty with their lives. I had written you earlier that my men were endangered through me, and if lost, my mad schemes would be the cause – and, thus, it had come to pass. I would be held responsible if the ship found its way to calmer waters. How could I possibly relate this incredulous tale; no sane man would believe such a fantasy? Those who listened would shake their heads in disbelief and whisper of the "ravings of a lunatic," or of one affected by the "madness of the North." What tribunal, aware of the carnage and desertion from my vessel, would keep me from the gallows? No, my only course was to end my life and, simultaneously, the life of the monster. I must burn my ship and destroy all evidence of the horrors perpetrated upon it. Yet, even as the vile creature hovered over me, I shivered in fear that somehow the fiend might live and my death, and the obliteration of my crew, would be in vain. Charged by that thought, the faintest glimmer of courage inched its way into my icy veins and I summoned what diminishing hope for life was left within me.

The monster's leering smile turned to a hideous scowl and he returned with lumbering steps to the body of Victor Frankenstein. I raised myself upon my elbows and watched as the creature retrieved the small volume he had thrown upon the corpse. The book appeared as a thimble against his massive chest. He opened it and began reading, issuing forth incantations similar to those I had heard as I stood outside the door.

"Are you aware," he finally said to me, his voice as constant as the waves that washed by the ship, "of the works of Cornelius Agrippa, Paracelsus and Albertus Magnus?"

I shook my head, not wanting to converse with the murderer.

"Come forth, wretched fool," the creature said. "We only have each other for discourse and yet several days before we land at a suitable port. The dog is a faithful companion, but he will not speak." The monster chuckled at his pun.

I lowered my head, averting my eyes from his watchful gaze.

"Long have I sought the company of man, though I am rebuffed in every encounter. I struggle to remember my creation –

31

a period confused and indistinct – yet now so close to what may be the end of my days, the agonies of my existence continue their torment. The blows continue to fall even as I curse and revere my creator. Why did I live? Did he create me for his own evil edification? Did he imbue me with life to see me die or to watch me kill? Can you answer those questions, Walton, as your *own* existence slips from your grasp?"

"Victor Frankenstein was a good man," said I, still looking away from his offensive countenance.

"Then why . . . ?" he screamed in fitful recrimination and then rushed toward me. He clutched my throat and forced me to look into his hideous face. The rotting smell of death nearly made me swoon. "Then why do these thoughts torment me, burrowing through my brain like conquering worms, and stirring the fiend within? Is it the laws and actions of men, including my creator, or some other foul defect unbeknownst to your middling race, that leads me down the path of wretchedness?"

I gasped for air and he released his grip. I looked directly into the watery eyes, which for a brief time were filled with melancholy rather than rage.

"Do you know the works of Agrippa?" he asked again. This time, his voice was suffused with an unexpected gentleness.

"Victor spoke of him," I replied.

"In his talks, did my father speak of the inevitable path his studies would have taken him?"

I shook my head. Victor, in telling his horrific tale, had made no mention of further scientific studies or what greatness he might have achieved. Instead, he was consumed with regret for the lives lost: his doomed wife, the darling Elizabeth; his sweet youngest brother, William; his devoted friend, Clerval; the innocent Justine, accused of William's murder; and his dear father – all in some turn destroyed by his hideous progeny. Victor had wanted no part of the power he had unleashed, save to see it extinguished by his own hands.

"My father had read the *De occulta philosophia*, Agrippa's defense of magic," the monster said. "But I recovered this volume, concealed within his coat."

He held the book and I translated the gold Latin lettering on its vellum spine – *The Transmutation of Souls*.

32

Once he perceived my comprehension, the creature continued, "My father's work remains unfinished. Do you understand, Walton, what fantastic knowledge this little book imparts? When I sat waiting for death on the pyre, I wished to shake off all thoughts and feelings; I waited for grim nothingness to slake my pain, until you told me of my father's journals – and, now, this book! Only two exist – this I learned from my reading in the hovel outside the peasant hut – and my father was fortunate enough to possess one. How strange, indeed, is the power of Agrippa's words."

The monster was gleeful in his discovery of the book. By fate's decree, Victor's thirst for the secrets of eternal life and the fiend's discovery had delayed my own death sentence. As long as the monster believed in the existence of Victor's journals, and that I possessed them, so would I live.

"Bear witness to the strange truth," the creature said and parted his black lips in a malevolent smile. He rose, taking the book with him and returned to the gurney bearing my friend's corpse. "Come, Walton. Observe."

I struggled to my feet, my knees nearly giving way as my spirit sank with the insistence of the creature's command. By degrees, my senses returned and I became acutely aware of the room in which I stood: the oak paneling, the tiller, the sternpost, all as familiar to me as the streets of London; yet these objects, so dear to the vessel, were bathed in an unearthly light that seemed to pour forth from the gates of heaven. The sea calmed, the insistent roil silenced by whatever supernatural power had been summoned into the room. The faint odor of the lamp drifted to my nostrils but was soon overpowered by the sweet smell of roses, as many as could fill an English garden. These observations washed over me as the creature bent over Victor. As my eyes adjusted to the powerful light, I comprehended the source of these sensual emanations: the slight volume of Agrippa the monster held in his hand. He gently lifted the blanket away and I stepped back in disbelief at what I observed. Victor lay in the same position, the gentle smile, the rosary wrapped delicately around his fingers, as I had witnessed hours before when the apparition appeared in the cuddy. The creature touched Victor's hand and, after that gentle greeting, a tear rolled from his eye. He looked upon the book and read a few phrases that were unintelligible to my ears, but the effect upon the corpse was immediate. A light of sparkling and yellowish hue surrounded my departed friend. Victor's creation, his voice rising in profound degrees, continued his reading, and to my astonishment, I detected a rippling movement beneath the cold skin – as if the muscles and bones of Victor Frankenstein were charged with energy. The corpse flashed with radiant life and the skull appeared to rise from the skin and gape at me with luminous eyes. At nearly the same moment, Victor's left hand tapped the gurney and I jumped in shock as I contemplated my friend's return to life despite his confinement by death. The monster continued his reading, filling his powerful lungs with air, until his voice boomed throughout the room, but the effect was temporary and the yellow hue dissipated in an electric flash despite his curses. Victor smiled at me – I supposed his last – and then settled back into the body that had carried him through life.

"My God," I said. "You have succeeded where Victor failed. You can raise the dead by the sheer power of words!" I made no mention of the apparition in the cuddy for fear the creature would make devilish use of his strange connection to the metaphysical, his ability to transmit supernatural powers. Now I was certain that he had been reading the Agrippa when I witnessed that shocking sight.

"Not so, not so, Walton," the monster replied. He sunk to the floor, exhausted by his efforts, and a deep sadness filled his eyes as he spoke. "You have seen the power of the book, but not its ultimate glory. You have witnessed my father's partial resurrection, yet *Death* has robbed me of the final victory. I have not succeeded – the sting has foiled my triumph as well as my father's. What wouldst I suffer if Frankenstein rose before me? Could I withhold the fury directed at my creator in exchange for the gratitude of a world removed from eternal darkness? These are questions I cannot answer."

"The transmutation of the soul – the body's resurrection –" said I, "would mean man could live forever."

"You possess a small mind, Walton," the creature replied as he rose from the floor. "The transmutation *is* the power of the soul – not the body. Souls, aided by the living who read from this book, can drift from vessel to vessel through eternity, choosing the recently departed to carry them in their journey through time." He stopped, gazed at his creator and then clutched the book and said, "And its holder may choose the wandering soul from *heaven or hell*. But other processes are needed in combination with the book. This my father knew. Come, if you doubt its power, I have one more sight to chill your blood."

The monster lead me like a child through the passageways of the ship as the dog howled above us; up the staircases to the mainmast and the forecastle where the bodies of my men still hung on the lines. Shocked beyond my senses by what I had observed and understanding the power of the being, I resisted any urge to attack. My mind reeled at the discovery made by Frankenstein's creation. In fact, I marveled at the genius he displayed; yet, I only had to think of my dear friend and the trail of murder and death left by the creature to allay any begrudging admiration.

"The bounty of my unrestrained fury," the creature said as he pointed to my crew. His eyes, which glinted in the lamplight, alternated between a chilling mixture of cold-hearted murder and remorse. "Thou may call me a charlatan, Walton, but I wept for your crew as I sent them to the beyond." He handed me the lamp and then read from the book. Above me, the bodies of my crew were suffused in the ghostly yellow light. All appeared to lift their hands and wave in spectral salutation to the two sentient beings who stood below. Mr. Chase's eyes flashed open and I jumped back in surprise. This unearthly vision had a strange effect upon me: I no longer viewed the men as dead – instead their bodies were carriers for the soul. The creature had clearly demonstrated an ageless truth of which I had always been skeptical, but this revelation filled me with elation, despite my revulsion for the horrific scene. My view of the world had been turned upside down, much as the beliefs of those who lived in the time of Copernicus, when the great astronomer challenged the laws of the solar system. After a time, the light faded and we stood on deck in the glow of the lamp.

"Return to your cabin, Walton, and do not venture forth; for when we make glorious landfall, you will spill my father's secret and take me to the place where he secured his writings. I, armed with such knowledge, will scale greater heights than Victor Frankenstein could have imagined." He lowered his head and his ragged locks framed the sallow features. He sighed and spoke in a voice tinged with melancholy: "Like all men, you see me as a monster. I know not what blind fury drives me to murder, but I should be happy to live in a sheltered place with a joyful companion far from the cities of men." He struck his massive fist against his chest. "Oh, couldst I hope for such a mate! If you, a puny man, could provide such happiness through my father's knowledge, I might spare your life."

With that, he bade me farewell and thrust his gigantic hand in the direction of my cabin. I quitted the deck and fled to my quarters to find the dog eagerly awaiting my return. I rubbed my hands over his bony ribs and he displayed his affection with excited licks to my neck. We settled in for the evening, he at the foot of my bed and I under the blankets, both bathed in the light of a single candle. I awoke, sometime after midnight I would judge, to the lumbering footsteps of the giant above. My candle was near extinction and its pitiful rays scarcely illuminated the room. The ship rolled over the swells and its gentle rocking belied the turmoil on my vessel. As the monster paced overhead, the dog flattened his ears and issued forth a low moan like a mournful prayer for the dying. It appeared that the beast, in some fantastic way, felt an endearing sympathy for the fiend who ambled fitfully through his nocturnal ramblings. As I lay fidgeting in bed waiting for an end to the monotonous torture, a plan of escape hatched in my brain. I shivered with each thought, knowing the creature could end my life upon his perverse whim. Thus, the dog and I slept with one eye open, fully aware of the precariousness of our existence.

September __, 17–

For two days, my dear Margaret, we sailed until the fresh crispness of the sea was replaced by the briny odors of fish and the muddy wash of shallow waters. Land, I surmised, was within sight. The dog and I remained captives within my cabin except for a common decency release of an hour in the morning and evening, when a tap on our door heralded the arrival of our pitiful sustenance. By the time I bounded to the now secured door, with the dog at my heels, our captor had made his silent escape, leaving the meager bowls of food in his wake. A few seconds after my return to the cabin, the door would close as if moved by ghostly hands and we would hear the wooden beam that held us captive drop into place. How the monster, so often a shambling horror, could move with such quick and stealthy intensity, I could not comprehend. During this time, I neither heard nor saw Mr. Sparrow, the other living being on board my vessel. My only indication of his presence was the sudden rapt attention of my animal companion, his ears pricked and his head cocked at some phantom lurking outside our door.

Because my quarters were behind the mizzenmast, it was difficult to judge my ship's proximity to land. The shallow light of day fell into the cabin only about forty-five minutes each morning as time marched toward fall with increasing darkness. Even as we proceeded southward, daylight continued its relentless retreat. One afternoon, at a peculiar angle through the gloom, I – or my imagination – conjured what I believed to be glowing campfires along some far-off shore. The flickering light thrilled me and my mind leapt in joy with images of Inuit huts, hearty meals of fish and seal blubber and the warmth of furs – or perhaps a whiskey with a band of English sailors taking a brief shore-side sojourn from their comfortable whaling ship. These romantic notions filled my head, but I knew my mind's machinations were far removed from the truth. And, as if in a prophecy fulfilled, the line of fires vanished into the dark, dense sea.

The dog and I suffered through another miserable night of cold and little food, and early the next morning, by my senses, the ship shuddered to a stop. The sweep of the waves against the hull was replaced by the thrash of water upon a rocky shore. I struggled to my feet and peered out my cabin window; the dim light turned the world into varying shades of gray. The interminable sea stretched to the north and west – whatever promontory had halted the vessel lay to the south and east beyond my vision. The time had come to act upon my escape or risk impending death, for the hour of my doom was at hand. Knowing the creature's propensity for inflicting pain and death, I could not trust him to honor any pledge to keep me alive until I led him to Victor's journals – the fabrication that had saved my life. The monster, at any moment, could turn upon me, and I dared not contemplate what devious device he might consider for my destruction – the visions were too horrible – but my tormented mind latched upon the terrible deaths of my crew, with perhaps a similar fate in store for me.

The hour pressed upon me; anxiety threatened to overtake me, for with each passing second I dreaded the monster's heavy tread. No food would be left outside the door this morning; I and perhaps the Inuit dog, if the monster were enraged for any reason, would breathe our last as he exacted his revenge. My bolted cabin door blocked my exit, leaving me one means of escape – to climb one deck above into the cabin where Victor had lain after death, and make my way through the ship without alerting my captor. Such a plan seemed nigh impossible considering an ascent up the stern, a plunge through the smashed window into the cuddy, and a speedy descent below decks to assure Mr. Sparrow's safety and, if warranted, an attack on Victor Frankenstein's creation. My resolve was clear; my fate decided. My chance to escape could wait no longer.

I patted the dog and assured the beast I would secure his release after executing my intentions. He wagged his black tail and surveyed me pitifully with his large brown eyes. Leaving the animal – my only true friend on this horrific voyage – depressed my spirits, for I could not with certainty ensure my success. Despite my unwillingness to leave the dog to the whims of the monster, I pulled on my woolen slops and taking care to protect my splinted thumb, unlatched the cabin window.

A chilling blast from the north-west smacked my face, rushed through the cabin and rattled the door. I fortified myself against the wind and with great difficulty climbed halfway out the window. The sea crashed against the rocks and stern – my vessel had been run aground by my captor. The destruction of my crew and ship sent my blood boiling, but the ferocity of my emotion was tempered by my circumstances. As my eyes took in the vertiginous view, my senses reeled at my undertaking. A slip of the hand – a plunge from this height would assure my death in the shallow waters. The cuddy loomed above in the swirling sea mist; my escape an insurmountable task achieved only by the miracle of God's good graces.

I reached for the wooden ornamentation that ran vertically up the stern. With careful movements, I could hoist myself to the cuddy by planting my feet against the windows, somewhat like a spider delicately balancing on the horizontal runners of his web. I rested my weight against the frame and it wobbled; I quickly reached for the runner and gripped it with both hands. Looking up, rather than down to allay my fear, I pulled myself up the ship using my feet as supports against the wooden slats. My left hand throbbed in pain, but I was determined to survive the perils before me. Fist-hold over excruciating fist-hold, I crawled up the runner until my feet reached the window smashed by the monster. Fortunately, the frame was intact and with a great kick of my legs, I dropped into the cabin. It, and its furnishings, stood solitary and glum, not an article moved since my encounter with Victor's apparition.

The cabin door stood open, beckoning me into the gloomy passageway. I searched for a lamp and found it along with lighting materials. Never was I so eager and my eyes so joyous as to behold a common lamp and the light it provided along my path. I stopped in the doorway to listen to the ship's sounds before I descended to the orlop. A shiver skittered over me as I held my breath and strained my ears. The quiet pounded in my head; the silence disconcerted me, for, beneath the calm, the dæmon lurked on *my* vessel awaiting his final revenge.

Without further hesitation, I bounded into the passage and began my descent: down three staircases into the bowels of the ship where clothing and provisions lay stored for the exploration of the northern polar region. Mr. Sparrow, the animal and I were in need of what food I could secure for our escape – in small portions no doubt – but perhaps enough to last until we could find another source of nourishment. When I reached the room, my heart pounded at the scene.

There sat Mr. Sparrow, my young lieutenant, naked among the stores of food and winter clothing. Like me, he held a lamp, but with one obvious difference. He scolded me and warned me to come no closer, otherwise he intended to drop the flame. The fire would ignite the cloth and foodstuffs and then spread to the gunpowder kegs the distraught man had secured against the wall.

"Please, Mr. Sparrow," I pleaded, "Gather your clothes and help me carry food for our escape."

"You cannot escape the monster," he said. "Look what 'e's done to me. Save yourself and the animal and let us be destroyed. There is no other way." He then lowered his head and muttered mournful phrases I could not comprehend. His ravings sounded to me like the gibberish of the lunatics who frequented the London docks. I knew there was little time for complacency and I begged him not to burn the ship – the scourge of the sea and the fear of all naval men – a transgression of the highest order for a sailor. If Mr. Sparrow carried through with his threat, I would have scant minutes to rescue the dog and escape before the vessel was consumed and blasted to bits when the gunpowder ignited.

"Go or you will die with us," he said.

With that he looked at me with tearful eyes and dropped the lamp. The oil burned brightly over his skin and then spread to his pyre. I cried out, but it was too late. As horrific as the immolation was, Mr. Sparrow did not scream. I will, until my final breath, remember the determination and serenity in his face as the flames consumed him; it was his awaited release to the ever-after, the moment when he could at last find peace from the devilish torments that had consumed him.

In a short time, the fire rose and filled the deck with smoke and a ghastly yellow hue. The heat and fumes increased with such ferocity they forced me, coughing and sputtering, up the staircase. When I arrived at my cabin, I was horrified to see the door sprung open and the dog missing. I called for the beast, but I was certain the animal had been spirited away by our captor.

My body shook in a strange mixture of anger and fear; I would not forsake my pledge to the Inuit dog despite my peril. Below, the flames crackled and lashed through the orlop. With little time to spare, I gathered my journal and Margaret's letters into my knapsack and then ran, with lamp in hand, across the cabin deck to the stairwell. There, I was detained by the lamp-oil keg which still remained where I had positioned it, a silent sentry against the door. With herculean effort, I pushed it from the entrance in one mighty blow.

I opened the door and peered into the gloom of the top deck.

The monster stood before me, the dog cowering at his feet.

"Thou wouldst make your escape on such a fine day?" my captor asked. His black lips quivered in the dim illumination and a ferocious intensity filled his eyes. He pointed at me and then swept his wrinkled hands toward the heavens. The stiff bodies of my crew still hung from the lines overhead. "What hast thou wrought?" he asked, and thrust his massive fingers toward my throat. His yellow skin glistened like rotting meat in the morbid light. "I hear rumblings below. Confess, or face your death."

"Not I, but Mr. Sparrow—"

Those few words were all I could utter before an expansive silence fell over the ship, as if all the air were sucked from the world; then, a thunderous explosion lifted the top deck like a wave and dropped it with a splintering thud. The monster was pinned beneath a jumble of timbers and I was thrown on my back a few yards away, my lamp flying from my hand. Before the giant could rise from his imprisonment, I scrambled to my feet. The cat-head off the foremast appeared the only reasonable path of escape. I sprinted down the deck, traversing the splintered beams and leaping across the broken expanses as smoke billowed from the decks below. I shuddered at the loss of my ship while the monster roared behind me. Perhaps Mr. Sparrow had succeeded in uncovering the creature's one terrible fear – fire. I turned and looked at the dæmon; with prodigious effort he dislodged the wood, rose and staggered across the quaking deck, more stunned than I by the force of the blast.

I swung from the cat-head, my knapsack in tow, and grabbed the large iron hook suspended from its pulley. Wrapping my feet around its ropes, I flew over the open water and dropped with dizzying force into the sea below. The frigid waves took away my breath as they washed over me. My feet hit the rocky bottom and I was relieved to discover, by fate's decree, I had landed in chest-deep water. I released the rope, thrashed to shore while pushed by the sea's force, and stood shivering and wringing the foamy ocean from my clothes. It was then I observed the indistinct form of another ship – a smaller whaling vessel – anchored due south off the tip of an icy peninsula. Already I could discern the tiny forms of its crew scurrying like ants toward my burning vessel. I was cheered by their arrival a few minutes later, the crew carrying muskets and other arms.

"What in God's name has happened?" a stout man with ruddy cheeks asked, looking in horror upon my ship. His uniform confirmed his position – he was the captain of the whaling vessel – and he soon directed his attentions to me while his crew gazed upon the hellish scene of flames and smoke that lit the small harbor.

"A tale you would not believe," I said, and was rocked on my feet by a windy swirl of embers.

The captain called for a fur coat from one of his crew and soon I was wrapped in warmth, even as my legs trembled with cold. I wondered what had become of my animal companion.

"You are Captain Robert Walton, the explorer, are you not?" the master asked with one eye cocked inquisitively.

I nodded and wished my name and profession had not been so soon discovered.

A second explosion rocked the stern of my ship, sending a shower of splintered beams and supplies cascading like fireworks into the bay. A beastly howl arose from the top deck, surpassing the clamor of the conflagration – the voice of Victor's creation echoed over the water. I cannot describe the sound other than to say it was as if all Satan's angels had been released from the depths of hell to sound their trumpets. Terror shot through the captain's eyes and I could scarce look upon his face for fear of revealing the truth of the horror aboard my vessel.

As if to taunt me, a few moments passed and then the unearthly face of the monster appeared near the forecastle.

"Good Christ," the captain said, pointing a pudgy finger toward the deck. "One of your crew has been disfigured by the explosion."

"No, sir, that is not one of my crew," I replied. "What you see is beyond comprehension. Have your men aim their weapons toward the deck."

The captain looked at me with questioning eyes, but complied with my request.

Seeing the firearms pointed at him, the monster howled again, but this time the cry congealed in a hideous mixture of rage, pain and despair. A momentary stab of pity washed over me despite my desire for his destruction.

As we watched, the monster's massive hands reeled in the cat-hook to its position on the forecastle. He latched a crate to its hook and gently lowered it to the water. When it reached the sea, the monster let out a piteous howl. The Inuit dog jumped from the crate and swam through the waves to shore. Unlike me, a shivering human, the animal shook the frigid water from his fur and yipped and cavorted about the rocks. I captured the dog and instructed the whaling master's crew to move inland, away from the ship. As they retreated, I heard the creature's voice above the chaos, "I will find you, Walton, and exact my revenge upon you and the last remaining Frankenstein! I will have my mate!"

A third explosion rocked the bay, and above the licking flames, I saw the tops of the three masts snap like twigs and collapse into the black smoke. The inferno split the hull and its timbers groaned and cracked as my vessel collapsed in a fiery rush into the sea. It blazed in a heap in the shallow bay and filled the skies with more light than the feeble Arctic sun could muster. After a time, the fire settled into a warm and almost comfortable glow as steaming pieces of my ship washed ashore. We watched for more than an hour before the anemic sun failed and the darkness and cold closed around us for the remainder of the day. Victor Frankenstein, his creation, and Mr. Sparrow had finally been delivered to their final resting places in these northern waters.

The captain bade me retire to the safety of his vessel, but before we departed I made one last survey of the shore. Amid the wreckage, I found a small wooden box. Inside it, lay a small book wrapped in a rosary, its binding damp but the handwritten text otherwise undamaged. It was *The Transmutation of Souls* by Cornelius Agrippa. I removed the rosary and the book from the container and placed them in my pocket. With that, I followed the whaling crew back to their ship, the faithful dog at my heels. On board the safety of this vessel, I recorded this last entry.

ROBERT WALTON'S JOURNAL

October 15th, 17—

With great effort, I put pen to paper despite the amiable surroundings and comforts afforded by my beloved sister, Margaret. I cannot rest, secure as I am, in her family's home on Warwick Street, London. The loss of my crew, my ship and the inquest weigh heavily on my mind, while the officers of great rank who comprise the panel offer grim-faced determination and little solace in their quest to ferret out the facts in the tragedy. The morning light does nothing to cheer me; the blazing hearth warms my body but not my soul. Even the normally refreshing sanctuary of my journal finds me agitated and melancholy; I find it nearly impossible to write as these events crush my spirit. By far the most crippling blow comes from the vivid memories of Victor's creation – I see his hideous face in my slumbers and when I do venture forth I see his grotesque form round every corner.

Thank God for the lively interactions with my sister; her dear husband, John; and my niece, Lila, and nephew, David. They have been the mainstays of my life and my singular sustenance during these tribulations. They deliver kindness and love every hour of the day – the children desire my constant attention. "Tell us more, Uncle Robert, about your journey to the north," they plead with that sad yet exuberant face only the young can muster. If only I could; the voyage is too painful for the telling. I extract what happiness I can from their lives; yet, I fear for their safety. What if the monster survived the conflagration and somehow made his way to London? Yet, after several trips to my destroyed ship, before the whaler embarked to England, no bodies were ever found, allaying my fear of the fiend's existence. However, Victor knew of the creature's craftiness when it came to pursuit; the fiend tracked him to the Orkney Islands, the desolate archipelago north of Scotland. How I would suffer if my dear family were harmed by the monster; I, again, would be the unwilling accomplice to death and destruction – this time to my dear loved ones – a thought too terrible in its consequences to bear. I took some comfort in the fact that the creature knew nothing of my family other than my name; this was short lived, however, when my arrival in London and the resulting inquiry became fodder for the papers.

Despite the hospitality of the whaling ship's master and his crew, my return to England was particularly difficult. Before departing, we spent two days anchored a good distance from the wreckage of my vessel. A native village thrived on a rocky bay south of the whaler – a fact unbeknownst to me in the hours after the fire. The crew exchanged goods with the inhabitants and there, after several pats and a tear from my eye, I relinquished the faithful Inuit dog to its people. There was no place for him on the voyage home and I was certain he would be happier in his homeland than in England. After our departure, the loquacious captain, obviously in the mood for intellectual stimulation beyond what his crew could offer, questioned me often about my exploratory voyage to the northern pole, and my scientific findings. The captain was kind and jovial, but cast a wary eye toward me when inquiring of my crew. I trembled at his questions and he knew soon enough not to ask of my loss or else witness my bitter anguish. Thank God in heaven, the fire, smoke and dim light had obscured the five bodies from the whaler's men and therefore left them in ignorance about the murders on board. With great effort, I convinced the captain that the creature who appeared on the top deck was the last survivor of my crew, a mutineer who had escaped from the ship's brig. With that explanation in mind the captain did not mourn, exclaiming the wretch deserved to die in the inferno.

The captain had read of my exploits in the London papers and I learned from him of the public fascination with our journey.

Vague rumors of a preternatural being racing across the ice also had made their way to the mainland. I asked him where the tales might have originated – he told me of stories circulated by natives that had encountered the beast and, equally surprising, reports of a European who had pursued him across the ice with fevered obsession. Plagued by my insecurities, I feared the monster was aboard the whaler, but no such sighting occurred, and as we neared England, the creature briefly relinquished his hold on my imagination and I, for a time, was able to rest peacefully.

However, upon landing, the disturbing visions resumed. These thoughts have unsettled me and when my nerves require it, I partake of a potion I procured from a sailor who suffered a terrible injury one windy day in my early voyages. He lost an arm to the sails when he became entangled in a line. I walked to his dingy home through a stout drizzle and we talked for hours about the terrible beauty and dangers of the sea. I left with my precious gift – a small supply – (he warned me to measure my drink because of its siren's call) and he, in turn, received my grateful thanks and some coin. A few drops of this magic elixir and I drift away; too much and the creature appears before me with his cold hands upon my neck and the stench of death infused in my nostrils. That unfortunate scene played out one evening after retiring to my bed chamber. My sister and her husband arrived in their nightclothes to find me sweating and inconsolable upon the bed. They comforted me and after a time I was able to find sleep.

The next morning, after John had left for his trade, my sister demanded to know the truth of my circumstances. I had yet to share with her the letters never sent and the journal she had never read. I was less than forthright in my confession, telling her of my sincere companionship with Victor Frankenstein, who had joined my crew (that was all I dared say about him), and how the deaths of my men and the resulting inquiry had taken a heavy toll. This explanation appeared to mollify her and, as a result, she has made it her duty to brighten my days. Despite her cheeriness, I know I must leave Warwick Street, if only for the safety of her family.

October 31st, 17—

With so little inclination and time to write, my journal has suffered. I must record one event, however, which strengthened my resolve to leave London as soon as the inquiry would allow.

Margaret was particularly happy on a day when the weather was decidedly dismal. I inquired about her joyous mood and she explained that we were "attending a cotillion of the highest social order" that evening. I protested strongly for a number of reasons: my bad temper, the inclement weather and, most of all, my total ineptitude for a new-fangled dance. She would hear none of it, and reminded me that John had worked exceedingly hard to procure the invitation and that as a guest in her house she would not abide my continuing melancholy. Therefore, I would attend despite my stated objections. I knew when to surrender.

With some trepidation, I dressed and, after the children were secured at a neighbor's – Mrs. Shelby's home – Margaret, John and I hailed a carriage which took us to an elegant residence in the heart of London. There we were escorted by coiffed footservants to a splendid ballroom where the festivities were already in progress. Everyone, including Margaret and John, were dressed in the French manner. I had never seen my sister look so beautiful – her brown hair was swept up in a fashionable braid; her eyes sparkled with merriment and delight as she breezed about the room in her green brocade dress. The stern authority of her household demeanor dissolved into gaiety and laughter as she tapped her ornamental fan in a coquettish manner.

As she and John danced the quadrille with the other couples that flooded the floor, I soon found the reason for her insistence upon my attendance. Margaret threw desperate looks my way – pointed in the direction of one Miss Jane Adams, a young woman decidedly richer in attractions than her common name. Miss Adams was in no manner a coquette; rather, she seemed to melt into the walls in her lovely blue gown. At my sister's continued insistence, I took the hint and asked Miss Adams to dance. She graciously accepted; however, she did nothing to stoke the fires of my heart. She was pleasant enough – a charming young lady – but I was too preoccupied with my troubles to find solace in her eyes, which corresponded to the color of her dress. At one point during the dance (which I stumbled through having only mastered a jig through the drunken courtesy of sailors), she remarked upon my career and "how exciting and fascinating it must be."

As we danced, it was not the admiration of my profession that stopped me cold, but the vision I saw through the windows that graced the exterior wall of the ballroom. The dæmon's hideous face leered at me through the glass. I stumbled in horror and Miss Adams, nearly plunging from a fall, gasped in shock. I could not discern whether she had been privy to the apparition as well, but I escorted her, with profuse apologies, to her seat and then made a hasty exit to the balcony where I surveyed the grounds in the cool, misty night. There was no sign of the creature; the earth was damp and moist but no footprints traced through the wet grass.

Margaret soon appeared at my side, scowling in disdain at my behavior. "What is the point of your undignified manners?" she asked with contempt. "Have I a ruffian for a brother?"

"No, Margaret," I pleaded. "You know better than to chastise me so." I looked at her and the fire in her eyes softened. "I must admit I am uncomfortable here, and little acquainted with society even less so with the gentle manners of women, so much of my time has been aboard ships; the inquiry drags me down like an anchor and, for a moment, I thought I saw . . . ." I could proceed no further.

"Saw what?" she asked with some sympathy.

After a time, as I took in the dark stillness of the trees, I replied, "The face of one of the dead."

Margaret sighed and patted my shoulder. "Oh, my dear brother, I am sorry. I was wrong to force you to come here. It shall not happen again."

"It is no fault of yours," I said. "I need to remove myself from the pleasures of your home – get out, enjoy life when I can." Here I stopped to weigh my next thought. "I should leave when the Board's work is done – return to Yorkshire or perhaps sign on aboard another vessel if the navy will have me. All my business is unfinished, Margaret . . . I do hope you understand." The web of lies I needed to survive were beginning to ensnare me: the fabrication of Victor's journals, the alibi constructed for the loss of my crew, my failure to tell Margaret the truth regarding my harrowing voyage.

She placed her hands on the railing and peered out in the darkness. "We will come down with the grippe if we are not careful – I understand your predicament, Robert. Please be assured that John and I stand behind you, whatever the need."

I hugged my sister and then said, "Yes, the weather is damp. Let us join the party." We returned to the ballroom, as the face of the monster danced in my head. Thereupon, I knew I would leave Margaret's comfortable home as soon as the Board permitted, and, on the morrow, I would write to Ernest Frankenstein to express my sympathy for the death of his brother. Such a gesture, after all, was the least a gentleman could do.

LETTER FROM ERNEST FRANKENSTEIN TO ROBERT WALTON IN CARE OF THE SAVILLES, LONDON

Geneva, November 30th, 17—

To Captain Robert Walton, England

Thank you for your kind condolences regarding my brother, Victor Frankenstein.

Although the tragedies my family has suffered over the preceding years have been immeasurable, your thoughts and well-wishes eased our pain and alleviated the mystery surrounding my brother's unfortunate death. To know that he died in pursuit of his scientific studies has lifted a great burden from my heart.

I have conveyed your sympathy to my family and our closest friends regarding Victor's final voyage aboard your vessel. However, I know in my soul, your words are less than the truth. I have been informed of the naval inquest and the strange circumstances regarding the death of your men. Imagine an entire crew wiped out – through your own admission – by disease and the hardships of your expedition! It is hard to conceive of such a fantastic loss, unless the Reaper of Death himself sailed aboard your doomed ship – perhaps a dæmon unleashed by my own brother? For this reason, I believe there is more to your tale than may have been told to the Board of Inquiry.

There is another reason for my letter. Of late, astonishing events have occurred at Belrive, my family's country home outside Geneva. These occurrences may have some relationship to the tragedy aboard your ship; in fact, I am certain of it. If you seek solutions regarding your recent troubles, you may find them at Belrive. It is my sincere hope you will consider a journey to partake of my family's hospitality, and, at your earliest convenience, aid me in a scientific quest. I am keenly aware of your fondness for exploration and adventure. My home and the surrounding grounds, should you accept my invitation, will be your own. I understand the difficult circumstances you now face, but know that the sooner you arrive at Belrive the sooner we may come to a mutual understanding of the importance of my brother's work.

It is neither boast nor threat to write that an unassuming trip to Geneva may change the course of history and the fate of mankind. I look forward in all haste to your impending visit.

Yours, this day, hoping for a favorable reply, in all sincerity,

E. Frankenstein

LETTER FROM ROBERT WALTON TO MARGARET SAVILLE OF LONDON

France, January 3, 17—

To Mrs. Saville, England

My dear Margaret, what can I write of the joys and pleasures of time spent with you and your family during the celebration of our Lord's birth and the introduction of the New Year? I look upon myself as fortunate to have you as my sister with all the blessings you and your family bestowed upon me during the joyous season. I reveled in the time spent with you, your considerate husband and my delightful niece and nephew; and, it was particularly precious considering the reason for my stay. You are a constant reminder of what I have relinquished for my love of exploration and what I may, perchance, consider for the future.

My life changed irrevocably the moment Victor Frankenstein boarded my ship, obsessed as he was with his scientific pursuits. His death and the deaths of my crew consume my thoughts to this day. In lucid moments, when the sharpness of all that has happened cuts like a knife, I retreat to a safer personal and psychological sanctuary; often, as you no doubt noted, to your side in the comfort of the blazing hearth. The stain of my failure was diminished through our discourse and I was able to achieve a slow recuperation under your hospitable roof. I much preferred it to the isolation I would have suffered at my home in the north, though I had no choice, as I was required in London for testimony.

Many nights at your home, I awoke to the terror of Death himself leaning over my bed, leering into my face, only to find my fevered imagination had played its terrible tricks upon my slumbers. I swallowed my screams, for I wished no disturbance to your household and, for the most part, was duly rewarded. For each morning during my stay you (and your family) greeted me with warm smiles, unaware as you were of the terror etched into my nightmares.

My dear sister, I must thank you for your steadfast support at the naval inquest. I know the proceedings have not been completed, but my questioning is through and I feel confident that no board of review would believe an honored Captain of His Majesty's Navy would sit idly by whilst his crew rushed to their doom. The sickness and terrible cold in the Arctic wilderness caused the demise of my men and my confession will remain constant. I issued my public apologies, and my temporary discharge from the fleet serves as my punishment. I am glad the matter is nearing its conclusion, for I cannot bear another grieving family and the hateful and suspicious looks directed toward me as the surviving member of the voyage. I am most grateful to the Commander and the Board for allowing me to travel as they complete their findings.

The road is smooth and a light snow is falling as I write. The brown French fields covered in their icy coat pass by my window. I have undertaken this journey to Geneva at the request of Ernest Frankenstein, Victor's brother. I wrote to him about Victor's death, only saying his brother's demise was the result of his scientific interests. Ernest's reply was strange in its tone and consideration – an invitation and yet a command for my knowledge – as if I was the sole person on earth able to answer questions about his brother's work. I may be – only providence can decide – but I look forward to the change of scenery, the chance to clear my memory of the inquiry in London, and, for you my dear sister, the return to your normal household duties, freed from the melancholy temperament of your brother. My lovers – exploration and adventure – have once again demonstrated their charms.

The French have allowed me to travel, despite our war, in the name of science; although I make this journey for many reasons, the primary being a call to adventure apart from the sea. Ernest has piqued my interest, but most of all I travel in deference to my dearest friend, Victor Frankenstein – may the good in his work be honored and preserved. In the meantime, until I return, be safe dear sister, and heaven heap its blessings upon you.

Your loving Brother,

R. Walton

ROBERT WALTON'S JOURNAL

Belrive, January 7th, 17—

I arrived at Belrive, on the western shore of Lake Geneva, as wind-swept snow drifted against the casements and a faint red sun slipped behind the western hills, sending a shiver through my body and a chill tumbling into my soul. I waited with some apprehension for my knock to be answered. When at last the massive oak door opened, an aged but cordial Swiss serving man bade me enter the country home purchased by Victor and Ernest's father, Alphonse. The limber Swiss, with his ruddy cheeks and sparkling eyes, took my bag as easily as I might carry an armful of provisions, and led me to an expansive great room whose windows looked out upon the frozen shore of the lake. My host, I assumed, rose upon my entrance and strode toward me with young and agile step. I recalled Victor's dear wife's assessment of his character: "full of activity and spirit . . . he is desirous to be a true Swiss, and to enter into the foreign service . . . he looks upon study as an odious fetter – his time is spent in the open air, climbing the hills or rowing on the lake. I fear he will become an idler, unless we yield to the point, and permit him to enter on the profession which he has selected."

Elizabeth's description did nothing to dissuade my impression of the young man who stood before me in the bloom of youth. His sturdy frame supported an attractive countenance set off by curling wisps of blond hair and lively blue eyes; however, he could not disguise an uneasy feeling of dread which I discerned in his gaze. He bore a remarkable resemblance to his brother, seven years his senior, but the elevated and gentle manners of Victor seemed displaced by a constitution that in Ernest teetered on mental agitation. Victor's scientific attitude and calm determination, though not forgotten, no longer haunted Belrive – the current owner seemed to have summoned his own ghosts as guests.

After a firm handshake, Ernest gathered my bag and introduced me to the two individuals seated across from a crackling fireplace. The first was a dark woman of remarkable beauty, Italian by birth I guessed; the second, a fiftyish, short, bespectacled man who puffed on a long clay pipe and watched my every step with interest. If Ernest in his movement and manner displayed his nerves, the woman, elegantly attired in an indigo gown and ensconced in a gilt chair, projected a subdued, almost melancholy air. I was entranced by her beauty: Her hair was of raven black, her eyes a deep emerald that glittered in the firelight as she looked my way. Her lips were sensuous and full, and in her demeanor I observed a thirst for life perhaps subdued by the confines of Belrive. She extended her delicate hand and I, with a solicitous bow, kissed it. Upon introduction, I learned her identity: Olivia Della Scalla, the young wife of my host. To my surprise, the second guest in the room was already known to me through Victor's tale. The wiry, somber man who sat next to Olivia was Maximilian Waldman, the distinguished professor from Ingolstadt who had guided Victor through his early studies at the University. Ernest bade me join the semi-circle facing the fire and after prolonged questioning about the duration and comfort of my journey, we at last retired to the dining room where a sumptuous meal of meats and autumnal vegetables had been procured for our enjoyment. The company was splendid, laughter rang throughout the room, and after several glasses of a crisp German wine any portent of gloom dissipated into the ether like mists from a fountain.

As the evening settled into its pleasantries, I drank an after-dinner brandy and watched through the room's frosty windows as the stars filled the nocturnal void. I had lifted my glass when the hot breath of a beast startled me in my chair. I whirled, nearly spilling the drink upon the lace tablecloth and unsettling the contented faces of my party. There, upon my left, was the largest wolfhound I had ever laid eyes upon, a gray-mottled bitch whose gigantic muzzle extended over the tabletop and whose steely eyes gazed upon the bony remains of the meat platter. She licked her chops and then rewarded my pounding heart and embarrassed laughter with her own devotion to my hand. Ernest, Olivia and the professor reveled in my discomfort before another less dramatic occurrence elicited chilling and agonized looks from them, followed by the bleak specter of despair, which, like a smothering fog, extinguished the room's gaiety.

The simple coughs of an infant had shaken the evening. Olivia excused herself with a nod and the three of us were left in an awkward and unyielding silence.

Thereupon, my dear sister, if you are so inclined to read this journal, the strange happenings at Belrive began. I sat, somewhat distracted by the hound and the intent stare of the professor upon Ernest, who had relinquished his glass and covered his face with his hands. A haunting, guttural moan arose from my host and when he uncovered his face, the young man's countenance had shifted from one of delight to despondency. A faint cry drifted from some far corner of the dwelling and left us all without words. How slowly time passes when encompassed by despair. Only the ticking tall clock in the great room interrupted our thoughts, which in my limited understanding, fixated on some unknown affliction in the house.

At last, after folding his hands as if in prayer, Ernest spoke and directed his words toward me: "My son of six months is dying of the grippe." His lips trembled; his voice was tempered by fear. "There has been too much death, too much sadness for the Frankensteins. We are cursed; yet, we struggle with the same demonic impulses. I fear for Olivia – she does not have the constitution of a Frankenstein."

"You fret too much, Ernest," said the stoic professor after a puff on his pipe. He swept a few gray hairs back from his temple. "Not for your child, but for your family. Your brother was my disciple and I had few doubts about his success, but who could have foretold the forces he would unleash. The modesty and deference he displayed toward me must now be repaid – he was a man of genius, however erroneously directed, whose labors will ultimately turn to the advantage of mankind."

I nodded my head in agreement in memory of Victor, but I remained uncertain of the connection between Ernest and the distinguished professor.

Turning to me, my host asked, "What do you know of my brother's work?"

"We were exceedingly close during his last days; in fact, I loved your brother as my best friend. He recounted all – from his birth to his pursuit of the . . . ." I could not continue for my mind shuddered at the very thought of the creature.

"Of the dæmon?" Ernest asked. The melancholy despair in his eyes was obliterated by an inquisitiveness which flashed upon his face and traveled like a spark across the table to the professor.

"Tell us of the dæmon," the professor said, bending toward the table, his eyes a-glitter with interest.

For the next three hours (for I heard the tall clock strike ten) I related Victor's strange and harrowing tale as closely as my mind could reconstruct from our time together. My host and the professor sat in rapt attention, occasionally sipping from their glasses whilst I spoke, until I concluded with the fiery destruction of my vessel, my escape from the monster and the inquest in London. I left one detail untouched – the powerful demonstration of *The Transmutation of Souls* – for I was not ready to reveal its secrets to Ernest or Maximilian, who had worked so closely with Victor. When I at last finished, they exhaled and stared at each other as if exhausted from my revelations.

"We knew Victor had succeeded," the professor said and rested his hands on the table. "He was the finest student ever to enroll at Ingolstadt."

"My father and Elizabeth looked up to him so," Ernest said bitterly, "whilst I lived in shame as the son devoted to nature, with no great talents to support me, and the brother who failed to protect . . . ." Tears glistened in his eyes and pain suffused his voice. "I have long believed it was Victor who brought death upon this house; but, I was the brother who lived whilst young William died. We were playing a game, hide-and-seek, when he disappeared. I was unable to find him – to save his life. A torrent of remorse has rained down upon me! If only Victor could take his vengeance from the heavens and punish the monster, but he cannot. It becomes my task to continue his work. Perhaps Victor hovers near and guides me in my efforts to end the miserable curse of death."

Ernest rose and bade us walk through the cold halls toward a room near the front of the house. As we approached, the soft crying of a woman issued forth. The scene that greeted us was one of utter despair. Ernest's young wife, Olivia, was seated in a chair but her hunched body hung over a crib like a dark ghost, her eyes intent upon a tiny form swaddled in blankets. A nurse stood nearby, hushing us with a finger to her pursed lips. A single candle lit the room and the embers from the dying fire cast a crepuscular glow. Maximilian and I huddled near the door until Ernest directed us into his child's room. Even from my distance, I could see the obvious discomfort on the infant's face – a boy, I learned, by the name of Wolfgang. His breathing was labored, his small chest heaved against the blankets while the fever of his disease drained the color from his cheeks. My soul wept deeply for Ernest and his young bride, knowing the child had perhaps only hours, at best days, to live, unless some angelic host entreated God for the infant's miraculous recovery. As if aware of my silent musings, Ernest grabbed my shoulders and said in a tormented whisper, "I will not let my son die, my friend. Through our efforts we will defeat death." When he released his grip, I marveled at the implication of his words and the insatiable ambition to conquer the natural world displayed by all the heirs of Frankenstein.

In the deep hours of the night, I was awakened by a soft scratching at my window. I became aware of this abhorrence by acute degrees – my mind first ignoring the encroaching sound through the fog of sleep; but then, shaking off my slumbers as the incessant noise grew, I threw off the blankets and jumped from bed. I shivered in the icy room and devouring darkness until my eyes caught a few sprinkles of light in the looking glass across from my bed. I crept toward the window as the shadows waved carelessly across it, the hoarfrost all but obscuring the view toward the lake. Through the glimmering rime, I caught sight of a shadow that froze me to the floor. The black hulk of a massive being drifted across the window and then evaporated as quickly as it had appeared, leaving me to wonder if my tortured imagination was descending into madness. I knew of only one being on earth to cast such a shadow, but I also had been fairly convinced of the creature's destruction in the northern bay, unless by some hellish miracle he had escaped death.

But even more chilling was the voice which entered my ears It was the mangled, distorted ruminations of the monster who called himself Frankenstein. "Walton, Walton," he hissed with the venom of an adder, "You consort with devils who will burn in hell. Frankenstein and Waldman are useless without the book Thou hast usurped its power – return it to me!" I lurched in horror toward the window and threw open the casement, a shriek of rage poised upon my lips. However, the overarching silence of the winter night extinguished the vengeful fires burning within and I cautiously extended my head past the sash. My heart pounded violently in my chest as I reeled from the shock I had received, but the cutting, cold breeze revived my spirits. I leaned against the casement and lowered my head, certain I had dissolved into lunacy, a man haunted by the ghost of Victor's creation. (Before bed, I had taken the last of the potion I had purchased from the old sailor; I was well aware of its narcotic effects.)

I looked round the window not once but thrice and saw nothing but the naked branches of the trees and the snow-covered fir boughs. I pulled shut the casement, returned to the middle of my chamber and cast my gaze once again outside, my senses acutely aware of every creak of the floorboards, every frosty shadow on the dark frozen terrace that stretched to the lake. In my travels, I had witnessed the trickery the eyes can play when consumed by exhaustion and nervous agitation. How long I remained stationary I cannot say, but the clock struck three and on the final chime the shadow of a gigantic figure draped itself a second time over the window.

Chills shot through me, precipitating mountains of gooseflesh, shaken as I was by the horror outside. I shrieked for the fiend to be gone. While not my intent, my shouts aroused the wolfhound, whose ferocious bark bellowed throughout the house like a hound of Satan. Soon, footsteps rang in the hall, followed by a tumultuous knocking upon my door. I shivered in the dark and breathed in frigid draughts, knowing I had foiled imminent peril while unintentionally summoning my host to my bed chamber.

What comment can I make, my dear Margaret, on the depth of my terror; yet, while suffering from this acute fear, I observed an odd lucidity, as if my brain were separated from my body. All sensory detail, from my arrival at Belrive, to my awakening in the terrible hour raced through my mind with startling clarity. You, my dear sister, when the time comes, may yet understand the truth of my confession, while other readers, yet unbeknownst, will dismiss this journal as the ravings of a madman. Protect my letters and journal, dear one, as they may be the only record of these horrendous events.

The knocking grew more persistent and after a few moments I found my fortitude restored. I opened the door to find Ernest and Professor Waldman before me, their faces floating like ghosts in the lamplight.

"What have you seen?" Ernest asked, and the immediacy of his question was reflected by his trembling hand and rigid expression.

"Nothing . . . perhaps everything," I replied, unable to confirm the reliability of my senses.

"Walton, you are a man of adventure and some science," the professor said, cinching the belt of his dressing gown about his waist. "Such an answer will satisfy only the feeble minded. Tell us the cause of your fright."

I bade them enter the room and they took their places in two sitting chairs on either side of the looking glass. I returned to the warm comfort of my blankets. Ernest stared at me with fiery intensity, his eyes, even in the unsteady light, betraying his immediate desire for my response.

"I thought I saw the shadow . . . and heard the voice . . . of the dæmon."

Ernest placed the lamp on the nightstand and his gaze shifted like a pendulum from me to the professor and back again. "I can vouch for your sanity. The creature has been at Belrive since November – haunting my family as he haunted my brother."

"Are you certain?" I asked incredulously. "You have seen him?" As I observed Ernest, any certainty I held in the monster's demise in the conflagration evaporated. I had wished for his death because the fiend's continued existence was too much to bear, especially in what I hoped was the protective shelter of London. A chill ran down my spine as I considered the evenings spent with Margaret and her family, gathered around the cheery fireplace while the murderous creature spied upon us with impunity from the damp and foggy streets, waiting, plotting in silence, to exact his revenge. Such frightful thinking was the primary reason I left the city. Perhaps I *had* seen his face as I danced with Miss Adams. Or had he shunned London, unaware of my presence there, and traveled to Geneva with a greater prize in mind? What purpose could he hope to achieve? I conjured one terrible thought – to snuff out the lives of the remaining Frankensteins.

Ernest nodded and for a moment cupped his face in his hands as if my question had overpowered him, adding a terrible weight to his crushing weariness. After a time, and with an encouraging gesture from Maximilian, he said, "I first observed him at Belrive when the November winds blew cold across the lake. In the beginning, I was convinced he was no more than a figment, a will-o'-the-wisp in the air, the shadow of a shadow. Often, at dusk, I observed a strange, hulking figure out of the corner of my eye, like a phantom on the hillside, but I was convinced, despite the acuity of my senses, no one was there. The copy of my brother's scientific findings that I had received from Clerval, Victor's trusted friend, – as they traveled through Europe with the monster in pursuit – provided the proof my senses refused to believe. Often, a specter would drift across the window and Olivia, whom I hoped to spare from this terror, would take notice of it as well. She calmed my obvious alarm, consoling me while suppressing any concern of her own. I feared not for myself, but for my wife and son, knowing what evil the fiend had rained down upon my family. 'It was only a branch moving in the wind,' Olivia would say and stroke my brow, and I would be quieted for a time. My concern for my wife grew because I knew of her love of walks upon our wooded grounds. What if she should wander upon this horror?

"As the days failed and the night overtook the faltering light, the sightings became more frequent; the monster delighted in his brazen wanderings. He taunted me! He never let me rest while I speculated upon his murderous intent. My suspicions were confirmed one late afternoon as the sun faded behind the western hills. I was enjoying the last of the pleasant fall days and I had ventured down the terrace to the lake. To my astonishment, I observed a massive form, concealed by a black cloak, crouched in a stand of brown rushes. I called out and slowly the figure turned until the hideous countenance was fully revealed – the fiend so despised by my family; yet, the obsession of my dreams. He held a bloody bone in his hands and his lips were coated with gore. He turned his gruesome face toward me and leered – the vision of his burnt and twisted features was enough to send me fleeing back to the house for reinforcement. I called for my servant and our firearms, but by the time we made our way back to the lake, darkness had consumed all and, with it, the creature."

"Burnt?" I asked, and shuddered underneath my coverings.

"Yes," Ernest replied, "horribly scarred with patches of red skin streaking across his sallow face. He is an abomination, but I could feel the god-like strength and power that emanated from him.

"I sent my servant back to the house to look upon Olivia, fearing for her safety, and I remained with the lamp to search the lake shore. Not far from the rushes, I came upon the creature's feast, the half-eaten carcass of a deer. I am a hunter, and I had never seen an animal so expertly gutted. The wind crackled around me and I jumped with the snap of every branch, certain the fiend would catch me in his grip and execute me with equal precision. After searching through the bare bushes and brambles, I ended my quest. I had turned back to Belrive when my eyes detected a shifting blackness in the woods to my left. I called out and the spectral form I had observed melted into the darkness. I faced the void and stared into the cold, deep woods. My lamp barely shed its paltry light beyond a line of birches but I knew the monster was there. I sensed him! He waited for me!

"After long minutes of staring into the forest, I was uncertain whether I could retain my composure much longer. I am a soldier at heart, but no military exercise had prepared me for this encounter. I seethed with anger, eager to see the fiend dead. Yet I marveled at my brother's work; I admired the creature's fortitude, his ability to survive in a world determined to end his existence. As you have attested, even my brother, his creator, spoke in wonder of his strength and ingenuity. Would that such superior characteristics could be bred into our race. Imagine the power of such an army? That thought held me enthralled as I searched.

"Then, without warning, the blackness shifted and before my startled eyes, the fiend rose like a towering devil in the dark. He lumbered into the lamp's circle and in his shadow I felt Death's presence accompany him like a handmaiden. I was unable to move my legs. I tightened my grip on my pistol, but did not fire consumed as I was with a strange mixture of revulsion and awe. He approached with one hand thrust from beneath his cloak. 'Thou art Frankenstein,' he spoke through his twisted mouth. The smell of blood and putrefaction poured from his lips. He bent closer to observe me, and the burned and blistered flesh beneath the hood of his cloak became visible in the lamplight. 'You bear a resemblance to my father who gave me life. Do you know of his work and studies?'

"I shook my head and he glared at me with his watery eyes. I had never encountered such an expression of rage. His gigantic frame shook and he thrust a finger capped by a blackened nail into my chest. The force of the blow nearly knocked me to the ground, but I held my own and stared into the face of evil."

"I know what he seeks," said I. Both Ernest and the professor listened intently. "He told me of a book by Cornelius Agrippa." I made no indication that the volume lay within my bag underneath the bed. Its protection was of prime concern for my safety; indeed, the security of the household might depend on its timely delivery to the monster.

Ernest rose from his chair and walked toward me. "We must have the book so we can decipher its secrets. Its magic must be powerful; otherwise, the creature would not seek it. It must never fall into his hands."

Maximilian nodded and then asked, "What is the secret he seeks, Walton? I know the answer lies in the dark arts, in the realm of magic and the supernatural. Do you know?"

"I cannot say, but if the monster obtains the book, we are destroyed," I said. "After his creation, when he lived in the hovel next to De Lacy, he learned there were only two copies of the Agrippa in existence."

"The secret of its strength lies within Victor's studies," Ernest said. "We have yet to discover it." Here he paused for a moment to look upon the frosty window, and then continued, "At my encounter in the woods, the creature told me, 'I know of your work. Thou hast followed in my father's footsteps – I can smell it in your blood. Let it be known, I still seek the mate I was promised. I am my father's son – as much a Frankenstein by birth as you.' I was revolted by the creature's words, but oddly enough, they tempered my fear. Through his remonstrations I felt a begrudging sense of respect for my family, but such confidence was short lived, as I pictured the carnage that might be wrought upon my wife and son."

Ernest stopped and stared out the icy window. After a time, he turned to me and asked, "Could I dare think of this monstrosity, this murderer who was responsible for the death of my brothers, as my nephew?"

I was stunned by the thought, but my silence betrayed my answer.

"He also told me that night he sought the book by Agrippa," Ernest said. "The creature said my brother's copy had been lost, but another might be obtained if I knew the location of Victor's papers and journals. With a passion bordering on madness, he allowed my family would live if I delivered the book to him, and then he mentioned two men who might aid me in my search."

I knew then why Maximilian and I had been summoned to Belrive. Ernest had bowed to the fiend's demands, but for what purpose: to save his family's life, or to continue his brother's experiments? I began to see the delicate drama in which the professor and I were players. We were pawns in Ernest's scientific plans and, equally so, in the monster's quest for a mate. Either of them, in alliance with the Agrippa, could wield his superior dominance over the human race. As I sat in bed, huddled against the cold, the precariousness of my situation became clear. If I delivered the book to either Ernest or the monster, I might unleash furies heretofore unbeknownst to the world; if not . . . either way I would surely die.

"The book is *The Transmutation of Souls*," Ernest whispered as if the secret might escape from my bed chamber.

As he ended his words, the scratching that had awakened me made itself known once again in the room. This time, however, it came from overhead, on the icy roof. We turned our heads toward the dark ceiling and listened as footsteps traversed from a far corner of Belrive until they were directly above us. Past the lamp's dim reflection in the window, chunks of ice and snow fell to the ground, and then the monstrous shadow again drifted over the window like a spider crawling down a wall. Ernest cursed and the figure dropped away. We ran to the casement and flung it open and there in the cold, blue snow, illuminated by the faint light of the stars, we saw gigantic footsteps leading down the terrace to the lake shore. An eerie howl emanated from somewhere near the water and the wolfhound, in response, bellowed from the great room, and her mournful call echoed throughout Belrive.

We stared at the tracks until Ernest and the professor bade me good night. I settled back into bed and tried to slip into an uneasy sleep, but my ears were attuned to every noise that grew within the house; and my mind marveled at how the creature could demonstrate such an apparition – for I have forgotten to mention, my dear Margaret – my bed chamber is on the second storey.

ROBERT WALTON'S JOURNAL

Belrive, January 9th, 17—

The morning after our strange encounter with the dæmon, the sun dawned bright in a clear and cloudless sky over Belrive. The snow sparkled like a blanket of diamonds and my anxiety and agitation from the previous night faded with the advancing morn. Even the household was cheered by the exhilarating day: The servant gathered wood and stoked the fire while the wolfhound reposed in front of the flames. The nurse cradled the precious Wolfgang at the breakfast table; the child's coloration, despite his illness, appeared somewhat better in the daylight. Olivia and Ernest busied themselves in the kitchen and, with the aid of the manservant, prepared a filling breakfast of porridge and cakes. Maximilian sat in the great room looking toward the lake as the lazy smoke from his pipe circled to the ceiling. I greeted him and sat likewise in one of the opulent chairs and watched the light sparkle on the icy shoreline, dissipating the long morning shadows as the sun rose higher.

The professor smiled, showing fine white teeth, and tapped his pipe on a ceramic bowl. Sparks raced around its edge and then vanished in the air. When he was through tamping the pipe for his next smoke, he turned to me and asked, "Where is the book, Walton? I know you must possess it or else the creature would have . . . ." He studied me with his gray eyes and in a firm, even tone said, "I would expect your days would be more precarious if you knew nothing of the Agrippa. Ernest feels likewise."

It was now my turn to smile before I answered. In the morning's perfection, I felt somewhat emboldened and certain of my own worth as a player in the drama. With such confidence behind me, I remarked, "My dear professor – what if I told you of the book's location and justly explained the depth of its power? What purpose would it serve?"

"I understand its magic – Victor wrote of its history in the experiments that were transcribed by Clerval," he replied matter-of-factly and then nodded in my direction. "I have not discussed that knowledge with Ernest, however, because even I am disturbed by its implications. My young charge has inherited the Frankenstein curiosity; he will soon understand the book's power, if he does not already. Ernest aspires to blot out the family tragedies, and live up to his brother's legacy; creating life is one matter – withdrawing souls from the ether is another. Regardless, the book would enrich *my* work and preserve the legacy of Victor Frankenstein. Perhaps I should carry it for safekeeping."

"But have you considered? – if *you* have the book, you will be at the creature's mercy. He has promised to spare the Frankensteins if the book is delivered, but could the same be said for you?"

Maximilian lit his pipe and blew a smoky circle into the air. After consideration, he said, "You may be correct in your assumption. Perhaps it is best Ernest and I do not know where you keep the book – if you have it, of course." With that, he issued a sly smile.

"A wise assumption, professor. I believe, in this case, discretion to be the better part of valor."

We continued our conversation, avoiding the unpleasant happenings of the previous night, but expounding upon the magnificence of Belrive and its grounds. After the professor had finished his pipe, the servant announced breakfast. The nurse gathered little Wolfgang, but before she could cover her breast and wrap the infant in his blanket, I was able to observe his tiny features. Whether or not the dim light in his chamber played any part in my assessment of his health the prior evening, I was cheered this morn by Wolfgang's renewed vitality. A faint blush spread across his cheeks and the pale complexion of last night appeared to have vanished. His tiny fingers clutched at the air.

The nurse spirited him away as Olivia, Ernest, Maximilian and I sat down to our hearty repast. Our conversation was genial and none of the cares of the evening shown in the faces of my hosts.

After we finished the meal, Ernest suggested the men take an invigorating walk in the hills west of Belrive. As it suited me to be in the countryside, and as I was keenly aware of Ernest's temperament, I readily agreed. The professor, as well, seemed heartened by the opportunity to be out-of-doors and after a half-hour of readying, we struck out from the house with the wolfhound leading the way. The dog led us through the fresh snow, at points in drifts over our knees, up the hillocks, through blinding white slashed by the vertical black stalks of naked trees. The effect was as ghostly and yet as serene as any landscape I had ever encountered. We traversed many a hill and descended into several valleys before we halted in front of a large escarpment in our path. An icy waterfall surrounded by large black boulders was situated to our right; the glacial blue of the ice attested to the purity of the water's source high above. The tracks of rabbit and deer mixed at the frozen pool with the large prints of a gigantic being. Ernest pointed to the footprints and the broken ice around the pool's edge where forest animals had come to drink, as most certainly had the dæmon. I envisioned the beating hearts of the terrified forest denizens, seeking to slake their thirst, ever watchful for the hideous being who observed their movements with hungry eyes.

The wolfhound, seeming to know her way, skirted the waterfall and bounded up a snowy trail that would have gone unnoticed by any human traveler unfamiliar with the terrain. As we ascended in a steep assault upon the escarpment, often aided by walking sticks we had fashioned early in our journey, we emerged upon a level plateau which gave us a favorable view of the surrounding landscape. To the east, and far below, Belrive rested on the lakeshore, tiny curls of smoke rising from its chimneys. The spires of Geneva and the dark snow-capped eastern mountains completed the panorama. To the west, the white hills, spotted with evergreens, flowed in undulating waves. But by far the most curious sight was a large stone barn (I have no other word for it) which rested a short distance from us on the plane. The structure was surrounded by fresh snow, with not an animal or human track in sight; its gray rocks and black roof imbued it with foreboding despite the brilliant sunlight which bathed its exterior. I looked at Ernest for an explanation; the nervous agitation I had observed upon my arrival at Belrive danced in his eyes.

Yielding to my curiosity, Ernest said, "This is where Professor Waldman and I continue Victor's work."

I stood blinking in the sun, now confronted with the truth of the young man's actions. The wolfhound, as familiar with the landscape as the comforts of Belrive, bounded toward the barn's towering oak doors.

"Let your eyes take in the sight, but hold your tongue to others," Ernest said in solemn reproach.

Oh, Margaret, how can I describe the exhilaration of the moment in the radiant beauty of the day, with so few cares under a cloudless sky – my pleasant thoughts transformed in seconds by the – dare I write it – madness of others? I felt as if I were following in Victor's footsteps; the work here would either lead to great benefit or miserable destruction. Of the former, I prayed for all mankind to receive.

Ernest led the way to the entry where the wolfhound already stood. The professor, in an attempt to placate my raw emotions, patted me on the back. The structure took on an even more sinister appearance as we approached: The black doors were girded with iron beams, the windows laced with bars, a trio of gleaming rods rose from the roof like spikes on a Horseman's Axe.

"Not even Olivia knows of our work," Ernest said as he withdrew a large key from his coat pocket and placed it in the iron lock. He turned it, the bolt clicked and, with great effort for a young man of his strength, he pulled open the door.

Great God! What a scene lay before my eyes. I knew from Victor's confession what studies he had undertaken, the essence of the strange and harrowing life that led to his demise – his broken soul, its melancholy sweetness extinguished by an insatiable passion for the completion of his experiments. To see it carried out again by his younger brother sent shocks coursing through my body; yet, in my short acquaintance with Ernest I had no doubt of his quest to surpass his brother's reputation and somehow erase the loss of William, whose death hung over him like a curse. Victor had sworn never to reveal the secret of his creative process to any being, intent as he was upon protecting the world from the terrible power he had unleashed. Yet, Clerval had unwittingly released another Frankenstein upon the world! As soon as the massive entryway swung open, my suspicion that the monster knew of Ernest and Professor Waldman's work was confirmed; the dæmon was waiting with stealthy intelligence to carry out his own design for a mate. The devious creature would strike when his purpose required it. How simple it would be for him to let Ernest and Maximilian perform their tasks, observing from afar, through his heightened senses, their mistakes and victories, so he could strike with perfect impunity at the zenith of their powers. With these thoughts in mind, I doubled my intention to protect the mysterious book by Cornelius Agrippa, in order to assure our safety.

Large wooden crates from the University at Ingolstadt lined the walls. The contents of several were revealed: shining surgical instruments, salts of various bright colors, beakers, jars and other containers similar to those found in an apothecary's shop. A large coil, constructed of some bright luminous metal unknown to me, spilled from one of them. In the center of the room, an enormous wooden platform hung suspended over a vat resting upon the stone floor. A sickening yellowish blue liquid filled the vessel and dispensed an unpleasant acidic aroma into the air. Metallic lines, intertwined with rope, traced overhead like a spider's web but found their confluence above the platform, which rocked slightly when Ernest touched it, so delicate was its balance. At the far end of the room sat a silver metal container blackened at the bottom by flames, made even more mysterious by the barn's interior shadows which concealed its true nature. The ovoid shape, a generator of some kind, rose nearly to the ceiling, at which point circular tubes stemming from its base curved like hideous tentacles upward and then downward to the platform.

"How?" I asked, incredulous at the sight.

"We – Ernest and I with the aid of Victor's work," Maximilian said. "Of course, none of this could have been accomplished had it not been for the unfortunate Clerval." Maximilian's voice was filled with pride in his accomplishment. "Victor began construction of this laboratory in the months after Elizabeth's death, before he quitted Geneva to seek revenge upon his creation We cannot be certain what Victor had in mind when he began his work here. Revenge, perhaps, upon the dæmon who had murdered his wife."

"It's like a monstrous dream," I said. "Don't you understand why the creature has allowed you to live – all of us to live?"

"Of course," Ernest said. "We are in a race against the murderer and I intend, by heaven, to be heir of my brother's legacy. The monster wishes the same, but by allowing *us* to do the work. He has his own purpose in mind – a mate perhaps – and that is why he has allowed us to live. I think the creature distrusts his ability in the sciences."

I was astonished at the young man's confession and the strength of his determination. I was tempted to provoke my host regarding his assessment of the monster's predilection for science, but common sense prevailed and I held my tongue. As I surveyed the room's apparatus, I remembered Victor's words about my eagerness to ascertain the secret of his creation: "Learn from me, if not by my precepts, at least by my example, how dangerous the acquirement of knowledge, and how much happier that man is who believes his native town to be the world, than he who aspires to become greater than his nature will allow." I understood the wisdom of his words, heard and repeated, but I had yet to fully embrace them. My desire to secure the safety of Margaret and her family had driven me from London; but, if I looked deeply into my soul, my fascination with Victor's life had not waned, nor had my wish to see his creation perish.

"Your brother died a victim of his science," said I. "Victor pleaded with me on his deathbed to avoid the seduction of unbridled scientific passion and the sin of ambition. However, I understand the allure of his achievements – if they are used for the good of man."

"Of course," Ernest replied and removed his gloves. "That is why I contacted you. What better way to honor Victor's legacy, and avenge his death, than to destroy the fiend that killed him . . . and to create those who are better than his equal."

His words brought forth an overpowering sense of fear. "Be wary, Ernest," I said. "Much can go wrong."

Ernest sniffed at my concern and said, "We have no time for worry. Come, professor, we have work to do and the days are short. Walton, you are welcome to join us; if not, we will proceed without you."

I determined to remain an observer. Nothing I could have said or done would have dissuaded Ernest from his passionate endeavors. With the precision of a soldier, he began his tasks, and the professor followed with equal enthusiasm. I saw in Ernest the signs of the scientific curiosity and impatience displayed by his brother: Ernest's luminous blue eyes took on an expression of wildness, bordering on madness, as he began his work; yet, I was reminded that at breakfast his whole countenance had been consumed with joy at the sight of his son. I was not prepared to dismiss those merciful qualities of benevolence and sweetness residing in Ernest's soul which, if unabated, might dispel the ruder passions.

Ernest dragged a few logs from the shadows and arranged them around the metallic ovoid. He struck a fire and soon the air was filled with crackling heat and the hiss of steam. The tentacles above my head pulsed with energy and after a few minutes they dripped a continuous stream of blue liquid which flowed down the connecting lines to the vat under the platform. The warmth in the room, in stark contrast to the snowy hills surrounding us, increased sevenfold and I shed my winter coat, gloves and scarf. Ernest shouted orders to the dutiful professor who often corrected his younger charge in the correct placement of the scientific equipment and the timing of their work. I observed this scene with an odd mixture of curiosity and revulsion. I wrote you last summer, my dear Margaret, I would be cool, persevering and prudent in my journeys; but, again, I find myself drawn into the lair of the Frankensteins and the fantastic realms contained within it.

Ernest attached two of the connecting lines to the platform, whereupon the blue liquid flowed in gutters carved into the wood and then fell through holes as droplets into the vat. The young man then turned his attention to a large kas situated against the eastern wall. From the cabinet, he withdrew the body of a snow-white hare, as beautiful a woodland creature as I had ever seen. A circle of brownish-red blood spotted its mouth; whoever had killed the hare had done it quickly and cleanly with little damage to its tissues. The professor took the dead animal in his hands and placed it carefully in the center of the platform while Ernest hovered nearby with eyes that danced with excitement. The professor then took over the duties of the experiment while Ernest continued his observation.

"The placement and pressure of the lines is of the greatest importance," Maximilian instructed Ernest. The professor withdrew clamps from a nearby drawer and placed them on the tubes; he then inserted the end of the lines into a device resembling a syringe. The hare, its brown eyes dull and lifeless, lay like a white offering on the table. The professor opened the creature's mouth and, moving past the pinkish tongue and white teeth, pushed the instrument down the throat. The second needle was carefully introduced into one of the hare's long, hind limbs, the stiff creature as devoid of life as the slab on which it lay. At the professor's signal, Ernest unlocked each of the clamps in a series of timed bursts. This activity continued for several minutes until I observed a most wondrous change in the animal. A slight prickle in the fur crept over the hare, beginning at the top of the crown and by degrees descending to its hindquarters. It was as if an electric charge had entered the body and flowed through it encountering little resistance. As the silky white fur revived, thus did an equally astonishing effect transform the eyes: The dull brown vanished beneath a rising glimmer that overtook the pupils, ever-widening until the animal shook off its deathly lethargy and stared at us with intense fright. Ernest attempted to calm the hare as the creature's legs moved in a mechanically rhythmic motion.

"Now," Maximilian shouted, and the two men simultaneously pulled the syringes from the animal. To my great shock, the hare responded by rising on its shaky legs, then settled for a moment on its white stomach before jumping off the platform. The wolfhound, who had been curled near the fire under the ovoid container, rushed at the poor creature, but Ernest's sharp reprimand stopped the dog in her tracks. She backed away with a still wary eye on the hare.

"See," the professor said in a glorious burst of spirit, "we have achieved through chemical means what Victor knew was an inherent secret to life. Electrical stimulation may be a factor in the equation, but not the sole determinant. Let us see how long the hare lives."

I, who had been silent through their experiment, asked, "Was this the process Victor used?"

The hare took small jumps around the room, taking great care to keep away from the wolfhound.

Ernest looked in wonder at the creature and then turned to me. "Yes, in part. You know, of course, of Clerval?"

I nodded, fully aware of the tragic story of the man whom Victor had loved as a trusted friend and companion.

"Clerval and my brother traveled together before Victor settled in the Orkney Islands to create a mate for the monster – another misshapen creature he destroyed before he gave it life. While they traveled, Clerval, aware of the strain my brother endured, discovered and investigated Victor's writings. He copied them as best he could, when time permitted, and dispatched them to me as a record of his work. Clerval feared not for his life but for Victor's and wished his legacy to live on. How ironic he should die at the hands of the dæmon my brother created – and then for my brother to be imprisoned, accused of his best friend's murder!"

"We have expanded upon Victor's work," Maximilian said. "He understood the basic chemical and electrical properties, but had no time to study the magnitude of their implications. We are taking the single rose offered by Victor and attempting to turn it into a garden."

"Does the creature know you have Victor's journals?" I asked and a chill raced down my spine.

"He may suspect," Ernest said, "but they are secured and safe – as perhaps is the Agrippa." The young man stared at me intently. "If the dæmon is aware of what we do here, he cannot duplicate our work without a guide; therefore, he will keep us alive until he is certain that all the processes are in place – until we are assured of success."

"You place great faith in the creature's capacity for compassion," I said, aware that Ernest played a dangerous game with the monster.

Our conversation was interrupted by the professor's exhortations – he pointed to the hare. The pathetic animal had collapsed near the kas and vomited a stream of blue liquid upon the stone floor. We approached the twitching creature and watched as its limbs surrendered to death once again and the light in its eyes, by degrees, fell dark until extinguished.

"By God's grace," Maximilian said. "We shall succeed . . . but what element are we missing?"

Neither Ernest nor I could speak with any degree of certainty, so we stood by idly as the wiry professor leafed through Clerval's hand-written notes, searching for the answer.

We spent the better part of the day in the barn as Ernest and Maximilian experimented on other animals: a brown goat, a plump squirrel, a calico cat. My patience, and the determined enthusiasm of the others, was rewarded with sustained life, in particular the cat and the squirrel, which provided endless amusement for the wolfhound. Their antics caused such consternation that Ernest confined the two resurrected animals to cages where they, assured of their security, dropped into deep slumbers. By mid-afternoon the lowering sun had cast the barn into dark shadow, so we departed for Belrive. I left somewhat cheered by the success upon the animals; however, a lingering dread about the young man tempered my enthusiasm.

After Ernest secured the door, we walked toward the escarpment. Near its edge, the ever-observant dog turned her head and led us to a set of elongated footprints surrounding a stand of firs. The prints circled the trees several times and then led down an unknown path to the woods below. Ernest reached into his coat and withdrew a pistol. As we descended the cliff we regarded every shadow, observed every movement in the darkening woods because we knew the calculating vengeance of the murderous creature; fresh dangers awaited around every hillock.

ROBERT WALTON'S JOURNAL

Belrive, January 12th, 17—

My Dear Margaret, to you or any unintended reader, I issue a warning: Do not proceed with this journal unless you are able, beyond imagination, to surrender all belief in a rational world. The events of the past three days have strained credulity and tested the limits of my perseverance, as the family known as Frankenstein crumbles around me. The shock of this disaster has yet to settle in all our minds; yet, we are assaulted with horrors that seem to multiply with each terrible day.

Our return trip from the barn to Belrive, although oppressive because of the encroaching darkness and constant specter of the monster, was undertaken without incident. Ernest, in particular, seemed in bright spirits as we approached the safety of his country home with its cheery welcoming warmth and promise of a gracious evening of food and drink before retirement to a comfortable bed. The evening passed in good discourse and gentle civility before we bade each other good-night. My only unease during our repast occurred as I observed the beautiful features of Olivia as she attempted to preserve her manners as hostess while simultaneously acting as a nurse to her ailing son. The hacking coughs, which reached our ears from his nursery down the hall, had grown markedly worse during the day – a severe change from his condition at breakfast. Olivia discharged her duties as well she could: serving wine, making certain the platters were filled, encouraging all manner of conversation among her guests

77

She would rise, her black hair falling to the middle of her back, and judge the satisfaction of those gathered at her table. Her son's illness, however, took precedence over our needs. Olivia would run to him when his labored exhalations reached her attentive ears. Unfortunately, these coughing fits occurred several times during the evening. Her anguish took its toll – I noted that the luster of her eyes and her engaging smile faded as the night continued its march.

For my part, I had one important task to fulfill before sleep. *The Transmutation of Souls* lay concealed in my bag, too easy a target for the monster, or, for that matter, the ambitious brother of Victor Frankenstein. The volume would have to be concealed in a place of greater safety. My choices were twofold: to hide the book inside Belrive or find a suitable location on the surrounding grounds. Either choice offered its own risk. What if, by some twist of fate, Belrive was destroyed – and with it one of the two existing copies of Agrippa's work? I trusted not the monster – I had seen his terrible vengeance aboard my ship and knew of his predilection for sudden and swift catastrophe. An attack upon Belrive would likely destroy us all, and with it the Agrippa and perhaps even Clerval's copy of Victor's journals, for I was not privy to its hiding place. Likewise, to conceal the book on the grounds, I would risk detection by the monster's acute senses. The impossibility of the task caused me to despair; my thoughts were paralyzed by indecision. After much consideration, I decided upon the first choice, the second being too strained by peril.

After all had retired to their beds and the house was quiet save the noises that haunt all visitors in a foreign residence, I walked softly downstairs to the great room. During my conversations with Professor Waldman there, I had noted one flagstone about half-way up the fireplace that seemed out of kilter. If I could remove the stone and replace it without notice, I was certain the Agrippa would be protected from harm; the book would be high enough that the flames and smoke from below would have little effect upon it. A few minutes before midnight, I descended the staircase. I carried no lamp; only the stars and a half-moon conveyed light through the windows, casting hazy rectangular blocks upon the floor. As I approached the fireplace, an indistinct form rose before me and threw me into a start before

I realized I had disturbed the sleeping wolfhound. She, now familiar with me as a guest, raised no alarm, but observed me intently as I completed my task. The stone slipped out easily and I placed the Agrippa on its side and restored the structure to its undisturbed state. The whole incident took less than five minutes and I returned to my bed, assured of the book's safety.

Less than three hours later, I was awakened by a terrible scream that turned my blood cold. My heart pounding, I jumped from bed and gathered my dressing gown. Below, the wolfhound barked wildly amid the exhortations of the household. Above the din, I recognized the anguished sobs of Olivia; her cries echoed throughout Belrive, as agonized and tortured a sound as I had ever heard. Her pleas rent my heart with sadness.

"My child! My child! My little Wolfgang!" she screamed as if her very body would explode with grief.

I rushed downstairs to find Belrive's occupants fallen into a hush against Olivia's violent protests. In the far corner of the hall, surrounded by a circle of lamplight, I saw Olivia and her son enfolded in the arms of Ernest, who stared at her with disbelieving eyes and tear-stained cheeks. Olivia muttered words unintelligible to my ears and her husband drew her closer. Three others, Maximilian, the grief-stricken nurse and the Swiss servant stood in the doorway to Wolfgang's chamber. I approached softly, brushing past the wolfhound, and peered at Olivia. There, I saw the infant pressed against her, its body swathed in blankets; I knew the child was dead and a terrible emptiness washed over me. Unmitigated sadness scorched my soul – for I saw in the lifeless eyes the hapless form of any child taken by tragedy; his angelic face was caressed by the figure of Death, whose cold, bony fingers led the infant into the ever-lasting night. I thought of my niece and nephew and a chill shook me; I resisted the imagining of such a tragic scene knowing the safety of my dear sister's children was secured in London.

No words need be spoken, no verses written upon the death of a child, our grief is so great; however, after Olivia had been led to her bedroom and the fire stoked, I extended my sympathies. She sat on her bed, with the child in her lap as if guarding a treasure of precious jewels.

"I offer my aid in your time of sorrow," I told Olivia, whose incoherent manner belied any awareness of my presence. She swiped at her eyes and then dragged her fingers across the bedcovers. Ernest, who sat nearby in one of the opulent gilt chairs, rose in fury at my condolence, his passions equal to any I had observed from the monster.

"My son *will not die!*" he shouted with reddened face, the veins on his temples throbbing with anger. Olivia moaned, uttered a great sob and then covered her eyes with her hands. Ernest rushed for the infant and pulled the body away from his distraught wife.

I withdrew to the door, in respect for his grief rather than fear, and stood staring at the fire, stunned into silence by his emotions.

"He must not die," he repeated like a psalm until at last he sat again in his chair. With each remonstration, his voice fell until it barely rose above a whisper. The young wet-nurse huddled near her mistress and shook with each of Ernest's exclamations.

Olivia rose from her bed with balled fists and directed her fury at her husband, "Our son *is* dead!" She glared at Ernest and then collapsed on the floor next to the sobbing nurse. The young man placed the dead child on the bed and with the fortitude of a soldier, walked to his wife with raised hand. I cannot describe my horror at what I was witnessing, an intimacy too bald and tumultuous for anyone not of the family.

Maximilian took hold of Ernest's arm and muttered, "Ernest, really . . . ," It was all he could say before he was shoved away.

"Leave us," Ernest commanded. "You are guests in my home, not its owners. Nurse, procure a sedative for my wife."

Maximilian and I left the room. We spoke not as we ascended the stairs, for as witnesses to the drama below, we were shocked by our observations, as well as the terrible implication suggested by the distorted mind of Ernest Frankenstein.

The night passed in somber desolation; by fate's decree was I thrust again into the garden of gloom and despondency cultivated by the family Frankenstein. I might have quit the household the following morn, had I not been convinced the monster was aware of my every step at Belrive. He would display little sympathy for my plight or the family's grief in his quest for the Agrippa. Throughout the long hours until dawn, I tossed and turned in my bed while a soft moaning reached my ears – as if a mournful ghost walked the halls. The pathetic sound abated at last when the first gray light pressed against my window and, for a short time, the house was blissfully silent, until the Swiss serving man stirred below.

Neither Ernest nor Olivia joined the professor or me at breakfast. Maximilian displayed a countenance of the deepest melancholy and we exchanged little communication at the table; this suffocating atmosphere prevailed in the great room as I dutifully tended the fire for the servant (for I had little else to do) and the professor smoked his pipe and took up his pen and notebook.

When the Frankensteins emerged from their chambers, the clock was poised at eleven. Olivia's beauty was hidden by a dress of the deepest black capped by an ebony veil which covered her comely face. Ernest wore a jacket of military cut pinned with regalia and ribbons. He escorted his wife, both gliding like spirits, across the great room to a side parlor where they sat, unmoving, as stiff as subjects posing for a portraitist. Within a few minutes, the manservant answered a vigorous knock at the door. A thin, bearded man, whom I thought to be a priest, was welcomed into the house and he made his way to the frozen figures without as much as a nod to Maximilian or me. The scene would have passed as one of mournful humility and suffering had it not been for one peculiar occurrence. Immediately upon the visitor's arrival in the room, Olivia fell to her knees, as if in supplication. Ernest, aware perhaps of my acute attention to their distress, rose to close a panel of French doors, thus concealing their intimacies from the professor and me. In the instant before the doors were drawn, I observed, through the opening, the man offer Ernest an object which he had withdrawn from his coat. My eyes were focused, my senses acute; and, I was certain the visitor presented my host with a book – of what kind I could not say – perhaps a small Holy Bible for comfort on the death of little Wolfgang – but Ernest, with trembling fingers, slipped the man gold coins. It was nearly the half-hour before the doors opened again and the trio stood facing the great room. The professor and I had scarcely moved from our seats during this scene – I only to pet the obedient wolfhound and Maximilian to procure more tobacco. At one point during our hosts' encounter, an argument erupted in which Olivia's strangled voice and Ernest's reproachful cries filled the room. Then, all was silent before the doors opened.

Ernest imparted the somber funereal news as Olivia lagged behind, supported by the indolent visitor. There was something terribly appalling about the sight of our host whose tone and demeanor reflected an utter refusal to accept his son's death, while the beautiful Olivia struggled to stand.

"Burial will be at the stroke of noon," Ernest said with a flatness of voice even I could not fathom, considering the circumstances. "We shall gather at the crypt by the lake shore." And with that, the trio retreated to another chamber leaving the stunned professor and me with the wolfhound.

"This is highly unusual – the interment so soon," the professor said, and then sighed. "Perhaps I should make an attempt to produce mourning clothes – not that I carried any from Ingolstadt."

I regarded my own situation; I had no suitable garments in my bag – only the dark jacket I had worn under my greatcoat. Twenty minutes remained before the funeral, so the professor and I bade each other good-bye and ascended to our rooms. I combed my hair, splashed water from the basin on my face and donned my jacket. These small preparations were the most I could muster to honor the dead child and his family. The house was empty when I descended the stairs a short time later, but from the windows in the great room I saw a cluster of black figures huddled near the frigid waters of Lake Geneva. I opened the door leading to the terrace and followed the snowy trail before me. The wind had freshened from the south-west and a warm, almost spring-like, breeze took the chill away. Low, rolling clouds scudded overhead; the sun patterned the white trail with brilliant points of light that shifted in the blink of an eye into deep shadows. What did the day portend? The wind, the warmth from the southern climes, foretold stormy occurrences at Belrive.

When I arrived at the lake, the family, the servants, Maximilian and the stranger were gathered at a small marble crypt which rose on a gentle slope that afforded a magnificent view of the frosted shore and the sparkling blue waters beyond. I assumed Wolfgang's resting place had been hastily constructed by the servant; no other burial trappings were in sight. The simple structure consisted of nothing more than a stone rectangle placed upon the winter-hardened ground. A white cross had been scratched into the marble lid and six white roses, one for each month of his life, lay strewn across it. Here, little Wolfgang, would slumber for eternity. In the calm of the moment, I could think of no better place to rest while he awaited his heavenly ascent.

The service, such as it was, was blessedly brief; the infant had been taken from the home and placed in the crypt sometime in the morning, unbeknownst to Maximilian and myself. Ernest spoke a few words – barely intelligible to me – while the male visitor stood silently by Olivia. The lack of ceremony and the brief time before burial struck me as odd, but being unfamiliar with whatever faith the family followed, I could not judge. Upon consideration it was a blessing, for I believe Olivia would have collapsed under the strain of her grief had the service continued at great length. Ernest spoke his final words, nodded and the entire party left the site to return to the house. Olivia retired to her chamber, while Ernest, Maximilian and I ate a frugal meal with the bearded visitor, who departed after a hushed conversation with our host. Ernest then excused himself for the remainder of the day and neither the professor nor I had any further discourse with the young man. The two of us entertained ourselves in the great room – the professor writing in his journal (with an occasional conversation on some topic of science or exploration) and I tending the fire, browsing books from the family library and enjoying the company of the wolfhound while the servant attended to our every need. At one point, as the sun vanished behind the western hills, the professor touched my arm and pointed toward the window that looked out upon the lake. We both started, for we exclaimed to each other we had seen a beautiful phantom – the lovely form of Olivia clothed in black, wending her way on the path that led to the crypt. We never saw her return to Belrive. After a solitary supper and a long, strange evening in the dismal atmosphere, the professor and I, after our good-nights, retired to our rooms.

83

Belrive, January 15th, 17–

Here my tale takes a fantastic and catastrophic twist I would never have imagined or deemed possible had I not witnessed the horrific events with my own eyes. I swear to you, Margaret, by all that is sacred, that what I record in this journal is the truth, although you may believe I have lost my senses under the devilish influence of Frankenstein.

Sometime after two in the morning the day after the burial, I was awakened by a soft laughter which filtered through my window on the second storey. I started from my bed and looking out on the icy but darkened landscape, I caught sight of a woman standing under the sheltering branches of a large fir. I immediately recognized the figure as Olivia Frankenstein; she could not conceal her ravishing beauty even in the shadows of night. She hummed a song, an innocent tune like a children's amusement, as she stroked the branches of the evergreen. An odd light struck her eyes, and she tilted her head upwards, smiling and pointing at my window, as if she recognized my figure at the casement. She beckoned to me and I hesitated to call out for fear of waking the household. She wore a thin white nightgown and no shoes; her feet were covered to her ankles in snow. Ernest was not in her presence. I knew their rooms were on the other side of Belrive adjacent to the chamber where Wolfgang had died; thus, there was little chance Ernest knew the whereabouts of his wife unless he was in her company, but the young man was nowhere to be seen.

I feared for Olivia's well-being, but some distinction in her countenance gave me pause, as if she sought me out, the way someone mad appears to focus their attention on an individual rather than the crowd around them. The light that suffused her eyes, her slight laugh, beckoned me. What possessed her to be standing in the freezing night at this devilish hour? Why did she call to me? Perchance she *was* mad with grief, or perhaps she played a childish game, but that reason seemed unlikely – I judged her to be roughly equivalent to Ernest in age, but in my short time at Belrive I had seen little joy or playful animation in her face.

I dressed quickly in my day clothes and greatcoat, descended the stairs (past the slumbering wolfhound who slept near the dying fireplace embers), taking care not to disturb the others. I soon found myself on the terrace staring at naked footprints in the snow. Olivia had departed from the shelter of the tree, but I was able to track her movements. Despite the appalling hour and depth of the night, she had followed with great ease the trail laid the previous morning to little Wolfgang's grave. In my haste, I had neglected to procure a lamp, but the heavens and its roiling clouds were bathed in an eerie red glow cast by the moon's sulky husk and the dusky stars. From whence the light came I knew not, but its qualities reminded me of a lunar eclipse I had witnessed many years ago near the Southern Cape. Under this strange and astonishing circumstance, on this wild and eerie night, I pursued Ernest's wife. As the path dropped toward the lake, I caught sight of Olivia, her white-clad figure fleeing from her son's crypt.

What horror I found at the scene! The white roses lay shredded in the snow, their broken stems and petals scattered as if by demonic hands. But the crypt! The marble covering was fractured, the tiny wooden coffin torn apart and the body of little Wolfgang gone missing. As I gazed in disbelief, the tinkling laugh of Olivia drifted to my ears and I watched as she peered at me from around a tree and then disappeared into the dark forest. With this, I was certain Ernest's young and beautiful wife had jumped from the precipice of sanity into madness. What woman could bear such horrors – from the death of the child to the grave's desecration?

Leaving the terrible scene behind, I followed Olivia into the shadowy depths, marveling at how swiftly she navigated her way through the firs and bare branches that blocked an easy journey. Her path took her to the north of Belrive and then to the western hills, up the escarpment where Ernest, Maximilian and I ascended to the barn and where the professor and the young man had conducted their laboratory experiments. I arrived at the plateau in time to see Olivia swing open the massive oak doors.

Again, I was unprepared for what was to unfold before my eyes. The barn stood under the reddish light of the moon and stars, but a blue, electric glare poured forth from its barred windows. A river of white steam rose from the chimney and swirled away in the gusting wind. The door stood open as I approached; I knew not what hideous experiments were in progress, but as I stood at the entrance my heart raced at the sight within.

There, bent over the lifeless body of the infant was Ernest Frankenstein!

His face took on a sickening cast in the garish light, which was fueled by the ovoid's rumblings at the end of the room. Consumed by his work, Ernest paid no attention to his tormented wife, her gown wet and torn by her nocturnal perambulations, who stood shivering a few yards away from his hideous task. Sparks coursed through the lines and tentacles above his head, illuminating the interior with its ghastly glow. Ernest, quite unaware of my presence at the door, grimaced as he viewed the body of his infant son. Olivia collapsed near the kas, sobbing in her overwhelming grief; but her exhortations came, I judged, not from horror but from her mind's dissolution. Ernest continued his fiendish work as I watched, attaching the lines of flowing blue liquid to the infant's mouth and muddy right leg, exactly as I had observed during the experiment on the hare. To my amazement, my host withdrew a thin book from his garments and began to read mournful incantations over the body of little Wolfgang. At precise intervals, he abandoned his words, and, stretching his arms as best he could, opened the clamps attached to the lines, just as he and the professor had earlier demonstrated. This process, he repeated for several minutes, while the sobbing Olivia turned her gaze upward as if seeking an intercession from heaven. I stepped inside and the sweltering warmth from the fire swept over me; I walked on silent feet, Ernest and Olivia absorbed in their particular worlds.

I cannot describe the emotions that washed over me as I watched Ernest work upon the innocent who lay sprawled upon the slab. In viewing the tiny face, I was thrust back in time to the infancy of my sister's children, particularly the birth of my sweet nephew, David. At birth, how like an angel he had appeared: fine black hair, ruddy cheeks, a happy child savoring the attention of his mother while tottering on the verge of sleep. Here, likewise a child lay, but not in a cradle of dreams, but in the embrace of Death himself. I was horrified by the scene before me; yet, I understood the mad desire of the father to resurrect his dead son – but the price paid was too high, as witnessed by the wretched moans of Olivia. I could have flung myself at the madman, but what remorse would I suffer if he should succeed in his task? Was I to observe a cataclysmic change in the course of history, as Ernest indicated in his invitation to me?

In one terrible moment, a solitary electric flash rent the structure and sparked down the line to the wooden slab. As this fantastic event occurred, Ernest withdrew his hands and shouted a wild and incoherent utterance over the infant's corpse. For a moment, the young man blocked my view of the child; however, a few seconds after the words left his lips, he started in surprise. Olivia screamed and then covered her mouth with her hands. The glare faded and the room grew oddly silent except for the hiss and gurgle of the steam generated by the ovoid. Agitated as I was by the strange and wondrous scene before me, I could no longer control my emotions. The child lay as dead upon the slab as when he was ripped from the grave.

"Wretch," I shouted, "how dare you desecrate the grave of an innocent!"

Ernest wheeled, a hellish fury unleashed in his gaze; his gory hands clutched the book. "You would have me inter my son, to lie in the cold and unforgiving ground forever, when he can yet live? What a fool you are, Walton. Look for yourself." His anger abated for a moment and he stepped aside from the platform and bade me view the infant. Olivia rose and walked toward us, but the taint of madness swirled in her eyes.

I crept to the platform and bent over the baby boy, keeping a wary eye upon his father. Little Wolfgang's naked body lay sprawled upon the slab, his skin as white as the snow that covered the fields surrounding us, his lips a deathly blue, his blond feathery lashes resting upon eyes sealed by eternal rest.

"You have failed and despoiled a child," I said with unbridled disgust.

Olivia wiped her tears and stared at the infant, as if she bore unfathomable sorrows. Ernest started at her and said, "Move away, wife, this is not for your eyes."

His words were cut short by the strangled, hacking coughs of the boy. I looked in shock upon Wolfgang whose blue eyes fluttered open in agitation; his small hands stabbed at the air and his legs kicked wildly.

"You see, Walton, I have not failed," Ernest said, and swept his hand in a self-gratifying circle over the infant. "I have saved my son's life and altered mankind's legacy forever. The world will bow to Ernest Frankenstein."

I was about to reply to his grandiose assertion, when the infant rose on its hands and knees and leapt upon his mother's breast with a vicious intent to feed. Olivia screamed and batted at her child as the infant bit and clawed. Blood poured forth from the bites on her breast and the lacerations on her neck. The terrified young woman fell backwards on the floor, thrashing and sobbing in utter desolation and, then, as if resigned to death, her eyes rolling upward, abated her struggle. Her resignation only enlivened her mewling progeny to rip and tear at her face and gown, until she fell silent, battered and bleeding upon the cold stones.

"See what you have unleashed," I shouted at Ernest. "I begged you to be cautious–"

Ernest recoiled in horror. "–the words . . . Agrippa's words have brought this about. *This soul is evil* . . . ."

Ernest had obtained the second Agrippa; I recalled the small volume the visitor had passed to him the morning of the burial. But in Ernest's hands, the power had gone horribly wrong.

He rushed to Olivia's side and pulled the squealing infant from its mother. The child thrashed with unmitigated fury against him, and Ernest struggled to hold the demonic thing who twisted and bit at the air and would have struck at both of us had we been within reach of his short grasp.

Behind us, the door burst open and a blast of air rushed over us. We both turned to see the gigantic monster, whose face was alight with the recognition of Wolfgang's resurrection.

"Fiend!" Ernest scowled as his son wriggled out of his hands and rushed toward the monster. The creature's distracted attention to the mewling infant allowed Ernest to withdraw his loaded pistol from his coat, aim and fire. The ball smashed into the creature's shoulder with a dull sound, causing him to stumble backwards; his sallow face registered his shock when the missile struck. His hideous jaws opened revealing ragged, pearly teeth and dark tongue, and his terrible howl filled the room.

Ernest shouted oaths at the monster and attempted a second shot. There was no time for the young man to reload; the fiend gathered the infant in his arms and fled through the open door. Before he disappeared into the enveloping night, he turned, held the boy in front of him and said, "Behold, the child I will cherish and protect – who lives by my father's legacy. Ernest has magnified my joy by continuing his brother's work. How much I have learned from him and the good professor from Ingolstadt. All that was missing was the Agrippa – we shall see how the scene plays out!"

Thereupon, he lowered little Wolfgang into the snow. The infant snapped, glared and issued a hideous howl not unlike the call of a wolf, and, then, on all fours, struck out across the ground with hellish speed before vanishing into the shadows. The creature gritted his teeth, pulled the ball from his left shoulder and threw it upon the ground; thereupon, he followed the infant and was soon lost in the distance and darkness.

The fire surrendered its strength to the ovoid and its rumble faded with the dying flames. Ernest looked at me with great sadness, but said nothing as he gathered the prostrate form of Olivia in his arms and carried her out of the barn and home to Belrive.

ROBERT WALTON'S JOURNAL

Belrive, January 15ᵗʰ, 17—

What utter despondency fell upon the house of Frankenstein The catastrophe was complete. With the demonic resurrection and loss of little Wolfgang, Olivia and Ernest descended into madness. I observed the full extent of their wretchedness during the terrible evening, but not until dawn broke and my senses could affirm what I had witnessed, could I weigh the pathetic conditions overwhelming my hosts. The night had passed fitfully: I was awakened by every creak and moan, and the terrifying countenance of the infant rushed into my memory. I was dizzy with the remembrance of the events in the barn. I hardly knew whether I had the courage to describe it, my fevered mind was so filled with the terrible scene.

As I descended the staircase to breakfast, I looked upon the leaden lake and pondered how I might express my sympathy to the grieving couple. Ernest stood on the terrace looking toward the water and I debated whether to interrupt his reverie. After some consideration, and seeing no one else in the house, I gathered my fortitude and opened the door. He scarcely granted me a look and then continued his sullen gaze to the east. The warm winds of the past two days had been replaced by an icy blast from the north-west; gray clouds hung over Belrive like a frigid marble slab, as oppressive and dark as the owner's spirit. I stood next to him and placed my hand upon his shoulder; he shivered slightly and turned to me. I had half-expected him to attack, his grief swollen by anger; instead, a line of tears fell from his glistening eyes.

"You called my brother friend," he said to me in a trembling voice barely above a whisper. "You must help me, Walton . . . you must *save* me . . . and my family. This madness is tearing me apart." As he spoke, his young face contorted in agony and chocking spasms of despair shook his body. "If you love the name of Frankenstein, you will see to our safety. Do you not understand the depth of my sorrow? I was the one who accompanied my younger brother William on his last walk before his death at the hands of the fiend. Every day the sun rises I am swamped by guilt and remorse, all to be laid at the feet of that monstrous creature. Now, he has control of my own son. I will search him out and destroy him."

I was taken aback by this emotional display; yet, I knew Ernest had brought this tragedy upon himself. "I am grieved beyond words for your loss," I countered. "I will do what I can to alleviate your suffering."

"Then," he said, a mad fire flickering through his eyes, "you will help me track and destroy this murderer – this foul beast who destroyed my family and kidnapped my son. Now, I fear for Clivia. She slept not last night, so consumed was she with her child and the horrible visage of the creature. When I looked into her eyes this morning it was as if I were looking into the void."

I released my hold upon his shoulder, taken in by the power of his words. "Ernest," I said, with sympathy for the condition of my host, "you are aware of my desire to avenge your brother's death, but the creature holds your son. Your plan must be carried out carefully, or surely Olivia will tumble over the edge."

All semblance of calm fell away with my plea and he stood before me, unleashing his agitation like a volcano bursting forth, his face charged with an expression of the wildest rage. "He has taken my son for his evil intent," he shouted, "and he will destroy my Olivia!" With those words, he collapsed, sobbing, upon the snow-covered ground. "I fear she has already consorted with the monster in her wanderings."

I was shocked by this admission, but stood over him while he wept; and, after a time, his cries turned to a cackling laughter.

"We will destroy him, Walton – if it takes an army – you and I will create an army to assure his destruction. We will avenge my brother's death, take our sweet revenge in the name of Frankenstein and, thereafter, conquer greater worlds. Then my name will be vindicated."

"Ernest . . ." I said, and then thought better of continuing our discourse. Better to leave it for a time of consolation, solitude and calm. I drew upon one hope – I had reveled in the gentle manners of Victor despite his frequent and violent imprecations upon his creation. I, above all men, with perhaps the exception of Clerval, was able to find the good in my departed friend's soul. I wished the same goodness, with utmost desire, for Ernest and his beautiful wife.

The morning passed with the inexorable clouds strangling Belrive. Even the cheery fireplace appeared dull in the cold and gray, the manservant being the sole member who offered any warmth in the household. He called us to breakfast and Maximilian was the first to sit, his appetite unaffected by the night's events. Ernest, melancholy and despairing, sat across from me, and barely touched his meal, then departed with an abrupt bow, leaving Maximilian and me alone at the table. The professor and I conversed about the weather and other innocuous subjects until we were interrupted by great sobbing cries which filled the room. The light of recognition dawned early, for we knew the originator of the anguished sobs could be none other than Olivia. As quickly as the exhortations had arisen, they dissolved into the ether, but were soon followed by violent crashing sounds: breaking glass – smashed upon the walls and floor. Even the redoubtable wolfhound lifted her head and peered with agitated eyes toward the harrowing noise.

"Madness lives in this house," Maximilian said and put aside his napkin. He rummaged in his coat pocket for his pipe. "I suspect she is already gone – there may be no other hope than the asylum."

I shuddered at his diagnosis; yet, I knew his words bore the truth. "I fear for the family," I added, and the professor nodded, a consensus achieved without argument. I soon discovered the reason behind the professor's ardor for his hearty breakfast: He was blissfully unaware of what had transpired in the barn. His amazement grew in magnitude as I recounted the evening's events beginning with Olivia's appearance outside my window, Ernest's use of the Agrippa and the disappearance of the creature and the infant.

"Now, I am convinced of the woman's madness," he said. "What mother would not be driven to the brink by such horrors?" He rose from the table and summoned me to the great room, where he tamped his pipe and we sat looking out upon the steely lake. After a few puffs, he said, "Walton, I know not how much longer I can abide this house. If I were not in such an untenable position, I would have left weeks ago." His comment did not surprise me; his manner throughout the days since we had met had been dignified and reserved, yet I detected an anxious spirit. "And the truth be known, Ernest is on the verge himself – all the devils of Hades seem to haunt him." He stopped and stared at me with resolve. "There is more, much more, than Ernest is telling you, or for that matter, either of us."

"How so?"

"Ernest called me to Belrive under the pretext of examining Victor's work – the journals copied by Clerval." He relaxed for a moment and sank back into his chair, but when he continued a burning urgency filled his voice. "I had no idea Victor had stored such materials here – the tools he discovered for the creation of life. I was, of course, fascinated by the opportunity to study the work of my best student, who had taken my theories beyond my wildest imagination. In a few scant years, Victor transformed the work of doctors and metaphysicians who had struggled for centuries. Yet, Ernest wants to achieve more than his brilliant brother. He, like many of those with affection for the military, burns with a patriotic fervor. However, such a simple explanation would not do him justice. He is intent upon besting Victor's reputation and he is consumed with guilt over the death of his brother, William. How the events of last night must have shaken him. But Ernest is sly and resourceful . . . very sly, and I succumbed to his entreaties. His love for the military was unbeknownst to me until I arrived in Geneva. This obsession fosters a hardness that offers little tolerance for the failings of others." He blew smoky circles toward the fireplace while I waited upon his tale.

"Ernest offered to pay me handsomely to stay at Belrive during the winter, and when the University balked at my intended leave, he dug deeply into the family coffers. I don't know if you are aware, Walton, but Victor and Ernest's father, Alphonse, was a rich man – a frugal Swiss who lived considerably below his means."

I shook my head and waited with anticipation for the professor's revelations. Victor had not revealed all to me.

"My decision to come here was not without discord, and my severed relationships with the University were less than amicable. After I arrived, Ernest displayed his true temptations. I took what I could of my professorial resources and transferred them to the laboratory. In long hours against the failing light and cold draughts, I studied Victor's writings and compared them against the wisdom of the ancients and my own studies. Victor was so advanced, even I was humbled by his genius. I imparted what I learned to Ernest and the change in his countenance was swift and recognizable. The anxiety that had plagued him since my arrival dissipated; it was replaced by the energy of ten men. That was when the true work began, and, with it, the corresponding destruction of his family."

Another blood-curdling cry from the depths of the house rent the great room and the professor and I stared at each other glumly. A few shouts were exchanged, and then we heard Ernest call out to his servant. Soon, footsteps echoed through the hall, followed by the hurried slam of the oak door.

Maximilian continued: "In the beginning, we tested Victor's principles on the lesser species – worms, spiders, insects that might be available for our experimentation – but you see how far Ernest has taken them. I wanted to believe he was an eccentric bystander, a novice follower of science, a young man bored with his life; but, a mad passion has fueled his work. His obsession took its toll on Olivia and the baby. He resented her questions about his absence; he would disappear into his study – lock himself away for hours with his books and Victor's writings, all the while demanding that I carry on the experiments. Some days he barely touched his son, only to give him a quick pat in the morning; less devotion than he showered upon the dog. Olivia would tend to Wolfgang, and then take long walks in the afternoon. Where she traveled I cannot say, but often she was gone for hours. When the child became ill, I understood, without a word being spoken, that if the boy died, he would become a subject in our experimentation. I resisted such temptation and reacted with cold indifference to any mention of such work, stated or implied.

"One cold night, after returning from the barn, I found Ernest asleep at his desk. He had fallen prey to the evening and slumbered over his own journal. I could not help but read his transcriptions, which filled me at first with horror – before I questioned the sanity of his musings – I took them as the ramblings of a naïve young man, whose aspirations were equal to that of a child who wishes for extravagant presents."

Maximilian stopped and returned to his pipe which had grown cold. I could barely contain my curiosity. "Tell me, what did he write?"

"He wrote of an army . . . an army of creatures that could defeat the French and rule the world, with Ernest as their benevolent king."

"Defeat Bonaparte and the Directory?" I asked in a whisper, subduing my incredulity at this revelation. An army of monsters was beyond any sane man's dreams; however, my mind raced back to Ernest's entreaties of the early morning.

Maximilian looked at me and smiled. "I know what you are thinking, Walton. My exact thought when I read his journal. '*He is mad.*' And here is the other secret only you shall be privy to. I have purposefully delayed our work. Even I could not conceive of our astounding discoveries at the laboratory. Ernest is far beyond woodland creatures – and the terrible proof lies in what you beheld last night. We *can* bring back the dead. And, most frightening of all, I now believe that Ernest has the power to fulfill his dream."

I sat, stupefied, with nothing to say for several minutes. I cannot describe, my dear Margaret, the sensations that washed over me at the prospect of Ernest's insane plan of a monstrous force; my disgust was tempered, however, by the achievements the professor and the young man had accomplished at Belrive. If, indeed, they had discovered the secret to eternal life, would not the world rejoice? Would not the cessation of death – the triumph of day over night – be the greatest victory ever wrought by mankind? But with discovery comes responsibility – would this power, in the hands of its purveyors, be used for good or evil? My conscious dictated the choice I could accept.

"Is Ernest continuing his experiments today?" I asked.

"Most certainly," the professor replied, with an air of indolence. I must have registered some degree of shock for Maximilian rose, tapped the ashes of his pipe into the fireplace and then said, "I fear Ernest may no longer need us." He turned toward the window and looked upon the gray lake. "So you can see, Walton, the precarious position I have placed myself in, with no monetary support other than our young benefactor. You also chose to come to Belrive; your action rests upon your head."

His words stung me and I rose from my chair, agitated by the thoughts coursing through my brain. "Either Ernest or the dæmon may unleash forces the world has never beheld – or be able to conquer. We are in dire straits, professor."

"We are, Walton. The creature has spared us while we conducted our experiments; he now knows the extent of our abilities. He may look upon our lives with less favor now that Ernest has created life; certainly, the monster's desires extend far beyond beneficence to mankind."

"Correct, professor," I said, and momentarily assessed Ernest's accomplishments. "However, something went awry with the infant." I recalled Ernest's shock as he struggled with Wolfgang, *"This soul is evil . . . ."* "The words Ernest read over Wolfgang from the Agrippa must have been altered; or the book is a poor copy of the original." I paced in front of the fireplace before muttering, "If chemistry animates the body, the Agrippa animates the soul."

The professor, consumed with his pipe, halted his task abruptly and looked at me with inquisitive eyes. "You may be an adventurer, Walton, but you have a natural affinity for the sciences. If you dare admit it, you own the true book," he said. "The one Ernest holds *must* be false. He will not rest until he procures yours. Rest assured, he will obtain it through his cunning."

I smiled at the professor and gazed upon the flagstone which concealed my copy of *The Transmutation of Souls*. "I thank you, professor. I will take your expression of my worth as a compliment." And with that, I left him in the great room with the wolfhound as his sole companion. In my bed chamber, I looked out upon the snowy terrace that led to the lake and I saw the sad form of Olivia disappear into the forest. I made up my mind to follow her without letting the others know, and I made haste, for the early nightfall of January would impede my efforts.

ROBERT WALTON'S JOURNAL

Belrive, January 17th, 17—

My beloved sister, you would no doubt rejoice to learn that no disaster has yet befallen me, although with each step I take at Belrive a deep foreboding underscores my actions. Know your dear brother is guided by courage and resolution, while those around him descend into deepest despair. I hope to return to England soon, but, until I do, this journal must serve as a record of the history of Ernest Frankenstein and the unfolding tragedies smitten upon his family.

A cold rain had begun to fall when I left the house in search of Olivia. Armed with a pistol I secured from the manservant, and protected from the winter elements by my greatcoat, I descended the staircase. I knew the weapon would have little effect upon the creature, but, none-the-less, its presence calmed my agitated mind. As no one else was to be found, I called the wolfhound to my side – the dog was grateful and leapt about, nearly knocking me to the ground upon its release from the home. Snowy tracks led down the terrace to the final resting place of little Wolfgang, but I had no desire to revisit the site or speculate upon the whereabouts of the sweet infant who had been transformed into such a hellish creature. The wolfhound, sensing my task, led the way into the forest. Remembering Ernest's description of his encounter with the dæmon and the events of the previous night, I wondered if Olivia, despite her instability, had instituted a search for her son and the creature who vowed to protect him. The dog and I ventured into the dark woods north of the house; I was convinced the malevolent being had fashioned a home in the forest; Victor had described the monster's former dwellings in his tale. As I descended deeper into the woods, I also speculated upon why Ernest had not pursued the creature himself: perhaps he doubted his ability to kill the monster, perhaps he was too absorbed in his work or he harbored some strange devotion to his brother's creation. None of these explanations struck me as particularly plausible, except for a final thought, which filled me with dread: Could he somehow usurp the monster's power and use it for his benefit? Imagine a general of the creature's strength and size in command of an army of Ernest's making. Such speculation chilled me to the bone.

The woods closed around me as I walked through the white depths, slashed by the dark trunks of firs and covered by a canopy of deep green boughs. The snow crunched underneath my feet, sending out a warning to the beasts of the forest. I stepped over the tracks of deer, rabbit and other small animals, their prints filled with rain and melting ice. Alongside these trails, I followed the small, delicate footsteps of a woman – Olivia! I was filled with concern for her safety, uncertain of her path, or whether, on some perverse whim, the monster might drag her into his lair.

After a half-hour of hiking, I came to a small stream. There, Olivia's footprints vanished into the swiftly flowing water and I despaired of finding her. The wolfhound, however, bounded forward along the cold damp rocks, drenched by the mist, until she stopped in front of a row of boulders that marked a bend in the rushing water. I could see nothing in the semi-darkness but the branches which brushed over the rocks and blocked any encroaching light from above. The wolfhound suddenly slouched into a crawl and crept forward in a manner similar to the one I had witnessed when the Inuit dog encountered the dæmon. I leaned forward, peering into the murky depths, and without warning, found myself snatched across the water by rough hands of enormous strength. Thereafter, I knew my salvation was in God's hands because I was in the monster's clutches. I emerged on the other side of the stream, choking and sputtering, with massive fingers encircling my neck.

"Walton," he said gruffly, as I stood in the shadow of his gigantic cloaked figure. "We meet again under different circumstances. Thou didst desert me on your burning vessel. I would have dispatched you earlier if not for your claim of my father's knowledge. However, adventure never leaves your blood, and I knew thou wouldst, in some manner, lead me to his journals."

He released his grip, grabbed my coat collar and pushed me through the prickly branches of the firs. "I am sorry you did not die and end our misery," I said and attempted to reach beneath my coat for the pistol. The creature grabbed my hand in anticipation of my scheme and wrested the weapon from my waistband.

"This will do you no good," he said, and threw the pistol through the boughs. I heard it snap the concealing branches and splash into the stream beyond. "Hear me out before you plot your revenge; remember, I could have killed you now with ease. I made a promise to you and my creator."

"I thank you for your kindness," I said with little enthusiasm. He responded by pushing me through the forest until a crudely constructed dwelling of logs and sticks appeared in front of us. Misty vapors rose from the hovel and wound through the branches before evaporating into the slate sky. The door to the cabin was ajar and a pungent odor of smoke and putrefaction leaked from its opening. I steeled myself against the vile smell and stepped inside.

There, on the straw floor, was Olivia, her despondent form bent over a small fire in the dwelling's center. Her raven hair was matted and unkempt, and when she lifted her head, her emerald eyes glistened with tears. She was wrapped in a flowing black coat and started at my sudden entry, but despite her surprise, her delicate hands remained clutched as if in prayer. The creature stood by my side, and then with a sweep of his hand bade me to sit on the straw. I positioned myself near the door, away from the carcass of a stag that had been recently gutted.

"Thou didst leave me to die on your vessel," the monster said, and sat next to the trembling Olivia.

"Mr. Sparrow saw to that," I said. "You drove him mad. He paid with his life, as did my crew."

"Your crew deserted your ship; they chose to die upon the ice."

"Rather than at your hands," I countered.

"I am sorry for their deaths. I killed only those who would have killed me. In the months that have followed, I have attempted to subdue the beast within me – and I have found one who has sustained my efforts." With those words, he smiled at Olivia and then continued, "The bones of your crew and the ashes of my father are now scattered in the north. I was fortunate to survive near the Inuit camp and make my way to France in the bowels of another ship. I lived for days upon the refuse of the crew."

So, the monster had not visited London; some relief washed over me as the safety of Margaret and her family was assured. "Why did you not attack the whaler?" I asked.

"Because I was weak and injured and I knew no human would take pity upon me," he replied with downcast voice. "Only the Inuit dogs welcomed me into their pack. I crawled through the icy waters as the ship burned around me, half-blind as I was with rage and fright."

"Fright?" I asked, astonished by his admission.

"Yes, Walton, I fear death, for who would resurrect me? I will face almighty God for my sins. But there is a greater reason for my agitation – Wouldst I ever see in hell the woman who sits next to me? I could not face an eternity of loneliness."

He removed the cloak from around his head and, once again, I stared at the terrible visage I had last seen on the ice. Just as Ernest had reported, the creature's face was scarred and distorted by the burns he suffered. The effect of the red streaks which cut across his face was one of revulsion, but if I looked deeply into my soul, perhaps my heart harbored pity for his deformity, which any person would be loathe to suffer.

"No human would shelter you because you have acted like a murderous child who has not gotten his way," I said. "Often men walk through life with no understanding of the importance of a chance meeting. Heaven answered my prayers for a friendly companion in Victor, but had I known what consequences would result from his friendship, I might have left him adrift on the icy sea to perish in his vengeful quest."

The creature put his mummy-like hand on Olivia's shoulders and reproached me: "Your race thinks only of itself. I have changed, Walton. Here, beside me, sits the fair woman who has transformed my life. You have guided me to Ernest and the works of my father, and, with them, my mate."

I was stunned by the creature's confession. Could I dare believe the words the monster spoke? Olivia Frankenstein – the dæmon's mate? "You are as mad as Ernest," I said. "What makes you think–"

He cut me off with a wave of his hand. "From my first days at Belrive, I admired her. I discerned her unhappiness as Ernest began and conducted his experiments; she became an afterthought to his work. Then came the terrible illness of Wolfgang. One day near the lake, as she walked the grounds to calm her troubled mind, I overcame my hesitation and forced myself to take pity upon her. My face was hidden from view and I expressed my sympathy for her plight. I found favor with her and she likewise took pity upon my condition, as a poor man of the forest – swearing to keep my identity and whereabouts a secret from her husband. We met several times to converse.

"After Wolfgang died, she came to me, mad with grief, and I revealed my face and promised her that her son would yet live. Ernest took matters into his own hands, however, and now it falls to me to protect the infant as Olivia recovers from the shock of his death. I will fulfill that promise."

Olivia muttered in choked sobs as the wolfhound skulked in the door and crept to her side. Could I trust the monster's sincerity? He had let me live when he could easily have wrung my neck. His mercy had softened my heart, and Olivia's anguish had touched my soul; a draught of pity quelled my desire for revenge.

"He is good . . . kind . . . ," Olivia stammered as she wiped her eyes. "Please do not harm the man created by my husband's brother."

Attempting to temper any severity of voice, I said, "He is a murderer. He has slain members of your family and taken the lives of my crew." Olivia's well-being was close to my heart and I sincerely wished her no mental harm, yet I could not refrain from telling the truth. "Can you not see what has been visited upon Wolfgang by this madness?" I regretted my blunt question immediately, for Olivia clutched her stomach and her tears flowed in a profuse stream, more so than I had witnessed since the boy's death.

"Not so, Walton, not so . . . ," the monster said.

"Be done with your lies . . . . I have heard those words pass your lips before."

Great, heaving sobs poured forth from his massive frame. I contained my disbelief and with caution peered past the ragged locks that framed his scarred face. Indeed, great swells of remorse racked his body; even the wolfhound (the dog sensed the creature's sadness) looked upon him with sad eyes.

"I had no hand in the defilement of the grave," the monster professed.

Olivia folded her arms and shivered in the chilly air.

"I know," I said.

He pointed a gnarled finger at me. "The deed was done by her husband. *He* drove her to madness and used the Agrippa falsely upon the infant. Thou wouldst believe I hold court in the Palace of Satan . . . yet, as thou dost believe so dost the rest of your race." He turned from the flickering fire and rose upon his haunches. "Any weapon you brandish will inflict far less pain than I have suffered. I could crush you now, but my spirit is broken by the depth of my regret and sorrow for this woman who has lost her child. My days of hostility with you are finished, if you would but listen . . . ."

Olivia looked at me with such concern and encouragement I could not but help honor his request. The creature gazed at her with affection.

"Before you begin, tell me why I should believe any of your tales?" I asked.

Olivia cradled her arms as if suckling an infant and sang a sweet lullaby. When she ended her song, she said in a sweet voice, as much to the air as to me: "He tells the truth. He has not the power to lie – it is his greatest strength."

I considered her words with amazement. Olivia was correct: The creature had never lied to me, and I gathered from Victor's tale he had done the same for his creator with perhaps one exception – his promise of self-immolation. However, I was to blame for his failure. In all other respects, he had fulfilled his destructive and malevolent intentions with impunity; I had had no doubt that given the perfect moment he would end my life as well; now, it seemed, I was in his favor.

"The boy died of his own sickness," the creature said. "The child was buried and then that night, as she watched, unobserved by her husband, he removed the infant from the crypt and carried him to the laboratory."

What a scene the poor Olivia witnessed: The father breaking open the crypt of his dead child; fracturing the stone, shredding the white roses in anger, lifting the naked body from its inevitable decay. All the while, his grieving wife watched in mad and piteous horror, helpless against her husband's rage and domination.

Olivia rocked on the floor and began her gentle song again. The monster's words, as shocking as they were to me, affected her not. Surely, angels, in abiding love and serene comfort, sat by her side, so content was her demeanor.

"I had spoken of the Agrippa to her – if the child died," he continued. "Ernest ascertained its power over the soul, but had little benefit of its study. He wanted it for his own heartless work – he so eager to emulate his brother's studies – but *she* loved her child more than a *book*."

"I know what went wrong," I said softly so as not to distress the angelic woman.

A fiendish rage animated him and he clutched at the air as if to wring the soul from the ether; his face was wrinkled into contortions to horrible for the human eye to behold, but presently he calmed himself and said: "He failed – Ernest resurrected the child carried so cruelly away by death after so brief an existence, but gave him the soul of a devil! How could I not be touched by the destruction of such innocence?" The creature lifted his head and implored, by the look in his watery gaze, that I give support to his tale. He thrust out his grotesque hands, thus beseeching compassion. This action had a strange effect upon me; I drew near to consoling him, but when I looked upon him and thought of the horror and hatred he had manifested upon the Frankensteins and my crew, I searched deeply within my soul for any scrap of forgiveness. It burned but dimly within. If not able to forgive, I was at least able to see the good in the heart of the creature.

"It is true I am a monster," he said, "but canst thou not behold the halo of benevolence that dissolves my murderous passions? I am loved of the baser creatures, and I find my solace in the weak and small, for *they* are as I – trod upon by mankind. This soothing balm is the quality that carries me through my days; the water that cools the flames of my inextinguishable hatred." He lowered his hands and placed them in his lap, never taking his eyes from mine. "The child is a creature of the forest. He suckles like a Fury at her breast and eats the small animals he can find. The Agrippa . . . the visitor gave to her husband . . . the incantations are warped. The child has the soul and constitution of a dæmon . . . ," he dropped his voice to a whisper, "and he must die or soon he will kill without mercy. Compassion and pity touch him not."

We sat for a time observing each other and listening to Olivia's mournful song. Presently, a skittering sound raced overhead followed by a loud mewling like that of a bawling cat. Olivia gazed at the ceiling above our heads; the wolfhound leapt to her feet and sniffed at the air.

"Wolfgang is hungry," the monster said and rose from his place on the floor. He pointed to the thatched roof and indicated his intention to pursue the child.

She smiled sweetly at him and lowered his hand with hers and said, "He will feed tonight, but you must protect me."

"I will do so," he replied with equal sweetness, "and then guide you home." Then the three: Olivia, the wolfhound and the creature, quitted his hovel and stepped into the mist. I peered after them into the descending dusk. The rain had softened to scattered drops and the gray sky was dimming to black. As I left the hut, I saw the child, garbed in fur, pressed against Olivia's breast while the monster stood protectively at her side. The child hissed and glared at me with his luminous eyes. Olivia patted the fine blond hairs on his small head and continued her evening lullaby. They turned from me and I left them in the deepening gloom, overwhelmed by the emotions of the encounter. In all my days, since my first meeting with Victor Frankenstein, I had never anticipated the unlikely thought that overtook me – I had observed the creature anew and, astonishingly, felt some kindness and compassion toward him. He had become Wolfgang's father.

Jangled by the newfound emotions stirring within me, I walked back to Belrive in the company of the wolfhound. Of a few revelations, I was certain – Ernest was no longer the master of his wife, and the creature, perhaps, was the lesser of two evils.

All shifted in one rainy afternoon in a crude forest hut.

ROBERT WALTON'S JOURNAL

Belrive, January 24ᵗʰ, 17–

Madness holds dominion over the Frankensteins.

I have retreated to the sanity of my journal, as few other pursuits here exhibit any semblance of normalcy. I write from my bed chamber, looking out upon the snow-covered terrace that descends like a white flowing river to the lake shore. The ashen sky continues its stranglehold upon Belrive, and days go by with only brief sightings of the sun, so occluded are the heavens. The family is in disarray and Waldman is on the verge of quitting the residence. I believe it would take very little to convince the professor, based upon his evident irritation with Ernest, to depart for Ingolstadt. I, too, have harbored thoughts of leaving Belrive, but I feel my task here is incomplete. I left London with the intention of securing the safety of my sister's family from any attack by the dæmon, and, in that, I perhaps succeeded. The fires of revenge still burned within me when I departed from England, and those have been dampened by the creature's kindness. However, I have also come to realize I was proud enough, under the pressing weight of the inquiry, to seek a revival of my reputation and secure a place in history – an honor that reached far beyond exploring the world. Could I, perchance, be party to the fantastic work that would lift the curse of death? I should have taken heed of Victor's words and anticipated the danger that grows from such godless ambition, instead of succumbing to such hubris. These words are easy to write now that I understand the unyielding madness that courses through the veins of the Frankensteins. A strange twist – Ernest's willingness to play God has complicated my departure from Belrive – perhaps a reversal of my quest for fame. The science practiced here may be used for good or evil. I believe that Victor, despite the outcome of his experiments, sincerely wished his work to benefit mankind. Instead of condoning such lunacy, should I protect my race from those who would extend science beyond human boundaries? To men of good character, the answer is easy. Therefore, I will remain in this secluded home, bidding my time, until I am no longer welcome, or the threat of danger requires my action. The authorities are of no use here – the Swiss are taciturn about their police work, and what crime could I impart upon Ernest Frankenstein, a man of wealth and power in his district – the resurrection of a dead son whom I could not produce, or the provocation of a monster who would likely destroy us all?

The experiments conducted by Ernest Frankenstein have dropped his family into a morass so contorted and deep I have begun to look upon Victor's creation as a troubled ally. The creature's attitude has shifted, and in Olivia he has found his mate. In his hovel, I observed his attentions – as if she were his betrothed – and witnessed what appeared, upon consideration, her reciprocation. The monster, in his way, has become the father to her demonic child and she, in her madness, has accepted his comfort.

For days after my discovery of the creature's hut, Ernest and the professor kept to themselves, and I was not invited to witness their work at the barn. The wolfhound and the manservant were my sole companions, the nurse being dismissed by Ernest after Wolfgang's death. Often, I wandered the grounds in the snow and deepening cold, with the intention of being a curious observer, although most days I was alone with my thoughts by the fireplace. I determined that any intercession on my part would come when events turned toward catastrophe. At that time, I could do the most good.

The two men would excuse themselves from the breakfast table and return late at night. One morning, Ernest departed Belrive before Maximilian – and my question about the duration of my visit was gruffly answered by our host, "Our task is unfinished. Would you deny the world its great destiny?" Then, his eyes softened and he offered an apology and asked me to look in upon Olivia while he and the professor continued their work at the barn. I saw them little during the evening and rarely before I departed for bed. Olivia, with the skill of a magician, disappeared during the late morning and near sunset, presumably to feed her child. When at Belrive, she passed through the halls like a lost ghost, singing her sweet song; her gloomy nights passed with only furtive glances my way, imprisoned as she was by her madness. Each night, she likewise excused herself from my company to retire, I presumed to her bed chamber, rather than engage me in discourse. Her eyes betrayed her nervous condition as her gaze shifted about the room, and there was no contentment in her soul; her agony shone in the lunatic spark of her vision.

I must record two startling incidents I witnessed during my wanderings through the wooded grounds. I avoided the barn, although I was sorely tempted to encroach upon Ernest and the professor's work. Such a tactic would have ensnared me and perhaps forced me to drastic action earlier than needed. However, any faith in Ernest's benign intentions was shattered one day when I walked near the lake shore. There, bending down to touch the icy waters, as if they were discovering the texture and feel of liquid for the first time, were two of the most beautiful creatures I had ever encountered. Yet, despite their astounding beauty, I sensed a chilling malevolence. A male and female knelt near the rocks. They wore drab clothing that reminded me of uniforms, rather than the customary clothes one would see worn in the English or French fashion. Profuse black hair covered their heads and their muscular agility was plainly evident in their forms. But most startling of all were their eyes: soulless and black, surrounded by dark sockets. They focused upon me with an intensity which transported me into the depths of hell. No sign of compassion, no sign of life, or, indeed, of any emotion were evident in their gazes. My apprehension upon seeing these creatures was equal to any invoked by the dæmon. I looked upon beings with *no soul*. They were living corpses intent upon their own designs – or the design of their creator. They spoke not a word nor uttered a sound as they lifted their hands from the water and looked upon me with their blank stares. Effortlessly, they rose and without a second look my way glided into the forest like stealthy deer.

The next day I encountered a similar pair with the same sinister countenance in the forest north of Belrive; they did nothing to threaten me, but continued on in their study of the various trees and winter berries, before my approach came too close for their liking. They disappeared among the concealing branches not to be seen again on my walk. The sighting left me concerned and cautious, and I soon returned to the safety of the house. Here was proof of Ernest's work, I was certain. But who were these creatures and what part did Ernest wish me to play in his drama?

My suspicions were solidified one early morning when Ernest returned to Belrive from the barn. I had fallen asleep on a chaise in front of the fireplace, and the welcoming whine of the wolfhound, sometime after midnight, awakened me to my host's presence. His blue eyes were sunken and red at their corners, great swaths of purple lay underneath them; he was silent and uneasy in his disposition and his hands and clothes were splattered with mud and stained by the blue liquid used in the experiments. The young man started at my presence, surprised by my reclining figure.

"I'll be off to bed," Ernest said wearily. "You should too. Tomorrow will be an early day."

"For me as well?" I asked.

He shook his head and said, "Not yet . . . soon, but not yet." And with that he left me alone in front of the dying fire. I knew the reason for his assertion – he believed I was in possession of the book he sought – *The Transmutation of Souls*.

January 25th, 17–

The next afternoon, curiosity got the better of me and I ventured toward the barn; my restlessness and encounters with the unknown creatures spurred me to action and, after a small repast of bread and cheese, I found myself on the trail forged in the western hills above Belrive.

Oddly, there were no tracks laid down by the two men, but I soon arrived at the escarpment that led up to the barn. Aware that my own footprints would be visible in the newly fallen snow, I cut off from the trail and followed the circle of trees which ringed the structure. I wished to remain undiscovered, and with reasonable precautions, I felt I could maintain my intention.

Voices alerted me to their presence: I sunk deeper into the shadows and watched as Ernest and Maximilian, each hoisting a soiled cloth bag over their shoulders, appeared from an unknown path west of the barn. Ernest carried the oddly shaped bundle with little effort, but the professor panted, troubled by the weight of his task, his breath rising in great smoky puffs, as they trundled to the door. I remained hidden in the shadows, allowing the two men time to go about their work.

After a few minutes, I crept closer to the structure near the area where the ovoid churned inside, spewing a plume of white steam through the chimney into the frosty air. I pressed myself against the rough stone and peered into one of the barred windows.

To my amazement, and as much to my horror, I saw two torsos – one male and the other female – of gigantic stature, head to head upon the wooden table. Unimaginably, both were without arms and legs! The two corpses lay in deathly silence and, as I watched, the men opened their bags and withdrew the extremities for their gruesome creations. Clearly, these appalling limbs came from other unfortunate beings, perhaps murdered for their own attributes. Ernest, in his madness, was intent upon creating men and women of greater stature than Victor had conceived; a preternatural race to propagate his terrible army.

Intent upon their tasks, neither man would have observed my presence, but for an unfortunate slip on the ice. I grabbed the iron bars lacing the window and in my efforts stumbled against the casement. Ernest swung quickly from his work upon the female and with angry countenance cursed me. The jig was up and I was forced to submit to my host's interrogation. He was soon at the door, beckoning me inside.

"We have an interloper in our midst," the young man said with irritation. I offered no excuses for my visit as he wiped his blood-streaked hands against his breeches. "No matter," he said, "the time has come for you to understand our work and your role . . . ." He spoke these last words as a command with kingly

111

bearing. As he turned to enter the barn, his eyes flashed upon me with that uneasy feeling of dread I had observed upon my arrival at Belrive. The conciliatory and gentle manner often displayed by Victor in our conversations was absent from Ernest. Even Maximilian huffed at my intrusion, as my presence distracted him from his preparations on the male corpse; the professor's demeanor heightened my suspicions regarding his motives.

"Each day, our work progresses," Ernest said and bade me gaze upon the horrible sight on the table. Both specimens displayed an astounding physical superiority while enfolded in Death's embrace. A thin red slash, stitched with animal gut, ran up the bruised and purple neck of each, a marker of their demise. The male was supremely muscular, exhibiting a wide breadth at the shoulders and a narrow waist. His massive pectorals swelled and were covered with a dark coating of hair. Unlike Victor's creation, the man retained his finely chiseled face, much like that of a sculptural Greek god, with flowing dark tresses and fine black lashes. His female counterpart was equally handsome, her torso firm and without marks; her auburn hair lay spread beneath her muscled frame. Each reposed as in sleep, with no pain or discomfort upon their faces.

I watched in fascination as the professor withdrew the gigantic leg of a man and fitted it against the waist of the male before him. Then, he took a large needle from the table and threaded white animal gut through its eye. With precise strokes, the professor plunged the instrument into the limb and drew the needle through to the pelvis attaching the leg to the body. This he repeated with deft accuracy, spacing his intricate work in small equal intervals. But as the process continued, my fascination slowly turned to revulsion. Great God, what was I witnessing but the desecration of the mortal vessel? With my eyes, I saw how Victor achieved his *glory*, and a great shock coursed through my body. How the dæmon must have suffered when he arose that dreary November night, his dull, yellow eyes opened again from death, his breathing labored and his limbs agitated with convulsive motion. I became acutely aware of the pain that coursed through his body, the panic that overtook him as he struggled to make sense of the birth that withdrew him from the grave.

"Desecration," I muttered.

Ernest glared at me with disdain; my thought was impertinent at the least, if not wholly insulting to him.

"Desecration?" he scolded me. "You may be an adventurer, my dear friend, but you have no sense of history and right. Have you no idea what brews to the west of our beloved country? Have you hidden your head so far in the sand that you sleep while Napoleon's armies subdue the continent and we, in turn, become slaves of France? Desecration? This price must be paid!" He pointed to the corpses. "This man and woman – Saxons – will be the progenitors of a new race that will defeat the dictator and later rule the world – on my terms. I have purchased the finest specimens for my work, each perfect for my needs . . . if the limb is not to my standards, I acquire another. With these creations, I have exceeded what Victor dreamed of and removed the stain of William's death. The world will recognize my genius." Here, he shook his head as if throwing off sadness and stated, "I have willingly sacrificed my fortune, my every hope, for the knowledge I sought. One man's life or death is but a small price to pay for dominion over the foes of our race."

"I have seen your work," I said. "Are these soulless beings who wander through the forest a loftier achievement than any dared by your brother?" I stepped back from the table and looked away, astounded by his claim; such lunacy was far beyond the creation of life. What arrogance, what grandiose elixir drugged Ernest Frankenstein? Victor had warned me of the intoxicating draught, the fervor that consumed all who attempted to navigate the course he had charted. Ernest followed in his unhappy footsteps. I held my tongue from further provocation, although my spirit sagged under the weight of the unfolding events and my role in them.

"You will deliver the Agrippa tomorrow, when the experiment is complete." Ernest commanded.

I turned to face him. "You have the book. The visitor delivered it to you."

For a moment, extreme agitation overtook him and he trembled as I awaited his reply. In a quivering voice he said, "That book is flawed. The incantations have been copied erroneously. You have seen the result . . . ." Here, he paused and placed his hands over his face, and when he removed them his eyes were red and filled with pain. "I know you carry the book with you; otherwise, the dæmon would not have mentioned your name – it is your security against death."

"Ernest," I said, placing my hand upon his shoulder, "you are witness to the book's terrible power. Abandon this insane plan and cling to what you have. Do not make the mistake, as Victor warned, of abandoning your family for the sake of science. " I was forced to look upon myself, however, as I had brought, through my actions, the same forces to bear.

He brushed my hand away savagely, and, as if reading my mind, said, "Live by your own words, Walton. *That abomination* is no longer my son and I care not whether he lives or dies. You will bring the Agrippa to me tomorrow – all will be in readiness. I know not whether Victor used the book upon his creation, but my army will benefit from its magic."

The professor looked up from his work, studied me with pensive eyes and then resumed his tasks. I wondered if he masked his true intentions, whether he wished to flee from Ernest and the labor before him; but, this day, it was too late for any retreat.

I watched as Maximilian finished his suture and then wrapped a tight band of flesh around the stitches. Disgusted by the scene, I said, "I will leave you to your work," and then left the men in the barn. I had no intention of delivering the Agrippa to Ernest.

As I closed the door, my blood was chilled by the gigantic footprints that lead from the woods toward the structure. The monster knew of Ernest's plan and was, for the moment, allowing it to continue unabated. Clearly, Victor's creation had his own purpose in mind. If Ernest wished the creature to be a commander in his army, perhaps the dæmon harbored a similar hope. Would the monster succumb to the malevolent beauty of Ernest's creations or would he see them as threats to his dominion?

As I descended the escarpment, passed the waterfall, and walked through the snowy woods toward Belrive, my mind was filled with thoughts of Olivia, Wolfgang, the creature and the experiments in the barn. As I approached one particularly dense thatch of brush, I spotted a small, gray animal with sharp teeth and reddish eyes and I started, convinced I had seen the infant scurrying through the forest, rather than any inhabitant of the woods. The sight heightened my agitation and I strode with increased vigor toward Belrive, certain the uneasy truce between the monster and Ernest Frankenstein was about to dissolve into war.

ROBERT WALTON'S JOURNAL

Geneva, February 3ʳᵈ, 17—

How I long for safety, my dearest Margaret; to find myself ensconced within the confines of your comfortable and welcoming home – for now I am fleeing for my life. But for the Board of Inquiry, I would make my way to Yorkshire, to the peaceful countryside rather than to London. I write by the light of a single candle, ever watchful of the shadows and movements around me. Rarely have I experienced such desolation, such gloom, all precipitated by the events of the past week; and, for two days I have sequestered myself like a common criminal in a tiny hostelry in Geneva until I can make my way to safety.

In the anxious night after my last experience with Ernest and the professor at the barn, I was awakened by a gentle knock on my door. I recall the event clearly because my sleep had been interrupted by strange and abhorrent dreams of clutching hands, blood and terrible darkness. The twelve-stroke chime from the tall clock had barely faded from my ears when a soft rapping roused me from my bed. I approached the locked door with apprehension (I had requested a key from Ernest's manservant), because of my uncertainty of what might lurk outside my chamber. A voice whispered my name and I recognized the speaker as Maximilian. I unlocked the door, peered around its edge, and to my surprise I beheld the professor clothed in his winter garments with bag in hand.

"May I come in, Walton?" he asked with the sincerity given to a formal request.

I bade him enter my chamber, which he did most willingly and with haste. He took a seat near the looking glass as I stood silently waiting for an explanation of his midnight visit.

Whilst I lit a candle, Maximilian rubbed his eyes and sighed. The yellow light spread over his face and illuminated his piercing gaze, which was replete with anguish. When I seated myself at the foot of the bed, he spoke: "I must be quick, for Ernest will discover something is amiss." He stopped for a moment to fortify his courage and then continued, "I am leaving Belrive – tonight. It is no longer safe to stay, and, if you are wise, Walton, you too will flee."

His tone unnerved me, yet I understood the depth of his fear and the veracity of his plea.

"Ernest is mad," the professor said. "He will kill anyone who stands in his way, and with his creations behind him we are lost. Perhaps the world is lost."

"But you have aided him," I said, now fearing for both our lives, knowing Ernest would seek Agrippa's power and fulfill his threat against me.

"I had no other income. I have been a fool for money, and played Ernest's game for far too long. Besides, what scientist could resist such temptation? – and proclaim his discovery of the secrets to eternal life. Ernest has perfected the chemical and electrical formulas – all he needs is the book – the second half of the equation – and he will destroy all to get it. He needs the Agrippa to impart the souls into his creations."

"I will never surrender it to him."

"Then, you will die."

"He does not understand its power."

Maximilian smiled weakly and said, "That is where you underestimate Ernest. He is driven beyond reason. He has studied the version he procured, and, like an exemplary student at the University, has marked the passages he needs. He will compare them against your book. He has learned the incantations and intends to use them. By all that is holy, he shall succeed!"

Maximilian leaned forward to retrieve his bag and then started in his chair. His eyes grew wide in terror as I strained to discern the source of his alarm. "Blow out the flame," he whispered roughly. I obeyed his command and the room was plunged into darkness. "I am too late," he said.

The door flew open and there in the ghostly light of a solitary candle stood Ernest, his face contorted in anger and splotched with blood; he held a carving knife in his gory hand. The professor leapt from his chair and swung his bag at the young man; the candle flew across the room and fell extinguished upon the floor. The knife clattered near the professor's feet. Maximilian rushed past Ernest to make good his escape; the enraged young man swung at the gentle professor with both fists, but only succeeded in knocking him into the door. Maximilian yowled in shock, but through fate's good fortune, he escaped into the hall and disappeared from view. I crouched near the bed, aware that the real subject of Ernest's attentions was the book, and, thus, its owner.

I lunged for the knife, but Ernest was too quick; even in the darkness his wicked smile shone as he wrapped his fingers around the handle. Like a Fury, he was upon me, the instrument held so close to my neck I could smell the iron blade.

"The book," he commanded as blood dripped from his face and fell in cold drops on mine.

"I gave it to Waldman."

"You lie . . . but you will not save your skin. For you see, I will finish this work with or without you. You have your choice – and to help you decide –" He lifted the knife and slashed it across my check. I howled and my blood ran warm down my neck; Ernest's murderous intention was the equal of any purveyed by the monster. Luck had come for his payment and I had no coin.

"Where is the book?" he asked again and held the knife tightly against my jugular. My appeals had swayed the monster on the Arctic ice, but Ernest could taste my death; madness burned like fire in his eyes.

"Cut deeply and quickly," I said, "for I will never concede to your demand."

Ernest lifted the blade and drew it above my head; it rose, a menacing black sliver in the clenched fist of my host. I struggled against his agile and muscular frame, and I was his equal for a time. He dropped the knife and we both grasped for it, until by a devious maneuver he was able to overpower me and recapture the weapon. I closed my eyes and prepared to meet Death at last – too young, perhaps, but I considered my life fulfilled, of dreams imagined, many attempted and a good number accomplished. There was no reason to mourn – my only regrets were of not being able to shower affection upon my dear niece and nephew, never again sharing the loving embrace of you, Margaret, my dear sister; and, of late, to remove my name from infamy – all acts I was forced to abandon under the threat of the knife.

Yet, as I readied myself to be lifted by the angels to the glorious home of my Maker, a dull crack rang above my head and the taut legs and arms of my attacker fell slack; the knife clattered to the floor.

Maximilian stood over me, gazing upon the limp body of our host. The professor clutched a large candlestick in his hand. I rolled the young man off me; he lay sprawled next to my side.

"Thank you, but I believe you've killed him," I said.

"Give me credit, Walton – I am a doctor – I know how to render a man senseless without murdering him." The professor threw the candlestick upon the bed as I sprang from the floor. "We must both be away," he said with alarm.

"I must destroy the barn before I quit Belrive," I said, and began to gather my clothes.

"By heaven, I have saved a fool," said he. "Make your escape now!"

"Ernest's laboratory must be destroyed; otherwise, there will be more creatures to wreak havoc upon the world."

"I admire your courage, Walton, but there is little time. This madman will soon rouse from his nap upon the floor. I am off to Geneva. God speed, my friend. May we meet again under more fortuitous circumstances."

The professor gave me a nod and departed the chamber. I dressed quickly and withdrew my bag from under the bed. I bent down and observed Ernest: His breathing was shallow and he moved not a muscle. I placed a finger upon his neck to gauge his pulse; it beat strongly underneath the clammy skin. Each second removed from his misguided passions was an opportunity to fulfill my task. I removed the sash from my dressing gown and tied it around Ernest's hands. He shuddered and then sank back into oblivion.

I gathered my possessions, secured a towel to staunch the flow of blood from my cheek and descended the staircase where the wolfhound nervously paced in front of the fireplace's dying embers. Steadying my hands, I withdrew the Agrippa from behind the concealing flagstone and placed it in my bag. I then bade a silent goodbye to the beautiful and inconsolable Olivia, brushed my hands through the wolfhound's wiry coat and fled past the oak doors into the cold winter night.

I ran like a man possessed to the barn, trusting my knowledge of the forest and my intuition to guide me along the dark path. Once I ascended the escarpment, the bright electric glare emanating from the structure filled my eyes. A chill prickled over me as I watched the steam from the chimney swirl in white pinwheels against the cloud-darkened sky. Victor's dream to end the curse of death had been carried to the extreme and I felt ashamed that I had participated in Ernest's folly for my own selfish purposes. No, never, I decided! Never would I allow the foul creations bred of Frankenstein to roam the earth! In my agitated state, I swept aside the danger of my situation. I arrived at the barn doors to find them unlocked; I heaved them open and stepped inside.

So strange a scene lay before me, I can hardly describe its wonders. The interior was filled with hissing steam and a garish blue light. Under the glare of the electric, sparks flew across the tentacles overhead, while the tubes bubbled with the chemical elixir of life. There, upon the table rested the two gargantuan bodies whose construction I had witnessed. They breathed not, but appeared as souls in peaceful repose, clothed in identical rough jackets and breeches, similar to the uniforms I had observed on the strangers in the woods – Ernest in his mad desire had outfitted his new *soldiers*. Revulsion filled me as I gazed upon the corpses. I was uncertain where best to begin my destructive task; however, I looked upon the silver ovoid, the flames licking its base, and decided to snuff out the experiment at its source.

I was about to smash a log into the tentacles streaming from it when I was interrupted by a foul curse. I stopped, dropped my battering ram and faced the enraged figure of Ernest; blackish blood, this time his own, ran from the top of his head and down his cheeks to his shirt soaked with gore. He held a pistol in his right hand and I was convinced of his sincerity to use it.

"You will be their first engagement with a mere human," Ernest said. He approached me with cautious steps; the overpowering blue light had turned his eyes of similar hue to piercing orbs consumed by hate. "My wife has gone mad, Walton. She hastened to my screams, released my restraints, and took pity upon her dear husband." Here, he laughed and forced me to a wall opposite where the creatures lay, and, thereupon, pulled an iron cuff and chain from the kas. He threw the apparatus, along with a key, at my feet and bade me attach them to my wrist. I had no recourse, for the pistol was pointed directly between my eyes. He attached the chain to a ring protruding from the wall, retrieved the key and my captivity was assured. Confident of my confinement, he walked with renewed vigor to my bag, opened it and with a triumphant wave withdrew the Agrippa. "One would never confuse you for a spy," he said with glee. "You have no powers of imagination." I could only watch helplessly as he continued with his terrible experiment.

With the book in hand, all was in place for Ernest's malevolent plan. He searched its pages before opening it to a selection obscured from my eyes; then he placed the small volume near the top of the table. He secured his pistol and then worked deftly, (much as I had seen him and Maximilian experiment upon the animals) inserting the tubes into the mouths and legs of his creations, attaching the lines that showered him and the table with sparks. I watched in horrified fascination as Ernest scurried about attending to his subjects. In bursts, he released the clamps from the tubes whilst the smell of electricity filled the heated air. The brackish liquid poured into the mouths of the prostrate creatures and dampened the legs of their breeches. The excess dripped through the holes into the vat below the table. A glaring arc of light jumped from the ovoid to the confluence of tubes above the platform and a rain of sparks fell upon the three. I saw the fingers of the male twitch – at first in infinitesimal movements, and, after the seconds ticked away, the fingers clutched and clawed at the wood with terrifying ferocity, kept only in restraint by the iron cuffs that bound him. Soon, the female, chained as well, followed

121

in similar fashion. My disgust for Ernest and his mad quest turned to pity for the poor creatures who lay before him. They coughed and spewed the foul liquid from their mouths, and had Ernest not removed the tubes at the appropriate times they would have drowned. The male was the first to act, and with hellish speed thrust out his arms as far as he could reach, barely missing the neck of his creator. Ernest screamed over the hiss of steam and snap of sparks – what his words were I cannot say – but the male, like an obedient automaton, resumed his prone position. Ernest then removed the tube from the female, who lay twitching and shivering on the slab.

Ernest, his eyes glazed with fiery intent, walked to the Agrippa and bent over it like a priest. His tunic and breeches were coated with blood and stained from the chemical elixir that poured life into his creations. His fingers crept to the book and traced a passage; I knew not what he was about to recite, but I was certain his intention was to pluck the most ferocious souls from the bowels of hell – as would be his choice – and drop them into the beautiful, but monstrous, vessels stretched out before him.

He opened his mouth to speak.

The window behind Ernest fractured in a rain of shards and Victor's creation was upon him, grasping for his neck while the young man tried desperately to elude the monster's attack. Ernest escaped in large part because of the slippery blood that covered his body and clothing; he found his pistol, retreated toward the wall, all the while keeping his weapon aimed at the head of his gigantic assailant. The automatons clawed at the platform but could not escape their shackles.

"Thou wouldst follow in the footsteps of your brother," the creature said in a voice suffused with rage. "But thou wouldst destroy me and the world for your gain. This I know."

"You could lead them," Ernest pleaded. "Think of the power you would hold. Mankind would trouble you no more."

The monster considered Ernest's entreaty for a moment, but then pointed to the door.

There, stood Olivia in a white gown whose hem was darkly stained. Her infant, swathed in fur, clutched at her breast and cast his demonic gaze upon his father. Olivia's left hand held a weighty bag, from which dripped a foul liquid.

"I have struck at your *army*," the dæmon said and retrieved the vessel from Olivia. He reached into the bag and pulled the severed heads of the male and female creatures I had earlier observed near the lake shore. Their soulless black eyes were swollen with death, whilst the gore drained from their necks. It was a sight I never imagined to witness, nor one I wish to behold again.

Ernest, upon seeing the heads, flew into a rage and hurled curses at the monster, and also at his stoic wife, who calmly fed her child. The young man cocked the hammer of his pistol and the creature shook his massive hand in warning.

"Your son will kill anything that denies him warmth and sustenance," the dæmon said, eyeing his adversary warily. "What devil does not?"

Ernest was unmoved by this plea and pulled the trigger.

The blast echoed throughout the barn; the automatons moaned and strained against their constraints but were held fast to the table. The creature, anticipating this attack, drew up the severed heads to the level of his; the ball struck the forehead of the male, splattering blood upon the monster, but leaving him otherwise unharmed. Ernest's assault, however, precipitated an amazing effect upon the possessed infant, whose eyes shone with hellish rage as he sprang from his mother's breast, evidence enough that Wolfgang viewed Victor's creation as his protector. He scurried across the stone floor and leapt upon his father.

Ernest beat at his son with all his strength, but failed to dislodge the savage devil from his head. He swung his pistol wildly, but under the onslaught, the blows glanced off his attacker.

For a moment, Wolfgang relented in his vicious assault, turned his head and glowered at me with his hideous countenance. I shrunk toward the wall, petrified of the abhorrence that had been the sickly little boy. The infant had already ripped shreds from his father's left cheek and now clutched at his neck. My heart despaired at the scene: The child bore no resemblance to any living creature, imbued as he was with the strength of a man. His small fists were covered with blood, and hammered relentlessly upon his father; sharp incisors, ready to devour flesh, had formed in the mouth of the bloated and bruised face. He had grown beyond normal measure in the scant few weeks since his death. Pity and disgust raged through me as I pulled at my cuff; what of the heavenly love and innocence offered to the world upon his birth?

Ernest howled in great pain and, in his attempt to dislodge his son, ran from the blinding glare of the barn into the cold winter night. The monster was powerless to stop the scene, apparently for fear of injuring the child.

The male and female on the table attempted to rise as their creator fled, but their cuffs held fast. Like the others I had observed, they held no life in their eyes. I discerned their desire was to follow Ernest – they were slaves to their creator, and, unlike the dæmon, were utterly without mindful direction of their own and, I assumed, devoid of free will. The first half of the equation – the chemical elixir – had been successful; the second half – the importation of a soul through the Agrippa – remained unfulfilled.

I bent forward as far as my captivity would allow and peered through the room's mists into the night, as the monster observed the creatures on the platform. My strained vision was rewarded only with vague shadows that pitched and yawed like a floundering ship. A cacophony of howls and curses mixed in the terrible night with the agony perpetuated on Ernest by his son. Olivia, unbeknownst to the creature, rushed into the dark. There was a great crash against the massive doors and they swung shut with violent force. Thereupon, a sharp crack split the air and all fell silent like the tomb.

I called out for Ernest – uncertain of his fate. A sound like the flapping of a thousand wings spread over the room, drowning out the hiss and crackle of the ovoid, as if a great flock of birds had flown over the barn; then the rush evaporated and all was quiet again.

With a slow creak, the doors opened. Never will I be able to purge from my memory the scene I am about to recall.

Olivia stood in the doorway, her white gown now dripping with the dark blood of her infant. In her arms she carried the lifeless babe, his head mangled in its furs, a single wound piercing his heart. Ernest had managed to load and fire his pistol, thus taking the life of his own son. The creature rushed to her side, shaken as he was by the sight of Wolfgang. How a mother mourns the death of a child – yet a second time! Olivia was shocked beyond her senses. She walked slowly to the platform, her face numb with grief, her eyes swollen and black under the light.

The creature flew into a rage, his tears now flowing over the dead infant. Without a word, he secured an iron stake from the kas and, looming over the male on the table, plunged it through his head. The male shivered and died. The female shrieked in horror as the monster proceeded with his gruesome task. The creature showed no remorse as he stood over the female; she hissed and grasped at the air as the monster raised the stake. With a swift blow, he plunged it into her brain. The creatures now lay in deathly repose. Another task remained for the monster, however. He ripped the restraints from the table, thus freeing the two bodies for disposal; he lifted them one-by-one and dropped them into the vat underneath the platform. The liquid churned and bubbled as it covered the flesh, and within a few minutes no evidence of the short lives of Ernest's creatures remained but their ghostly bones.

Olivia, in her grief, lay the child upon the table and sank to the floor. Whilst I observed the mother, the monster walked toward her, his scarred face contorted in pain. The creature bent over Olivia and placed his massive hands upon her shoulders; thereafter, I could not discern his tormented face through the ragged black locks that concealed it, but his tears fell freely upon her body. For several minutes, Olivia writhed upon the floor clutching her raven hair and pulling with abandonment. Her cries and curses alternated between anguish and maniacal laughter; I was convinced she had descended into complete madness at last.

I lifted my arm and my confining chain clattered against the stone wall.

The creature started, stared at me with his watery eyes and then rose slowly to his full stature whilst surprise clouded his gaze. I cowered against the wall, uncertain as I was of his motives, as he approached me.

With a violent snap, he pulled the chain from its ring, then took my arm in his hands and wrenched open the cuff from my wrist. Having done so, he dissolved into spasms of grief.

"Witness Ernest's love for his son," the creature said through his twisted mouth. He thrust out his hands as if pleading for my understanding. "I will destroy him; this I vow as I stand before you."

"He has fled?" I asked, seeking a confirmation of my instincts. My heart thumped wildly as I looked upon the dæmon, but I was overcome with his concern and love for Wolfgang and Olivia. I had no choice but to observe the scene because I was in his power, but I felt, at that moment, the creature would not have objected had I walked from Belrive never to return. I viewed him as a man, not as the monster given life by Victor Frankenstein. The many descriptions I had concocted for the fiend: monster, abhorrence, horror and dæmon – foul curses I had already volleyed against him – seemed inappropriate names for the being who stood before me.

"He has fled into the western hills," the monster replied, "but he will return to Belrive. Ernest hast not yet fulfilled his true powers, and that time will come. At present, he would suffer defeat in a battle with Frankenstein." As the name left his lips, he raised his fists to his broad chest.

Olivia cried out and clutched the wooden platform, sending it rocking over the vat as the lines sparked and the tubes spilled forth their magical blue contents. The infant's head lolled in an eerie cadence with the table like a child rocked in a cradle.

"She is mad and I mourn for her," the creature said and wiped his eyes.

"Nothing can be done," I said and walked toward the crying woman.

"Still thou art the victim of a small mind, Walton." The creature stared at Olivia who had collapsed, sputtering upon the floor.

"I must die . . . I must die . . . and be with my son," Olivia cried out, and as quickly as her screams faded her tremulous voice tumbled into laughter.

"And so she shall," said the creature.

"What horror do you contemplate?" I asked.

He bent over me and the odor of death filled my nostrils, but in his eyes I observed a gentle manner, a compassion far beyond affection. "Her only hope of salvation is death," he continued in a whisper. "Dost thou not admire the beautiful Olivia? She, of all on the earth, has been my guide to the fair emotions of your race. She alone has brought joy and grace to my life whilst the world rails against me still. Her resurrection will be the reward for her benevolence; her feelings of kindness and gentleness have overcome the agony of my wounds." Here he stopped and wiped the tears from his eyes. "She has carried her grace from heaven. From her, I have learned goodness and the power of redemption. I have no desire to lead an army. I only require a mate – my love – the promise my creator never fulfilled. As I have felt hatred and revenge, so I now feel – love – for the woman who suffers at our feet. To her son, I will bestow the same."

In light of Victor's failings, I understood the creature's tenderness for Olivia and Wolfgang, but wondered of his capacity for his gruesome undertaking. "You would slay her in order to bring her back to life?"

"Yes, and you must aid me, for I cannot carry out this task alone. I must follow the steps exactly or all will be lost and Olivia will die. There is hope for her child – his brain has not been pierced, although he is cradled by Death – he can be rescued from the bitter darkness and restored to health." The creature lifted the infant with reverence and moved the small body to the position where the male had lain. Olivia moaned and covered her eyes with her hands.

He then returned to the young woman, rested on his knees in front of her and addressed her in soothing tones. She gazed into his eyes with longing and caressed the ragged scars on his cheeks. It was as the monster said; this display of love and companionship was as natural as any I had witnessed. He had, after all, protected her child, only to see it destroyed by the father. But in an instant, despite his sympathy, she turned like an enraged beast, screaming epithets at the creature and slamming her fists against his chest. Her attack did no physical harm, and the creature responded with a loving touch and Olivia sank into his arms. He rose and placed her limp body on the edge of the platform.

"Walton, you must calm her whilst I carry out my work," said he. "Hold her arms whilst I . . . ." He was unable to speak for a time. "She must not thrash . . . . she may injure herself."

I studied the sobbing Olivia and considered my role in the drama about to unfold. At the exact instant the monster had lifted the young woman to the table, next to her son, a strange thrill washed over me as if I were watching the birth of a distant star, or witnessing a strange event heretofore never recorded by the historian. I could have fled to Geneva, refusing the creature's request, but what of the resurrection of Olivia's glorious spirit? Having sparse contact with women while dedicating myself to exploration and the call of adventure, I knew little of love. Was it possible the monster could be my instructor in the mysterious affairs of the heart? I was stunned by this thought and shivers raced over my body. The creature's murderous intentions were expiated whilst his attentions and devotion were showered upon the woman *he loved*. My presence could only help the beautiful Olivia and the child, and thus, I found myself caught up in the emotions of that strange and wonderful night. In my heart, the spark of forgiveness was forged and – without warning – Victor Frankenstein's creation had become *my friend*, and a new enemy had taken his place.

"What exquisite passion is this," the creature said. "Make haste, we must complete our work. Hold down her arms."

I complied with his request and took her pliant limbs into my hands. She did not rail against me; her body seemed resigned to its appointment with eternity. The creature took his place at the top of the platform near her head and slowly lowered his gigantic hand over her mouth and nose. Olivia started, but struggled little; her body tensed and shook, and in a few minutes the pale flush on her cheek drained away leaving her skin pallid and blue under the electric glare. She had died with simplicity and grace. The monster withdrew his hand and shed a few tears as he looked upon her peaceful form.

"The tubes, Walton, hurry!" he commanded. "Place the elixir in their mouths." The creature re-positioned Olivia upon the table and with a gentle touch opened her jaws. He then withdrew a syringe from the cabinet and attached it to a similar tube which he inserted into her leg. I followed the monster's instructions and did the same for the child, whilst he rushed to stoke the fire under the ovoid. Soon, the room crackled again with the pop and hiss of electricity while the blue light built to a blinding glare. He drew two electric lines near to the tubes and shouted, "Release the clamps." I did so and the blue liquid gushed into the mouths of Olivia and her son; he simultaneously acted upon the instruments in his hands.

The creature raced to the head of the platform and, picking up the Agrippa, read several Latin incantations in a firm, determined voice. This he did for several minutes as I worked with the tubes and the electric, until he ordered me to step away from the platform. With a great shout, he delivered a final exhortation and the confluence of tentacles above the platform took on a heavenly glow until the room was bathed in a buttery yellow light that rivaled the sun. This intensity grew until a bolt of immense force rushed down the lines into the twitching forms. That manifestation ended the shower of electric, while the steam generated from the ovoid dropped considerably. The creature clamped the tubes and withdrew them from the bodies. I stood, shaken, by the scene before me.

Olivia and her child were bathed in a warm angelic light that encased them like a cocoon. The creature stepped back as he gazed upon the bodies wrapped in the encompassing force. I stared in disbelief when, after a few minutes, the natural skin color returned to their cheeks and both regained their healthy demeanors. Never had Olivia looked so beautiful and serene, as life flowed into her once again; even her son's blood evaporated from the white gown she wore. The child gurgled and grasped at the air with his hands. It was if the smallest angel had descended from heaven and made himself a home within the infant's body.

The creature bent over Olivia, kissed her lips and spoke her name softly. Her eyes fluttered open and a gentle smile spread across her face. She rose from the platform like a dove taking flight. The creature fell upon his knees in grateful appreciation and kissed her hands. This gesture Olivia received with equal grace and bade him rise. She spoke my name in her sweet voice as I gazed upon her in wonder. She waivered not in her walk and with quiet determination gathered the infant into her arms. "My son has returned," she said with grateful reverence to the monster as the child clutched her face with delight. "You are my savior and husband." Olivia's lustrous black hair fell about her shoulders, her lips were red and full; the power of her resurrection had vanquished the sad instability of her mind. The creature had drawn the gentlest souls from the ether and placed them within their bodies.

The dæmon handed me the Agrippa and said, "Protect it, Walton. Let it never reside with the enemy. I have what I desired most in life – a mate." He stopped and placed his hands upon mine. "I will always thank you for your kindness. Our hostility must be put to rest."

I marveled at the beautiful woman and child in front of me and nodded my assent.

The creature placed his hand on Olivia's arm and led her toward the door. I gathered my bag and placed the book inside.

As we stood near the entry, the creature said to me, "We must end this madness. My life is now complete and my hours of despondency and solitude are over." He stepped inside the room and with one push from his mighty hand overturned the kas and the crates left behind by the professor. He took a lamp and threw its volatile oil upon the walls and scattered it likewise upon the spilled contents; then he removed a flaming log from under the ovoid and tossed it upon the rubble. The noxious vapors ignited in an explosive flash and spread quickly throughout the structure. We made good our escape, shut the doors and secured them.

As we descended the escarpment, crashes and explosions rent the barn and a strange orange light filled the darkened sky and cast eerie and menacing shadows on the snow. At a turning point in the path, Olivia and the monster bade me good-bye and veered north into the dark woods. I was certain they would be blessed in their newly found companionship.

I walked through the hillocks, until I reached the path that ran near Belrive. Keeping my distance from the structure, I observed its dark and grim presence. It sat, overlooking the lake, a gloomy specter and dark testament to obsession. As the house fell away, I looked back and in a second-storey window saw the form of the servant silhouetted by a lamp, the only presence in lonely Belrive. I gripped my bag and increased my pace down the snowy trail. In the dark woods, I detected movement as a coating of snow shifted and fell from the fir boughs. Underneath them, luminous black eyes shone with ferocious intensity – of what nature they were I could not say. However, the frightening sight jogged my memory; I then remembered that Ernest had created six beings, but only four had been killed by the monster. This troubling observation was punctuated by the terrible howl of the wolfhound, as if the animal were aware of the unholy creatures who had taken up residence outside of Belrive.

THE TIMES

London, April 5ᵗʰ, 17—

The proceedings in the case of Captain Robert Walton have been successfully resolved in favor of the officer. After months of investigation, the findings were announced by the High Commissioner Board of Inquiry, Admiral Ronald Edward Petite, Esq.

For those who cannot recall the famous Captain Walton, the board was assembled to find the facts in the case of the H.M.S. Prosper, whose crew was lost under his command. The ship was destroyed in a conflagration off the Greenland coast and the good Captain was the sole survivor of His Majesty's expedition to the Arctic lands.

Admiral Petite asserted his faith in the Board and its findings, telling this newspaper there was no evidence to dispute the Captain's claim that his crew had perished from excursions upon the ice and from a strange disease of the northern latitudes. Captain Walton and a few crew members of the whaling vessel that carried him home to England corroborated his story under oath.

For his part, Captain Walton expressed his gratitude for the findings and vowed to put the past behind him, bearing always the burden of the losses. He had no further words.

We find the expedition's circumstances strange and confusing, but must bow to the Board's judgment. The question remains, however, how Captain Walton managed to steer a ship from the northern waters to Greenland with no crew and yet survive the grueling journey; and what of the blaze on board? According to the Captain, an ember from a kitchen stove ignited a fire that spread to the ship's store of gun powder.

The crew members' families may find the Captain's testimony less palatable than the Board. Whatever Captain Walton's fate, he will live the rest of his days in the tragic shadow of the Prosper.

ROBERT WALTON'S JOURNAL

London, June 4th, 17—

One-year-and-a-half of our Lord has passed since I lifted my pen to write in this journal, and what blessed relief it has been: a time of rest and enjoyment in my country home and wonderful visits with my beloved sister, Margaret, and her family in London. But, of late, circumstances have titled toward the strange and I must make note of my several encounters – I have fresh incidents to record.

The dreary inquest ended in the spring of last year, absolving me of any blame in the deaths of my crew – and for this I am forever grateful to the Board and the wisdom of its members. Still, I have suffered under the oppressive weight of the proceedings, and my reputation has declined, as well as my constitution. There are those who blame me still for the tragedy onboard, and, there is some truth in their reasoning, but as time churns onward the event grows blessedly faint in my recollection. Likewise, the horrors of Belrive touch me now like a distant nightmare that has faded into benign oblivion. Yes, I still see the shadowy figures in the woods as I departed, but the forms are faint and indistinct. I never turned to the authorities – Ernest would suffer no regret in connecting me to the destruction of his property and, likewise, Maximilian figured too intimately in the young man's work to cast sole blame upon my host. And, if so reported, what could I prove? The monster and Olivia surely would have disappeared into the forest with their son, and Ernest's creations would be as stealthy. Yet, with me, I carry the Cornelius Agrippa, protecting it from the hands of my enemy.

Despite my past misfortunes, the company of Margaret, John and their two dear children; David, my nephew; and Lila, my niece; has cheered my days and restored the depths of affection for a family well loved. Their comfortable home on Warwick Street has been a haven, a retreat for the weary, for this tired adventurer. I have had to spend little savings due to their generosity. How my mind, in my dotage, will be blessed with the memories of those sunny days in St. James's Park, with the sun flashing off David's sandy-brown hair and the cheerful smile of Lila, pointing and laughing at the park's bovine occupants who share their good-natured captivity with the casual stroller. Never have I seen two happier children upon this earth, nor more obedient and respectful of their elders than David and Lila.

On one particularly beautiful afternoon a few days ago, when the sun hung brightly in the sapphire sky, the puffy white clouds drifted overhead and the light flashed yellow against the green leaves, David set me aback. Quite out of the blue for an eight-year-old, he asked, with an interrogative tone reminiscent of a barrister, "Are you a murderer, Uncle Robert?" After my incredulous look, he repeated his question. Little Lila eyed me suspiciously despite her distracted attention to her doll.

"Nonsense," I replied and tried gamely to smile whilst pretending to gaze at the other park goers. "Why would you attribute such a foul deed to your Uncle? And at such time as you know I was held blameless of any wrongdoing?"

"I've been told," he replied with the innocence of a new-born babe.

"By whom?"

"A chum."

"Well, it appears to me you are in need of a new circle of friends. I have harmed neither man nor beast," I said, hoping my nephew would end his inquisition. "And I never intend to do so." Like waves upon sand, his curiosity dissipated, and he transformed into the child he is – his attentions were soon absorbed in the waddle of a duck and her ducklings as they made their way down the path. I pondered with amusement and, yes, consternation, at his gall, as my nephew and niece followed their avian companions.

Between their giggles and delighted laughter, I became aware of movement behind us. No threat, no danger alerted me to peril: call it intuition or what you may, it raised the hackles on my neck and sent gooseflesh rippling over my body. In one horrible instant, with the children running ahead of me, the memories of Belrive swamped me and I felt as if I might drown in their terrible waters. I turned and the sight chilled me to the bone.

There, behind me, was a couple of the most immense stature, extraordinary beauty and composure that had ever been my pleasure (and horror) to witness. Their clothes were of regal cut, not as crafted for royalty but rather for the military; the gentleman held a gold-tipped walking stick; the lady led two magnificent children by her gloved hands. Their stately gait bespoke of their power and dominion, as did the unearthly intensity of their dark eyes. They and the children studied me and held me with their looks as if I were an object to be captured, imprisoned by their gaze. In a fit of panic, I called for David and Lila to halt and stood facing the approaching couple. They passed us by with neither a sideways glance nor spoken word, but the specter of Death froze me to my spot as they walked on. It was several minutes before I regained my senses and, dazed, sat on the ground, hugging my dear niece and nephew.

"Let's be off to home," I said to the children and, tousling David's hair and picking up Lila, we left St. James's for Warwick Street. Along the way, we passed another couple equally as handsome and atavistic, with the same forceful gaze, and, without doubt, I knew we had been visited by the progeny of Ernest Frankenstein. How I feared for the safety of my niece and nephew; indeed, how I feared for our dear family. But how could this be? How could these monsters roam the streets of London? Or was my nervous agitation worsening – this beautiful sunny day in London had not been the first where I had questioned the fragile nature of sanity. When I fled Belrive leaving Ernest to his mad design, I constructed my doubts, like an illusion, about his capacity to unleash his horrors upon the world. I suffered from a naiveté endemic to the natural state of man: I rushed away from the terrible scene building a conclusion in my mind. I would secure my survival and Ernest would fail – his creations would die. much as the woodland hare had collapsed upon the barn floor after its resurrection. Such would be the fate of Ernest; and he, and his "army," would suffer the indignities of any broken man with grandiose dreams. The name of Frankenstein would die an ignoble death. But as I entered your peaceful and cheery home this day, dear Margaret, I knew my brief respite from the terrors brought on by my friendship with Victor would take yet another abhorrent twist. As any man faced with hardship and difficulties, I steeled myself and recalled my early days in the expedition to the northern lands (as I wrote to you) when my courage and resolution were firm, but my hopes fluctuated and my spirits were often depressed. The long and difficult voyage I considered finished was but interrupted. Dangers of the direst nature demand all my fortitude and I look to heaven with an imploring heart to save not only our lives, but ensure the well-being of mankind.

This morning, Margaret, with a quizzical but resolute expression, handed me a letter. As I touched her hand she smiled, but her joyous expression waivered as I took the missive. She excused herself from the room and I took in with interest the writing on the parchment envelope; it was addressed to Captain Robert Walton, care of The Saville Family, Warwick Street. The hand was strict and formal and there was no return, but the note had been posted from London. Dread rushed over me as I considered the source; I tore open the flap and read:

My Dearest Sir:

I have failed in my efforts at hospitality. I am acutely aware of my insufficiencies after your abrupt departure from Belrive; but, be of good cheer, a reunion of sorts is imminent. You will be a guest at my invitation – perhaps you have observed the other hosts who have watched you and the children cavort in St. James's Park. They know your every movement, as well as the travels of those you hold so dear.

It has taken some time to rebuild my new family. After a few days alone with my two remaining creations, I ventured into the cold woods in search of solitude, and my dog led me to the forest hut. There, I found a still smoldering fire, but no sign of the inhabitants. The monster you aided, Victor's creation, has fled with my former wife. She is dead to me,

137

as is our son. I know not, nor little care at the moment, where they make their unholy tryst. I have blessedly endured their absence, but the dæmon will, in due time, bow to my will. My plans go on without them, however, as with you, my creations will find them and extract the appropriate price.

Belrive still stands; however, the joy I once found there has evaporated and the house sits ghostly and empty. A distant neighbor has taken my loyal wolfhound and she lives in care and comfort unfettered by the woes that have been heaped upon me. The barn and the work I so cherished were destroyed by a suspicious fire on the night you departed. I surmise you may have had a hand in that, but it is of no matter. Victor's journals, so lovingly transcribed by Clerval, survived in their hiding place and have aided me immensely in my work. You would be stunned by the number of sons and daughters I have fostered and how quickly and forcefully they grow; but soon you will have your chance at first-hand observation.

I prattle on too much for the confining structure of a letter. Suffice it to say, I am in London. I find the English better hosts for my work – so much more than the despicable French who, ultimately, will be crushed as they have crushed others under their tyranny.

And, one last point. There is another reason I have ventured to London. It is the matter of a book by Cornelius Agrippa. My children languish from the lack of its knowledge. Be assured I will wrest the volume from you and use it to my (and my family's) full advantage.

Until we meet again, with all sincerity, Yours Truly,

E. Frankenstein.

The signature was written in blood.

The letter shook me to the core. Despite the bright rays of sun slanting through the window, I could not shake the terrible foreboding and crushing doom that spread like a pall over me during the day. My sister, after numerous inquiries about my health, and cognizant of my mood, prepared a lovely supper for us that evening. Night had not yet fallen when we sat to eat: John was in a jovial mood, reveling in decent business that had come his way despite the ongoing war with France and other insecurities; the two children were amiable and behaved as always, their bright eyes sparkling in the warmth of their parents' attentions; and Margaret was at her best relishing her duties as mother and wife.

I meant no alarm when I announced to my sister, "Perhaps it would be good for you and the children to get away from London." Certain of some past trouble come to haunt me, Margaret looked at me with inquisitive eyes, but suppressed any exclamation of concern.

"Why should we leave London?" she asked calmly.

"The summer's approaching – Yorkshire would be so cool and comfortable. It would be a chance for David and Lila to learn about country life."

"But, dear brother, June is the best month to be in London," Margaret replied. She took a bite of her roast and then said, "Perhaps in late July or August when the heat grows oppressive."

John nodded and sipped his wine.

I hesitated to carry the conversation further for fear of upset; however, not long after the supper dishes were cleared and the children sent to bed, Margaret knocked softly upon my door.

"Now, what's this about?" she asked. "You've been out of sorts since the post arrived this morning. Something is wrong and I deserve to know. You must share your tribulations with your sister."

Out of respect for her wishes, I could not withhold the truth from her. I also was unsettled by her intent gaze, which was drawn to the scar upon my cheek – inflicted by Ernest on my last night at Belrive. Thus, I revealed all, including the letter's contents, to her. At length, she sat on my bed, looking in despair at the correspondence in her lap, occasionally wringing her hands and clutching at her dress. After much urging from me, she finally spoke: "I will not endanger the children. I will agree to your proposal; however, you must stay and protect John. The children and I will leave – for our summer holiday – on the morrow, as soon as transportation can be arranged."

I placed my hand on her shoulder and she shivered under my touch. She rose and with defiance in her eyes, said, "He *will not* get the best of us." With that she left the room and closed the door. I retired to bed, but I was haunted by her sobs as she made her way to her chamber. For my part, I resolved to find the one inhabitant on earth who could match the strength and cunning of my pursuer – Frankenstein's dæmon.

ROBERT WALTON'S JOURNAL

London, June 5th, 17—

The tears flowed from my dear sister when she departed late the next morn from her home on Warwick Street. I comforted her as best I could and whispered in her ear my intention to protect her household and husband from harm. For the good of the children and John's peace of mind, Margaret insisted that my trials and the ensuing consequences be held in mutual confidence – and I readily agreed, for there was no good reason to upset the stability of her husband, or alarm my niece and nephew without cause. I showered my blessings upon the stage-coach and its travelers as they turned from view, the last memory of my sister being that of her lovely face shining from inside her bonnet and the generous wave of her hand that signaled her good-bye. It is my sincere hope that she and her children will be safely ensconced in my Yorkshire home after several days journey. Heaven bless my beloved sister and her children!

In late morning, long after John's departure to his business, I made my way to the Legal Quays upon the Thames as some instinctual spirit urged me forward. There, I found the company of a number of fishermen and I was soon engaged in spirited conversation with many of the seafaring souls, a few of whom I had accompanied as a lad on whale-fishing expeditions to the North Sea. This discourse served me well and soon my sagging spirits were elevated enough to accompany a few of the men to a serving establishment for a pint of ale. After several, one of the sailors unfamiliar to me swaggered my way and put his hand roughly on my shoulder.

"Yer the gentle-man called Cap'n Robert Walton, ain't ya," he slurred through his intoxicated state.

I nodded, but said nothing, not wishing to make my identity known to everyone in the tavern.

"Aye, my brother paid a high price to serve aboard yer cursed ship," he said, and I feared my life might be threatened as his hands drifted toward his pockets. His eyes reddened and swelled at the thought of his dead brother, but instead of a knife or other instrument of death, he withdrew a yellowed slip of paper and clutched it in his fist.

Of course, the memories of my ill-fated voyage flashed through my mind, but those thoughts were reserved for my personal hell and could not be shared with anyone other than my trusted sister. I, of course, was assailed by the degradation and despondency the sailor's presence stirred within me. I extended my hand, but he rejected my offer of friendship and stared at me with sad eyes. After a time, I asked the brother's name and the man replied, "Stafford." I remembered the young sailor who had served as an under-mate aboard my vessel. I offered my condolences, making mention of the terrible disease that had wasted the crew, and was about to turn away from him (for I had no further stomach for the company) when he thrust the paper into my hands.

"Take this," he said, pressing my fingers around it. "I don' believe in spirits, but I believe in evil. I prayed I'd see ya someday to give ya this message." He drew me to a dark corner, and his eyes glittered in the lamplight cast from the far side of the room. "I heard tales from the whaling crew that delivered ya back to England – strange tales – stories no right man would believe possible. One of them says to me, he saw men hanging by their feet from the riggings while the *Prosper* burned. Course, who was he to go against the testimony of a ship's captain when such strange goings on would judge a poor sailor mad? Maybe all that smoke and fire clouded his vision. And not one mention at the inquest of such a 'orrible occurrence. Strange indeed."

"The northern lights can play tricks on the eye," I said, hoping the man would come to his point and allow me to escape the now suffocating confines of the tavern.

"My brother died," he continued, "and it's been eatin' at me since. And now I have the company of the Cap'n who knows the truth. What really happened on yer ship, Cap'n Walton?" He swayed a bit and reached for his half-drained pint.

"You can read the results of the inquest – it was made public. I have nothing further to say on the subject." I attempted to push past him to the door, but he stopped me with a thrust to my chest from his beefy arm.

"Not quite yet, Cap'n." His lips hung upon the appellation and his inflection laid a curse upon my title. "This 'ere sailor also says there was stories of a gigantic being that raced across the northlands, killin' all in his path. Ya know nothin' about him, I suppose, Cap'n Walton? Ya know nothin' 'bout a monster that might have come aboard yer ship?"

"I know of no such being," I said, and with the telling of that falsehood, my stomach turned over; I could not abide much more of this sadistic questioning.

"Look at the paper," he commanded.

I opened the yellow sheet and read the crudely printed word, *Hoy*. "What does this mean?"

"It's an island in the cursed Orkneys," he replied. "Not fit for man, but perfect for a murderer. They say a monstrous creature who covers his face with a black cloak lives there with a beautiful woman. That mean anything to ya, Cap'n? I thought I might travel there myself to see the sights."

"I wouldn't suggest it," said I. "You'll be chasing after phantoms."

He snorted and took another swig of his ale.

Chills rushed over me because I knew, quite by accident, I had found my answer. Of all the places on earth, the creature might inhabit, the Orkney Islands would be a suitable home – isolated, inhospitable to all but the hardiest of beings – there he could live out the rest of his days in seclusion with Olivia and not be hounded by the tyranny of man. Geneva, the ice caves of the Arveiron, the summit of Montanvert, were familiar to him but too close to the calamities of Belrive and Ernest's destructive plan. No, the creature knew the islands – Victor had pledged to create the monster's mate there, but then destroyed the female companion and thus sealed his own tragic fate – so to the archipelago the dæmon would be drawn.

"I am deeply sorry for your loss," I said and brushed past the sailor.

"Be watchful, Cap'n," he shouted after me, alerting the tavern to my hasty retreat. "The phantoms might come for ya, too." Thus, he clutched at the wall and his voice dissolved into inebriated laughter.

Once out of the room and back on the docks, my head cleared and I resolved immediately to quit London the next day and secure a sea voyage to Hoy. I required the services of a privateer, which would take me speedily to the isolated islands. There, I would beg the creature to return to London to defend my sister and her family and to aid me in my efforts to save the world from the destructive forces of Ernest Frankenstein.

Hoy, June 12th, 17—

The wild and primeval island of Hoy lay before me, its ancient crags and sea spires thrusting from the water before us in a rush of spray, its forbidding mountains breaking through the mists like enormous sentinels. There, I sought the creature who calls himself Frankenstein.

Several days earlier, I bade John good-bye, urging him to caution and abstention from any night-time ramblings. He looked askance of my pleas, and, with a wave of his hand swept back his hair in defiance, whilst awaiting further explanation from me. I informed him of my decision to travel to the Orkney Islands, a scientific voyage to combat the northern illness as I termed it, and recounted a few details from the tavern incident. There were people who wished me harm, I explained, despite the inquest's outcome; drunken sailors and mournful fathers who held no compassion for me or any member of my family – a cure for the disease might quell their anger. This seemed to mollify him, however, my tone brought on a general agitation, and I believe he sensed the vague peril that might befall his wife and children. For that, he may have wished me removed from London sooner than later, and, of course, I could not blame him.

I secured the services of a crew and privateer, a refitted merchant vessel, suited for attacking the Spanish and French. The Captain was not entirely amicable to my voyage, preferring to sail south rather than north with the intention of gaining bounty from enemy ships, but my generous offer of gold turned his head. We sailed down the Thames on a brilliant day, the sun sparkling in our eyes. As we rounded the river's mouth and pitched toward the North Sea, the weather became rougher and bereft of any semblance of calm: the turbulent ocean slapped against the heaving ship and the salt spray filled our nostrils and eyes, obscuring our vision of the near shore. At points in our voyage we traversed roiling banks of mist – the clouds from the heavens trembling low over us, breezing through the masts. For several days, we churned northward past Scarborough, Sunderland, Dundee and finally Aberdeen before entering the untamed and desolate waters carrying us to our destination.

We arrived at Hoy shortly after five in the morning, our ship coming to rest in a wide bay nestled beneath a large hill streaked with pink and white. Our vessel caused some excitement among the village inhabitants; those going out for the day's fishing had issued an alert. The captain lowered the skiff, taking a few crew members aboard, and we set ashore amongst a crowd on the sandy beach. The Orcadians, drab though they may have appeared, were animated and generous with their hospitality, one speaking perfect English – my ear lost in the others' rough dialect. I asked the gentleman I could understand – a shopkeeper by trade – if he was aware of any tales regarding a gigantic being said to be living on the island.

"With a beautiful and angelic woman named Olivia?" he asked without hesitation.

My heart leapt at this news and I immediately asked him to guide me in my search. He pointed to the north-west toward the hills and the encompassing moorlands. "A half-hour's walk from here, you will find the man you seek. He lives a life of seclusion with his wife in a stone house. I have never looked upon his face." Here, he turned away from the others and spoke to me in a hushed voice. "They say he is deformed and monstrous, and hides his grotesque features beneath a cloak."

"And what of his temperament?" I asked.

"A gentler man never existed. He carries the new-born calf to a place of shelter, hauls wood and water to his neighbors in the depth of winter, lifts grain with the strength of ten men and does not complain. Curses never pour from his lips. The people treat him with respect and gratitude, and he bestows the same upon them."

I was astonished at the admiration accorded to Victor's creation. With Olivia, he had found his mate, the security of a home and obvious contentment; I was certain my plea for his return to London would be ill received. Why leave paradise to jump into hell?

Thanking the man, I turned to the Captain and bade him await my return to the ship by no later than sundown. I expected my discourse would be short upon my meeting with the dæmon. Taking my leave of the crowd, I ascended the beach and found a narrow path that led into the green and restless moors.

The walk reminded me of the far reaches of northern England: a wild, desolate place where a man could gain his soul or lose it according to his constitution. The effect upon me was almost gladdening and I reveled in the heath and the touch of mist that hung in the bracing air. Therefore, with some sadness I approached the end of my journey, the rough stone house occupied by the creature. The structure sat on the crest of a windswept valley with the looming hills in the distance, and looking back, I could see the rolling ocean and the black dot of the ship resting on the wide bay.

There was no sign of life save a solitary lamp that burned in the window. As I walked to the door, several dogs crawled from their sleeping places and barked a friendly warning; and three cats, one black, the others calico, stretched and eyed me with distrust. Overall, the scene was one of calm and delicious peace, so far removed from the bustle of London and Ernest's threat that any man would have been a fool to spurn such a tranquil setting.

With great anticipation, I knocked upon the entry.

After a few moments, the rough-hewn door opened by slow degrees and the hooded figure of the creature stood before me, his massive frame blocking the entry to the room beyond. His face was covered except for his eyes, which upon sighting me grew wide with recognition. I knew not what to expect, a dagger or an offer of friendship; instead, he kept his gaze upon me and with a wave of his hand invited me in.

Near the fireplace stood Olivia, more radiant and beautiful than when I had met her upon our introduction at Belrive. She, with a generous smile, turned from her cooking and offered her hand, which I kissed with genuine affection and gratitude. Surely all the angels of heaven had bestowed their blessings upon the creature's companion. He, in turn, called the joyful animals inside and they gathered about his feet as content as supplicants before the Cross. There was no sign of little Wolfgang. My heart grew sick with worry – my favor (and I could think of no better word as a guest in his home) would surely be refused. What lunacy even to ask! No good, only harm, would come to him if he agreed to my undertaking.

Olivia sat in one of the crude wooden chairs in the center of the room and bade me sit as well – so different from the opulent furnishings of Belrive; yet, what man would not trade his wealth for the happiness found in this simple dwelling.

Olivia spoke first: "Welcome to our home. Please break the fast with us."

I readily agreed, not having partaken this morn of any of the miserable sustenance aboard the privateer.

As Olivia rose to prepare the meal, the creature pulled back his cloak and revealed his countenance, the object of disgust and horror to so many men. To my astonishment, his features had softened during his time with Olivia. The terrible scars and burns that blighted his visage remained, but appeared less loathsome, less severe, inspiring pity rather than terror. We sat for a time in discourse upon his journey to the Orkney Islands and his reasons for settlement. They were as I judged: He had visited the islands during his pursuit of Victor and found them suitably inviting; his contact with men would be limited to the small local population; and, less likely in my reasoning, but of great importance to the dæmon, was a specific mental consideration. On this archipelago, Victor Frankenstein had destroyed the promised mate and stoked the creature's horrific revenge, including the later murder of

Victor's lovely bride, Elizabeth. In this setting, the creature, tempered by time and love, could repent for his actions. The monster found upon his return with Olivia, a penitence for his dream fulfilled, atonement for his past sins. He considered it his duty to make amends with all inhabitants of the island – human and animal. Here he would create the family and companionship he so desperately desired.

Olivia served a meal of oats and baked bread, churned butter and fresh milk; her food was like manna to my mouth and I savored every morsel. After the dishes had been taken away, I withdrew Ernest's letter from my coat and handed it to the dæmon. He read it with interest, but I found it hard to gauge his feelings as he held it – save a tremble in his fingers as he returned it to me.

"You can see why I came," said I, "why I had to find you."

He nodded. Olivia moved her chair to a corner near a small rectangular object covered by a blanket.

"Ernest will destroy my family and he has vowed the same for you and Olivia," I said, hoping to appeal for the protection of his companion. "I have seen his minions in London. They found me – and they will find you, if you do not act. You must be on your guard. Ernest makes no idle threats."

He slumped in his chair and covered his face with his massive hands.

"You are the only one who can meet the enemy face-to-face and survive," I continued. "Without your intervention, he will fulfill his plan and create his army. Every day's delay assures his success." There was but one other reason for the monster to act, that being the vow of revenge he uttered in the barn upon the death of little Wolfgang. I reminded him of this curse and he shook his head and pointed to Olivia. She lifted the blanket from the object next to her. My eyes could not make out the form in the dim light, until I rose from the chair and peered, with astonishment, into the wooden box. It was a cradle and inside slept the most handsome child; his luxuriant blond hair and lashes added to his beauty and perfect form. There, with his mother and protector by his side, slept Wolfgang, a boy upon whom the world, obsessed with its scientific curiosities, would shower innumerable blessings – science would clamor for the child whom twice had died and endured two reincarnations. What fortune for the infant!

"This is my son – no longer does he belong to Ernest," the creature said with great humility. "Olivia is my wife."

"He is my husband," Olivia said gently, and I had no doubt of her veracity. In her madness, she had depended upon the monster to protect her child, and now the gentle soul that inhabited her looked with loving favor upon her disfigured husband. His countenance, which terrified the strongest of men, was inconsequential to her. She alone was able to draw out the goodness that resided within him.

I offered my congratulations, but my tone was subdued by the thrust of my journey. The dæmon would never leave his son and wife to fight an army created by Ernest, who ultimately sought our destruction. Would the creature flee the Orkney Islands with his family or stand to fight? I dared not ask it – I would not ask it of any man, except those under my command in the service of our country. Those men knew the risks when pledging their allegiance to our nation.

"I am sorry," I said. "I understand your obligations. I will return to London."

The monster looked upon me with sad, watery eyes.

I rose to leave and with despairing heart contemplated a long, slow walk back to the ship. My journey to Hoy had been doomed from its inception. I gathered my coat and said my good-byes. Olivia kissed me upon the cheek and the creature offered his hand. The strength emanating from his grip shocked me and, sensing this power, I wished to convey one final request in my fevered desire to secure him for my cause – but instead I turned toward the door where the cottage lay robed in the morn's brilliant light.

The creature followed me over the rough stone entry, closed the door and covered his face with his cloak.

I waved to him and began my descent toward the ship.

The creature bade me to stop; his eyes softened in an expression of kindness and a thin smile creased his lips. "Our son," he said, "is no longer called Wolfgang. He is Robert – in gratitude for the man who helped save the lives of my wife and child, and freed me from the shackles of destruction and revenge."

I knew not what to speak; instead I walked away from his solitary and peaceful home. From my vantage point above the bay, I looked toward the sea and upon the small speck of the privateer that had carried me from London, and I dreaded my return, but it was my duty; my family was in my trust and the hands of God. After several yards, I turned back to the house. He stood in the doorway, his dark figure shining in the blazing light.

"Thank you, my friend," I shouted. "I will think of you often and I will address you by the name you desired – Frankenstein. Let that be my acknowledgment of our friendship."

He said nothing, but nodded, and I was soon out of sight of his house and on the hoary path back to the ship. As I neared the bay, I spotted another vessel, glistening in the distance. I inquired of one man who told me that visitations to Hoy from foreign ships were few. The second, he said, had been curiously circling the bay all morning, but had not dropped anchor. The sight of the marauder shook my confidence in a peaceful return to England; I asked my local companion to carry a message to Frankenstein.

"Frankenstein?" the man inquired with suspicious eyes.

"Yes, Frankenstein . . . who lives on the ridge with Olivia. Tell him a ship has arrived for him. He will understand. This message comes from his friend . . . Captain Robert Walton."

And with that I departed to find the crew of the privateer, which would carry me, I prayed, without incident to my Yorkshire home and the company of Margaret, and her children.

LETTER FROM ROBERT WALTON TO FRANKENSTEIN OF HOY

The Wolds, June 17th, 17—

To Frankenstein, Hoy, the Orkney Islands

My friend, I hope this letter finds you in better spirits than those that have possessed me since we last met. I write because you are my final hope and, once again, I plead – no beg – for your intercession in a matter of grave concern not only to me, but to the world.

Despair has ripped the life from my soul, tears fall from my sad eyes daily and my mental agitation borders on chaos. Never can I rest, perchance nod for a few moments, before the terror that fills me returns with overwhelming fury. I beg your forgiveness for the length of this missive, but you must know my terrible tale and not be spared from its horrors, lest you consider the situation dire only in my imagination.

The awful news is that my beloved sister, Margaret and my nephew, David – the dear child – have been taken by Ernest's creations! I can only surmise that this is his diabolical plan to lay his hands upon the Agrippa, which I have so cautiously guarded since its use upon Olivia and your son. And, of course, I will never willingly again relinquish its power. I would ensure its obliteration by tossing it overboard into the tempestuous sea, but I am nowhere near its destructive waters. I cannot throw it from the stage-coach; it may fall to the wrong person or perhaps be swept up by sentries from Ernest's army, but the truth is, this small book, which has been the bane and pride of my existence, is the only object that assures the life of my sister and my nephew. Ernest will stop at nothing to secure it so he can deliver the hellish souls that suit his scheme.

When last I saw you, I asked one of Hoy's inhabitants to deliver a message about a second ship circling the bay. I trust this communication was received by you and no unfortunate consequences occurred as a result of the strange visitors. I was eager to leave the island for Yorkshire, but the crew could not be swayed, even for the promise of extra gold. We remained in the bay overnight before departing; the sailors wished some time on land before returning to sea. I kept watch on the other vessel, whose route was marked by the torches on board, until the wee hours of the morning. At dawn, the ghostly ship had vanished, but I felt its presence as surely as if it were anchored next to us; therefore, I was certain of its imminent threat.

The next day the weather had turned and the bay was choppy and the voyage portended no better. For two days, our ship was buffeted by the cold and dangerous waters as we pursued our southerly route, past Scotland to the north of England to Spurn where we anchored until we could ride the Humber's high tide into Kingston-upon-Hull. There, I departed the privateer and left its crew with a moderate amount of coin to continue the journey to London, or wherever the avaricious captain would steer his ship. I secured a horse from the local livery and soon was off amongst the roads to the Wolds. My black steed was fleet and after a grueling day's ride over the low green hills spotted with trees, with little time for rest, I arrived home to find the door open, the glass shattered and the interior blackened by flames!

I called out for my dear sister and her children, but there was no answer. How can I describe the moment's panic – the corrupt machinations of Ernest Frankenstein had come to bear their terrible witness upon me. In my rage, I overturned the charred cabinets, threw my uncle Thomas's books, I had so admired, upon the remaining embers, laughed maniacally over the destruction of my life's trappings, which meant so little to me whilst the lives of my precious ones remained in the balance. I sat sobbing upon the stoop, when to my ears I detected the faint cries of child. At once, my heart leapt at the sound and I moved round the corner and gazed upon the blackened stones. There, amongst the cover of the lilacs I saw a small hand creep forth. I rushed to the greenery and gathered my terrified niece in my arms and smothered her soot-covered face with kisses. Shocked as she was, she appeared unharmed except for several small scratches upon her limbs.

"What happened, my dear one?" I implored of the shivering and crying Lila, although her answer already lay within my agitated mind.

She clutched at my coat with her small hands and looked into my eyes. "Oh, Uncle Robert, I hid through the night in the trees and then came back to hide under the bush. I managed to escape from *them*." Upon her final word, she burst into tears and for several minutes she was unable to speak. I stroked her hair and face and eventually managed to coax her back from her fearful state.

"Who were they?" I asked. "They cannot hurt you now – I promise."

Her brown eyes grew wide in wonder and she said, "The people we saw in the park – like the man and woman we saw when David and I followed the ducks."

A horrible thirst for vengeance filled me; Ernest had made good upon his threat. My heart beat fast for his blood to be spilt, and the murderous intention sent shocks coursing through my body. I swore by God, I would not rest until my family was safe and I had witnessed Ernest's death. My nephew had asked me in St. James's Park if I was a murderer, I had recoiled from the appellation; but, as I looked upon my distraught niece who suffered like a frightened angel in my arms, I relished the thought of killing Ernest Frankenstein. It was the second time in my life (the first being my pursuit in the Arctic of the creature) I harbored such terrible ambition.

When she had calmed a bit, I asked, "Where are your mother and David?"

Lila covered her eyes with her small hands and brushed away tears. "They dragged them into a carriage – and they were gone. Mother and David fought – he kicked at one until I got away."

"Hush, you've said enough. You must be hungry and tired." Lila nodded and snuggled against my chest. "Would you like to take a ride on my horse?"

"Oh, yes, Uncle Robert! I want to see, papa, mama and David in London. Please don't leave me!"

I carried her to the front of the house where my steed waited; the evening was growing short and darkness was falling. I was afraid Ernest's automatons might return and wreak more havoc upon my small charge. I lifted Lila to the horse's neck and told her to grip his mane tightly until I could mount. With a kick, we were away to the comforting safety of the village inn far down the lane, where the fire at my home would have gone unnoticed.

I write tonight by the light of a single candle as I watch over my small cherub who sleeps so soundly near the window. The stars circle overhead and all appears right with the world, but I know such a thought is a dangerous illusion and cannot be embraced. I ask you – again, implore you – please come to London and aid me in this war, for Ernest has delivered the first blow. We shall either find solace in victory or peace in death. The choice is ours, one we must soon make or risk the downfall of man to science. I ask you as a friend to share my tribulations, for without your courage and strength we may lose all.

On the morrow, we are off to London and an uncertain future. I cannot leave Lila alone in Yorkshire when she begs for a reunion with her family. All blessings follow us in our journey.

Yours truly, with much anticipation for your reply,

R. Walton

ROBERT WALTON'S JOURNAL

London, June 24ᵗʰ, 17 –

Victory has slipped from my grasp and my darkest hour is upon me.

I am alone in my struggle against Ernest and I fear his numerous minions are carrying out the devil's work. Terrible fires have burned in London and the city is besieged by woes of the greatest magnitude. Murder is rampant, particularly among the poor, and disease and pestilence ravage the population. Even our King is ineffectual against the despair and destruction that has gripped us; his madness, his inability to see the tragedy, is a metaphor for the calamities that befall us. Can no one see with the eyes in their heads? Cannot the population which so calmly strolls the streets perceive the terrible curses, which any day may rain down upon them?

I have taken refuge in a public house not far from Warwick Street, being exceedingly careful to avoid detection by the creatures. There has been no time to soothe the soul or dispel the mental agitation which fills me to the point of constant distraction. I cannot rest, cannot take solace in my past voyages whose hearty glow elevated me to heaven, for their steady purpose acted as an aid to tranquilize the mind. I have none of that now. Even my memories of Margaret, her ready smile and steady hand do little to assuage the burning fires that stoke my revenge. One could say that the devil who inhabited Frankenstein has fled from that creature and found new vessels in Ernest and, in my fury, me.

Lila and I departed the Wolds by wagon after I gathered what few clothes I could from my ruined home and placed them in a trunk, which was filled to bursting. Upon return to the lodge, I implored the proprietor to send word to my neighbors to secure my dwelling until my return, for I had urgent business to attend to in London, not the least of which was the reunion of my niece with her father. I paid the innkeeper to board my black steed until my return, for Lila, in her few hours with the beast, had grown quite fond of the animal, and, I likewise, looked forward to a day when I could ride over the countryside upon the gallant horse. By mid-morn we were away by stage-coach with the Agrippa concealed safely within my bag. On this journey, I added a weapon to my possessions – a pistol which was given to me by my Uncle Thomas and unscathed by the conflagration. I kept it hidden within my coat, my hand at the ready should the need arise.

Wishing to spare Lila further emotional distress, I inquired about her playmates who might reside near Warwick Street. Lila was eager to see her father and learn the whereabouts of her mother and brother, but I cautioned that in order to see them we must first play a game – one in which she would have to be a good girl and follow my instructions for several days until I could surprise her with their return. I did not want, unwittingly, to deliver her again into the arms of Ernest's army. To my suggestion of a game, after much coaxing on the journey, she finally acquiesced. After several days, we arrived in London to the horrors I described earlier.

We searched for my niece's friend, Dora, and, after what would have been a pleasant walk through the neighborhood under better circumstances, we arrived at a modest dwelling several blocks from Warwick Street. A somewhat terrified woman, Mrs. Shelby, answered the door to which Lila had directed me. Upon sight of my dear niece, the good lady burst into tears and welcomed her with open arms. The matron covered her with kisses and exclaimed, "how fortunate, how glad," she was to caresses the girl once again. To my joy, a young lady of nearly identical age to my niece ran to the landing and, with equal affection, demonstrated her fondness for Lila. I could not have been happier at that moment, for all seemed according to plan, until Mrs. Shelby instructed the children to play upstairs and ushered me into the parlor. I then remembered the woman who had cared for David and Lila the evening of the cotillion so long ago.

"A plague has fallen upon London," Mrs. Shelby said in a hushed voice, and pointed out the window to the sun-splashed streets. "It is a curse from the French," she continued, displaying her loyalty to the Crown. "Have you been to Warwick Street?"

"No, that is why I came here straight away – so Lila would not suffer any more than she has. My dear niece has spoken fondly of your Dora." I explained to Mrs. Shelby as best I could the events that had transpired in Yorkshire, without any mention of Ernest Frankenstein and his malevolent plan.

"It was terrible, one night; so terrible my husband and I thought it was the end of the world." She gazed at me in wonderment.

I nodded, eager for her to continue her story.

"The sky was ablaze with embers and we gathered as much water as we could in pots and pails. My husband even made his way to the upper storey – poor man – he's not fit for such activity – leaned over the window ledge and doused water upon the shingles. We could see the fire on Warwick Street and hear the screams. The neighbors told us what happened – at least what they saw from their windows."

Here, she paused in her tale as if judging my interest. I, of course, could barely contain the revulsion filling my throat; yet, I knew I must hear her out, for only in the telling would I ascertain the gravity of the matter.

"The Saville house was on fire. Poor Mr. Saville was at home – we knew that Margaret and the children were in Yorkshire. There must have been twenty of them, who dragged him from the house – dear man – in his nightclothes. He fought like a banshee against these – *soldiers* – well, I don't know what else to call them. The last we knew, he was spirited away in a carriage as if devils were delivering him to Hades. The house nearly burned to the ground and since, we've been scared to venture into the street. It's all my poor husband can do to get himself to his labor every day. These fires keep popping up in London . . . ."

Her description of the terrible night sickened me. What little hope was there for John if he was taken by Ernest's creations – a strong presumption of death filled me. Mrs. Shelby looked at me expectantly, as if I might enlighten her in these dire matters, but I held my tongue and only expressed my appreciation for any offer of caretaking for my niece.

"She can stay as long as she likes," said Mrs. Shelby. "She'll be wonderful company for my Dora – she always has been. It's such a sad state of affairs these days. This war will be the death of us if it doesn't end soon."

With that, I called out for Lila who stood at the top of the stairs; I wished her farewell and promised a speedy return. I then offered my good wishes to Mrs. Shelby, bade her farewell and set off toward Warwick Street. Oh, the horror of it! I could barely contain my rage as I viewed the catastrophic scene of the Saville house: the pungent odor of smoke leaked from the standing timbers, the stone foundation and walls were blackened and besmirched with grime and soot. The neighbors' houses had suffered in the onslaught as well; the whole of deserted Warwick Street looked a shambles with shuttered windows and bolted doors – even the neighboring church stood silent and dark as if praying to an absent God.

I pushed open the fractured door and tested my footing on the blackened floorboards. There, in the entry, where I had been welcomed so many holidays with good wishes, warmed by the hearth and immersed in my family's charity and love, I gazed upon the remains of the destroyed dwelling. The china my sister had collected from generations past lay smashed in the broken cabinets; the paintings that had adorned the parlor crumbled in blackened frames on the stone walls; the fine silk furnishings and draperies were reduced to charred mounds of debris. The sun poured through a hole in the roof and fell in golden patches on the stairs, confirming my suspicion that the floor above was equally devastated. I took a few cautious steps inside, examining the overturned tables which had lined the hall.

My ears caught a noise and I stopped and listened, but was soon convinced I heard only the rustle of the wind through the eaves. A few steps farther and I heard it again – what should I call it? – my electrified nerves sent shivers racing down my body. It was a skitter – I can think of no better word to describe the horror that crept above me.

In my agitation, I called out the name of my brother-in-law, but he did not answer. What madness possessed me? Mrs. Shelby had informed me of his tragic fate. The slow, crawling thing over my head, the drift of ashes through the cracked timbers, shook my nerves and rattled my body; but little-by-little, in tiny flashes, blackened fingertips curled around the stair post above. I screamed, not in horror, but in desperation that the hand might belong to our beloved John, but it retreated upon my call and I thought, perhaps, I had suffered a nightmarish hallucination.

At my peril, I stepped toward the staircase.

My decision was a strategic blunder, for sensing my presence, the hand, fingers out-stretched, flesh, sinew and tendon trailing behind, leapt from the staircase, the hideous projectile set in its course for my throat. The grasping fingers missed their intended target, but struck me with force in my chest, and unable to clutch at my shirt, fell to the floor and wrapped itself around my boot in a hideous grip.

I shook my foot in terror and the already weakened floor crumbled around me, causing shards of blackened wood to pierce the hand's burnt flesh. This painful infliction did nothing to halt its deadly movement; it wrapped its fingers tightly around my calf and then crawled up my leg. All was in line for a catastrophe of the most delicate nature when the floorboards collapsed, hurling me into a dark pit beneath the house and somehow wrenching the fiendish hand free of my thigh. I could not see the devilish thing, but I heard its demonic scratches from underneath the timbers. I scrambled out of the rubble and kicked my way to the entrance and thence past the broken door to the street. Save for a few splinters of my own and some insignificant rips in my breeches I was none the worse. A brief respite allowed me to think upon the attack I had suffered, for without the intervention of gravity the outcome would have been calamitous.

Whose hand had attacked me? After a few minutes of needed composure, I drew this conclusion: The severed hand was from one of Ernest's male creatures – which one I could not say – separated from its owner in the assault on Warwick Street, but quite able to live and function without the aid of its body.

Whether the hand's aim was to kill or capture I knew not, but this realization gave me added concern because of its dire implication – the bodies of Ernest's creations would have to be rendered useless, destroyed completely, or, like certain reptiles, the creatures would regenerate and continue their attacks. Such an army would obliterate any other enemy, let alone a single man charged with their destruction. I doubted that even the dæmon could hold dominion over such a battle. Fear, like a sickness, spread over me and I stumbled down the street overwhelmed by the pressing weight of it all. I thought to take refuge in the shadow of the church, but even its cold, dark exterior seemed imbued with evil and despair. How I longed for my dear sister and her family. When I embarked on the expedition to the northern lands, I wrote to Margaret of my concern whether I should ever return alive – whether I would meet my dear ones once again in reunion, as, in my youth, having traversed immense seas and rounded the southern capes of Africa and America, and by God's graces returned safely to England. Then, I had expected success and could not bear to look upon the reverse of the picture. How I longed, during the time of those voyages, to read any letter from England – my connection with home – for they kept my family close whilst I reveled in my adventures. Now, standing in the midst of Warwick Street's destruction, I doubted my capacity as an adventurer and as a man. Through my explorations, I had torn my family apart.

Leaving Saville house, I walked past the church's holy doors and a small boy emerged from the shadows and clutched at the air in front of me. The movement startled me, considering what had just occurred, but his actions also brought back unpleasant memories of Lila hiding in the lilacs to escape her hideous tormentors. He was not to be feared, simply a street urchin seeking coin; however, in my agitated state I could offer neither pity nor charity, and had neither the time nor the inclination for beggars. But the child was insistent and threw his arms around my legs. I reacted forcefully to this assault and wrenched his limbs free. He looked upon me with a piteous gaze and my heart softened.

"I am to give you this or they will kill me," said he.

So strange were his words for a street child, I readily ascertained the cause of his alarm, and his formal manner of speech. He handed me a carefully folded note.

I opened it and read the prescribed details. I reached into my pocket with shaking hand and gave the boy a coin to which he displayed slavish devotion, but after a few moments, he, with eyes widened in horror, looked past me toward an indistinct figure that prowled along the distant corner. In an instant, the child turned and ran in the direction from whence I had come, past the church and the smoldering remains of Saville house.

The note was from Ernest Frankenstein requesting my presence at a specific address in London's East End, the next night before the stroke of midnight. I should arrive alone, it instructed, with the Agrippa, and surrender it to him – otherwise I would witness the excruciating deaths of Margaret and David before experiencing my own.

ROBERT WALTON'S JOURNAL

London, June 26th, 17 –

This entry may be my last.

I have lost all hope of victory, but I will endeavor to record all I have seen on what may be my final day on earth, before my appointed meeting with Ernest Frankenstein. The die is cast; I must suffer my final judgment. Fate has summoned me to this reckoning; Margaret and David must be saved, for if their blood is upon my hands – which surely it will be if I do nothing – I could not live, yet breathe, in good conscience. I have, after all, by my very existence and my friendship with Victor Frankenstein brought this madness upon my family. If I surrender the Agrippa to Ernest, all is lost; the same applies if I do not act. So, my time upon this beautiful earth will see its end for I fear I have little hope of winning this battle, even with the aid of Victor's creation. For all I know, he still enjoys his comfortable home in the Orkney Islands with Olivia and his son.

This final day dawned sunny and warm, unusually hot for London, which serves as an omen for a stormy evening ahead. My first task, after securing a morning meal, was to visit my niece at Mrs. Shelby's. Little Lila was thrilled, and showered me with hugs and kisses, even wiping tears from her innocent face. Mrs. Shelby had dressed her for the morning in a violet pinafore and the outfit complemented her honey-brown locks. Lila, of course, made numerous inquiries upon the whereabouts of her family, and I was suitably vague in my response because it pained me to offer the child hope of ever seeing her beloved parents and brother alive again.

"Our game is still on. You must be strong and await its finish," I told my niece, and Mrs. Shelby patted her head and nodded her agreement. Dora told Lila she wished she could play such a game with her parents, whereupon Mrs. Shelby muttered and frowned.

"Your father, mother and brother will be home soon and you will have a grand new home on Warwick Street with lots of playmates for company," Mrs. Shelby said to Lila and her words appeared to comfort my niece. Dora had broken the news of the Saville House fire the day before to my niece.

I knelt before Lila and took her, as light as a feather, into my arms and kissed her tender cheeks. In reciprocation, she clasped her hands around my neck and asserted she never wished to let me go, and her plea nearly broke my heart.

"Be brave. I will come back for you," I told her, and then gave her a kiss good-bye.

Mrs. Shelby and I ushered the two girls upstairs to play and then returned to the parlor where I spoke in firm tones about the gravity of my task. I did not want the poor woman and her family involved in my business, but I indicated she might not see me for several days, and if not within a week, she should inquire after me at the public house where I was staying. I begged her to rescue my meager possessions if necessary – particularly my journal and letters, which I had faithfully transported with me during all my journeys – and keep them safe from all usurpers. This was all I could say to the alarmed woman – all I could promise. I departed with one look back upon the house and there spotted the downcast face of my niece in the upstairs window. I waved to her and blew a kiss and wondered if I should ever see her again.

As I made my way down the street, I became increasingly aware of a smoky haze that drifted over the city. This came not from wood for heat or cooking (as the day was warm from its onset) but from spotty fires ignited, I presumed, by Ernest's army. Black plumes of smoke swirled like dark columns into the sky. For what purpose these tragedies were conducted, I knew not; however, I suspected they were maneuvers for his minions – attempts to terrorize the public into submission, as would be his later plan with the French and the remainder of the Continent. He could use this training ground to test his creations in their encounters with the British military, as well as hone their stealthy escapes.

But of greater concern to me was the presence of a legion of Londoners, male and female, that walked the streets with impunity, their glistening looks, their blissful smiles so rich with malevolence. I observed them, when I could, from my hiding places along the street. They strolled in clothes of impeccable form, each member handsome beyond description; their hair was luxurious and black, their eyes equally dark and *devoid of soul*. They did not directly meet my gaze; however, the hate that suffused their being was fixed upon me, of this I was certain. These automatons wished my death; and, I knew from whence came such hatred and vengeful spite. Yet, they did not attack. Why? The answer lay with Ernest Frankenstein: *He commanded these creatures with his thought – they carried no soul from the Agrippa – and, for now, I served Ernest better alive than dead until I should deliver the volume to him.*

I hailed a carriage to carry me from St. James's Park to the address written by my adversary. If I could not defeat him, I could at least discern some strategic advantage by visiting the site of our soon-to-be encounter. As the driver wound through The Strand, past Fleet Street, St. Paul's, to The Keys and The Tower, skirting a few burning buildings attended by fire brigades and shouting neighbors who carried pails of water, my thoughts fell to my dear sister and her family. The creatures could have Margaret and David sequestered in any of the structures I passed this day, awaiting the bidding of their master.

I arrived shortly before eleven in the morn at a large stone building in sight of The Tower, near the western end of Wapping Docks and the confluence of Hermitage Street. The structure itself filled me with dread as I contemplated its severe lines and dark windows dripping with grime and soot. The door was fit for a medieval castle, so solid were its oak beams and iron hinges – the intimidating effect, so similar to the barn at Belrive, suited Ernest's mad designs and assured me the address written on the note was an honest one.

The surroundings were quiet and still – not a soul in sight. I knew that if this was Ernest's laboratory no amount of concern and caution could protect me from his army. One ace tilted the game in my favor, however – the Agrippa rested securely hidden at the public house and no one, not even Mrs. Shelby, knew of its whereabouts. It would only be found if the planks were taken apart one-by-one and thus its safety, away from my ownership, was assured. Therefore, this late morn I had few thoughts upon my own life, but instead suffered along with my family awaiting their final fate.

I pulled at the handle and the massive door swung open. There, to my astonished and terrified eyes sat fifty or more of Ernest's army in repose along a banquette. They, men and women, stared at me with indifference despite the evil intent that seemed to flow from their bodies. The dark depths of their souls knew no limit. I stood frozen to the spot awaiting their attack at once, but it did not come. They watched me with their beautiful malevolent faces, but did nothing to harm me; nary a hand raised nor a word uttered. To my utter horror, the length of the building was filled with the same abhorrent creatures, some yielding weapons, others standing, watchful and remote, as if a spider waiting to pounce upon the fly. Perhaps three hundred or more of them milled about the lower level.

Wide stone stairs disappeared in the darkness to a second-storey. The path was menacing, but I could not forgo its exploration despite my fears. What if my sister and nephew were captives in this gruesome structure? Death could not sway me in an effort to secure their freedom.

A milky haze of mist and fumes greeted me at the top; the mixture was so thick I had to wave my hand in front of my face to see a short distance. I walked cautiously, and with good reason I found out, for no sooner had I entered a few steps into the cavern-like atmosphere than my head struck tentacles that descended from the roof to a vile creature hanging in front of me. I retreated in disgust.

There, before me, suspended in a glass container of immense size, was an infant – but a child like no other I had seen. The baby – a girl – of massive proportion, seemed to grow before my very eyes. Through the blue liquid she stared at me with sullen discontent and scraped her fingers against her transparent prison, and the murderous intention in her gaze was perfectly clear. A breathing tube ran from the smoky vault overhead into the container and, with this as her aid, she inhaled and exhaled in perfect breaths. Her hair waved like seaweed in the watery womb, and the whole effect was of a fantastic nightmare.

A breeze wafted through the dank air and split the haze, as one of the fully grown males appeared out of the mist and stood by the container; it was then that my eyes, with the aid of a few dismal rays of sun which filtered through the dirty windows, beheld numerous cocoons suspended from the beams above. This was Ernest's breeding ground for his army, and I was powerless to destroy it until Margaret, John and David were safe and held in my loving embrace.

Thus, in the cloudy gloom I walked, each step suffused with trepidation, as I passed through the labyrinthine maze of lines and birth globules, each filled with creatures of various sizes. Oh, how despair filled my soul! How could I hope to win a battle against such an army? Standing near each container was an adult, at the ready, a caretaker or sentry to the new-born. My nose and eyes burned from the acidic air, but the creatures appeared oblivious to their surroundings. With each step I found new terrors, the cocoons larger, their inhabitants stronger and more developed until I happened upon one where a young man the size and constitution of a sixteen-year-old emerged from his watery conception with a forceful kick of his feet. The glass shattered and the creature, naked in his birth, slipped from the container into the arms of a waiting female. She ignored my presence and attended to her duties, drying the liquid and birth matter from his body, cleansing the floor and preparing another vessel to hang in its place. The man-boy stared at me with his coal-black eyes, and a hiss, not unlike that of a cat's, emerged from his lips; the intensity of his hatred bored through me to my very innards. I stood placidly, suppressing the fear and revulsion that consumed me, until I could discern his plan. Presently, he turned and walked away into the mist as if receiving a silent command from a source unfamiliar to human eyes and ears. I moved past the busy female and followed the young man, who turned once in my direction and then with lightning step disappeared into the murky depths of the structure.

I had seen enough in a few minutes to shatter any courage or resolve I harbored for a battle with Ernest Frankenstein; however, I could not succumb to the tyranny of despair and tears and, therefore, with measured cadence resumed my exploration. My search of Ernest's haven overcame, temporarily, my capacity for fear. It was an eerie brew – one of terror combined with the thirst for adventure, a potent mixture that threatened to defeat me with any unfortunate misstep.

By slow measure, like a blind man, I found myself at the end of my quest. Looming in the half-darkness was a massive desk, flanked by long banks of tables which extended from each side. The male creature, whose birth I had witnessed, had already taken his place among the corps working for their master. The young man, attired in breeches and tunic of military cut, attended a vast milky white pool, which bubbled in a basin on one of the tables. These minions spooned the liquid – which smelled like ammonia liquor, and added its noxious vapors to the already foul acidic air – into cups and then poured their contents into waiting containers. The vessels were then dispatched into the fog away from my eyes.

Through the hazy distance, I perceived the hunched form of a man whose head lay in sleep on the gigantic desk – whether he was human or automaton I knew not, but as I drew near the hackles on my neck bristled in intuitive fear and recognition. In front of me reposed my adversary, and his slumber, I gathered, was the reason for my survival thus far. I dared not disturb his rest. His attendants eyed me with disdain and kept to their tasks. Margaret and David were not in sight; thus were my actions limited by their absence, for I could not risk Ernest's death when the whereabouts of my loved ones were yet unknown.

I had begun to find my way back to the stairwell when a mocking, sinister call echoed across the haze. I knew the voice well from my time at Belrive, and when I turned I could not believe the horror that rose from the desk and directed its frightening gaze at me.

Ernest Frankenstein had transformed himself into a monster.

The young man I had met barely two years before stood, and, with determined hand, pointed a gnarled finger at me. "I know why you have come, Walton. Your sister and nephew are not here, but they will be in our company at midnight, not before. Do you think I'm such a fool as to bring them here?"

I stared at the fiend who stood before me. The tentacles and lines that swirled above his head and spread like a web over the room ended in a confluence that disappeared behind his back. They were connected to his head and body. *Ernest was feeding his army: his life blood flowed from him to the gestating automatons, his thoughts to those already released from their confinement.* The creatures had truly become his children, but the consequences to his physical and mental state were evident. He appeared frail, much like a bat in his form; he had grown taller and leaner, more vampiric, since I had seen him last at Belrive. His fine clothes had been replaced by loose robes, which floated like wings across his arms. His profuse blond hair had grown thin and turned a sleek black, wild and streaked with gray; his eyes were deeply sunken in their sockets, as lifeless as orbs set into the pits of hell. His cracked smile was thin; his papery flesh stretched across his bony face. When he moved the tubes shook and rattled under the roof; all the creatures looked upon him as he stood and a devilish reverence shone in their dark eyes as they followed his movement.

"What have you done with my family, monster, and also with the loving husband and father, John? I will kill you on the spot if any harm has come to them."

Ernest's sardonic laugh filled the room; his voice was broken, yet piercing, and his eyes burned with indignation. In a rush, his minions were upon me; their speed swifter than that of the forest deer. They encircled me with glowing eyes, weapons of all kinds drawn and pointed at my shaking body. I was certain all Ernest had to do was to *think* of my death and his very thought would be carried into action – his will be done.

"I care not what has happened to the husband – he is of no consequence to me. However, the sister and nephew are a different matter. For them, you have a great and abiding love; therefore, you are a slave to your devotion." He shook his head and gazed upon me with mock pity. "They are well and will remain so until you deliver the Agrippa."

I could barely speak with the lances and daggers thrust at my throat, but I managed to call out in the most firm, resolute voice I could display, "You have my word. I will return before midnight with the book, but I will destroy it, unless you release them unharmed."

He drew his arms together and folded them across his chest. "Threats are useless . . . but the book is precious. You know its strength." He stopped and chastised me with his demonic eyes. "Bring it to me and they shall be released."

"John as well?"

"The husband, as agreed." Ernest sat and his creatures moved away from me in a slowly expanding circle. "Now, leave me. You know the appointed hour."

I turned to depart, but the monster chided me with one final warning: "And rely not on the military or any authority, or you will seal your family's doom." I looked back at his hideous form and he smiled. "And, be warned, the traitorous creature from Hov can no longer come to your aid. In your haste to destroy me, you led me to the vile dæmon and, thus, sealed his fate – he is dead and rests in hell."

An overpowering grief clawed at my heart and I nearly fell to my knees in despair, for Ernest confirmed what I had sensed – the second ship circling the bay had been under his command. My misguided effort to ensure my family's preservation had exposed Victor's creation and, thus, he had perished by my foolish blunder. All was lost with the death of my friend, Frankenstein – my ally, and sole hope for victory, was destroyed.

Rage filled me, but I said nothing and coursed past the surrounding creatures to the dingy stairwell. The light shifted as I made my way through the coils and hanging wombs; each container filled me with horror and my blood congealed as I surveyed Ernest's mad work. At the stairs, deep shadows fell across the grimy windows and the steps were plunged into darkness; far away lightning traced to the ground and the gentle rumble of thunder rolled over Ernest's laboratory. With the flash, I noted something which struck me as extraordinarily odd. A female was walking up the steps when the bolt struck. Her dark eyes, the color of obsidian, sparkled with the lightning and then returned to their terrible shade as quickly as the brilliance evaporated, as if the charge, for a brief instant, had disconnected her body from her master's control. But the effect was slight and I

168

could not weigh the truth of my observation against the agitated state of my mind – so much of what I have experienced since the fateful day of Victor's arrival on the ice has manifested itself like a nightmarish hallucination.

I descended past the female and the steps grew cold and forbidding; I wished to flee from the horrors that threatened me and my loved ones; a dark regret filled me as I pondered what events fate had thrown in my path. Never would I have sought Victor's friendship had I been able to foresee this day. As I reached the landing and was about to open the door, I looked toward the creatures who inhabited the lower rooms. Once again, they eyed me with indifference as if their master had forsworn his foe; they busied themselves with their work and paid little attention as I returned to the street. My burning lungs heaved in the oppressive air outside and I vomited upon the rough stones – my body shook and I knew I could never defeat the monster that resided inside this grim structure. In that despondent and pitiful mood, I made my way back to the public house near Warwick Street (making certain none of the creatures observed me) to rest before my final hours.

I have slept little in the feverish heat, and, forgoing rest, return to my journal for one last entry before I go to my death. I could not eat, could only doze before this battle, as my thoughts gravitated to my dear sister Margaret, her husband, my niece and nephew and what will surely be a failed rescue and their ultimate demise. My friend from the Orkney Islands is dead and I think upon the fate of Olivia and her child. Should they have escaped the harm that befell the dæmon, I wish them peace, blessings and a fruitful existence wherever they may be. May Mrs. Shelby find these journals and letters and save them for later generations, should my life cease.

Much of what I contemplated this afternoon and evening has been upon the meaning of my existence. Why was I put upon this earth? What journey have I been asked to take in order to arrive at this destination? I have never been a particularly religious man, but I have always respected and worshiped nature in all its forms – this includes all creatures, human and animal. At one time in my youth before my sailing days, under the tutelage of my gentle sister, I pledged that I would never harm a living thing. I soon released the folly of such thinking, for what, after all, is a living thing? Is it the beautiful flower that adorns the fields of spring, the jumping fish that provides sustenance from all the earth's waters: the untamed beast, providing nourishment and clothing, which runs free until felled by the hunter's arrow? How are such decisions made? The question arises: What tempts man to play God, to usurp powers intended for His divine plan?

For these questions, I have no answer, and as the hour of reckoning draws near, a strange quiet has overtaken me. Until I picked up the pen, regret filled me for tasks undone, for words unsaid and verse not yet written. But I cannot dwell upon my unfinished work for this is the vainglorious attempt to seek immortality and a path that leads to madness – witness the grotesque tale told so far. So, I will attempt a rescue despite all my misgivings and look to heaven for guidance, and the ordained route of my next voyage. That is all I can ask, and with faith I must be content.

The sun has fallen, the hour is after ten and my appointment with Ernest Frankenstein looms near. Roiling black clouds have converged over London, pushing the smoky haze from the fires ever lower; however, the crackle of electricity flows through the air and a cleansing rain may obliterate the hellish heat and lift the city from its despair.

For my part, I will take up my pistol in my family's defense against the hundreds of Ernest's army. I pray for his defeat as I march toward death.

It should be recorded – as my last wish – that I died after a life well-lived, a life not to be pitied or mourned. I will rest in eternity's arms knowing I did the best I could and until now never harmed another human being; it is with great sorrow I express my regret that the same cannot be said for my final evening upon this beautiful earth.

With all sincerity and good wishes toward mankind,

Captain Robert Walton

LETTER TO M. WALDMAN, INGOLSTADT, FROM MARGARET SAVILLE, LONDON

London, September 21ˢᵗ, 17 –

My dearest Professor:

I know from reading Robert's journals and letters that you among all men are acutely aware of the circumstances leading up to the death of my brother, Captain Robert Walton. Therefore, I write to you, hoping your knowledge and wisdom will shed light upon the madness that overtook him and the family Frankenstein.

I have said little about the events of the 26th of June past, for the scenes remain too terrible to my mind's eye and my heart remains torn to pieces by the overwhelming tragedy of it all. I beg your forgiveness for this letter's length – for the Night Sheriff of London has asked me for a written account of the evening to bring before an inquest. Dr. Trilling, my physician, has suffered questioning by the authorities, and relayed to them the delicate nature of my condition, asking for patience whilst I preserve my strength and take to my bed until I can safely record the facts. As a tonic for my agitated mind, this letter, in fact, may take days to write, so overpowering is my grief. To say the events of that evening and the resulting consequences were horrific is but the opening line of the play; you, above all, should understand my pain and concern due to your involvement with the dramatis personae. More often than not, I sit with tears in my eyes and watch the day fade into night with little to cheer me but memories, which bring in their wake unbearable pain as well as bitter joys.

You may know little of my involvement with my brother, but suffice it to say we held each other in the highest regard. I was his elder sister, his teacher of the arts (including his propensity for letters and journals), of the sciences, and the mentor who guided him through his early days. His life was cut too short, by his friendship with Victor Frankenstein and the evil perpetrated by Ernest, for my brother loved exploration and adventure and could have achieved many honors had he been able to live out his life to its full capacity.

This letter cannot describe how much I miss my dear Robert, and how I regret the words I spoke to him the night he died. For it was I who shunned him during the terrible battle and precipitated his demise – the brother I loved beyond words. My exhortations drove him to his actions and I will forever hold myself responsible; the light died in his eyes when I shouted in a rage accompanied by flowing tears, "*You are the one to blame for all this death – you have destroyed my family and failed me beyond measure with your broken promise! You vowed to protect my husband. It is you whom God should have taken!*"

But as I describe this tale, I must first lead you to the climax of that horrible night.

When Robert allowed me to read Ernest Frankenstein's letter threatening our family, my course was clear – I would quit London, with the children, for Robert's home in The Wolds, leaving my husband, John, in his care. To this end, I made my brother swear his allegiance and duty for I could not bear our separation without such considerations. Under such conditions, I willingly left our home on Warwick Street for the journey to Yorkshire, unaware of my brother's plan to sail to the Orkney Islands the following day.

My journey was pleasant and without incident, although the trip magnified my fears about the safety of my family. I, somewhat like a nervous cat, prowled Robert's inviting country home, watching every movement out the window, alert to every shadow, every brush of the limb against the house. The weather was mild, but the sunny and warm days did nothing to alter my gloomy disposition. Lila and David, on the other hand, reveled in the countryside enjoying the fresh air and the attentions of butterflies, squirrels and other woodland creatures that happened by our picturesque retreat.

About a week after our arrival, I was awakened during the night by a sound in the lane in front of the house. The noise was unpleasant, like a scratching and scraping of hooves on a road normally traversed by a neighbor's horse, or, less frequently, a wagon or carriage. But never at the stroke of midnight would such a sound be heard. I shot upright in bed and fumbled for the candle, but then thought better of lighting the wick and returned it to the bedside table.

I crept from my room and looked in upon my children. David and Lila slept, like angels embraced by God, on the parlor sofa. Unbeknownst to me, this was my final night of contentment as I took in their peaceful countenances, for I have been forever damned by the tragedy inflicted upon my family. Oh, that I could travel back in time and wipe these horrid events from our past!

Assured of my children's safety, I moved toward the door – the sky was starry but without light from the moon, so the house was consumed by the darkest shadows. However, as I made my way to the entry, the hair on my nape rose; some strange vibration in the air, a shudder that passed over the roof alerted me to a presence standing on the stone path that led from the lane. I felt this entity as surely as I was alive. In the dark, I could barely discern the latch; I started when my eyes detected a quiver in the bolt followed by a rattle. Could my vision and hearing have deceived me in the blackness? Of this I was uncertain, but my senses tingled in apprehension from the horrors I imagined outside.

Robert's cottage was his haven – so little of his time was spent in Yorkshire whilst his adventures consumed him – his small home was comfortable but crammed with many artifacts and antiquities from his travels. He had many books piled in the corners and on shelves, and most of these volumes came from our Uncle Thomas who fired the young Robert with his exploratory energy. You may ask why I bring such arcane details to light, but the strangest, most horrific scene occurred as I approached the door. An unearthly glow, a yellowish phantasmagorical aura, spread across the books, illuminating their spines one-by-one, as if the light itself sought out a hidden prize. The sight chilled me to the bone as I watched it creep across the room, its form at first vague and indistinct, but then building to a consuming force that filled the parlor. I prayed my children would be spared from this specter and I ran to comfort them in their slumbers. Only little Lila turned and smiled sweetly in her sleep, and for an instant I was once again soothed by my children's contentment.

How short lived was my happiness; horror mounted upon horror!

For there, in the ghostly light, I saw a vision my eyes could scarcely believe possible – terror fell upon me. Looking at me through the windows were scores of glowing eyes. They were orbs of deepest black suffused with hate and infused with the devil's own fire. Their gaze burned through me and turned my blood to ice. Words are but a poor substitute for the fear that shook me. Death, multiplied, was waiting to enter my brother's home and I felt, beyond doubt, the fiends outside had come for *us*.

I screamed and my dear children awoke trembling and in tears at their mother's voice. At once the door burst open and the creatures, forty or more, flooded the room with their hideous presence. The devils rushed to surround us and with their glowering faces and ghastly smiles, tore us from each other and dragged us from the room. My dear David struggled valiantly against the horde as did Lila who kicked and screamed as the monsters carried her away. I fought as well, but too many of the creatures had me locked in their infernal embrace and I could not escape. Our captors delighted in their evil duties as they spirited us away to a waiting carriage. The creatures, their maniacal laughter filling the night and overpowering the sweet nocturnal breeze, secured me first in the carriage. I was caught between two of them as others stood guard outside. But, my David! My small hero, who had been shoved into the carriage, kicked at the terror who held my daughter. The blow knocked the assailant aside for an instant, long enough for Lila to break free and run from the bewildered creature. How the hate filled his terrible eyes – but I felt by some strange power of communication, he was not there to kill; his purpose was to capture and to bring his bounty to London. Our destination was made clear to me during our journey. I was cheered by my daughter's escape, but despondent upon our separation; I hoped that she would find sufficient shelter in the neighboring woods. It would be many days before I would learn of her fate.

That night brings terrible visions to mind and my hand grows weak from writing. There is much more to tell you and I beg your patience whilst I rest, compose myself and return to this missive another day.

September 23rd, 17 –

I have sufficient energy to resume my story and pray for your forgiveness for my interruption. It is my sincere hope, Professor Waldman, you will act as an advocate in these forthcoming legal proceedings for I am certain you will respond in good faith when the truth must be told.

With my Lila gone and David and I locked in the carriage, our journey from Yorkshire began. We traveled at night, I assumed, to quell the suspicions of those passing in the road, and slept during the day under the shade and protection of a forest grove, under constant guard by the creatures. They were our sole source of sustenance and provider of wants, even those of common decency. Once in their possession, David and I became like a child's toy to them; their fascination was evident from the first day and they continued to stare at us with their dark eyes. How handsome yet how beastly they are, even the most beauteous of the women! As different as they are as individuals, they seem born of the same lineage, to share the same thoughts and ideas. Our second night in the carriage, though we were still treated like prisoners, their attitudes changed distinctly. We became an annoyance, comparable to a swarming insect intent upon human flesh on a warm summer night, and they paid us little attention the rest of the journey.

After three nights travel, we arrived in London. The carriage shades were pulled so I could not see out, but the muddy smell of the Thames, the clatter of carriages and the screech of the fishmonger signaled our morning arrival in my beloved city. My

175

hopes for any escape from the creatures were quashed when we reached our destination.

First, we were escorted from the carriage into a large stone building near Wapping Docks. Being a lady of some means, I had spent little time in the area, other than to see my brother off on his many explorations. The general vicinity is course and rough and not frequented by women of a decent sort. Knowing the dangers of the area, I shuddered at our fate.

Robert had told me of the evils and horrors of the Frankensteins, but nothing prepared me for what I was about to witness. I wished I could have covered my son's eyes to protect his innocence, but he was held apart from me as we were ushered into the dismal surroundings. The pungent smell of acid burned our lungs and we coughed until one of the creatures allowed us to place a handkerchief over our mouths. The air was acrid and thick with haze and we were forced up the steps into a large room equally as dreary. My brave boy kicked at one of our guards in an attempted escape, but the creature slapped him and my son recoiled in anger and shame for his failure. I cautioned David to do as he was told and that all would be well. We were guided through the mist and, to my astonishment, observed numerous glass vessels harboring life in all stages from fetus to child; all the children were beautiful, but suffused with a malevolence so palpable it crackled over my body as I walked.

Out of the mists arose a sight so fantastic, I can never erase the memory from my mind. A man connected to an array of tubes stood near the back of the room behind a large desk. A silver ovoid pulsed red and yellow against the wall and seemed to feed him and the lines that coursed from his body. He looked at me and smiled – his face seemed markedly older than his years, judging from the overall strength and vitality of his frame.

"Welcome," he said, "it gives me the greatest delight to see you."

"You must be Ernest Frankenstein," I replied with disdain. He eyed me with suspicion as I anticipated his introduction and delivered my answer. "I read your letter which threatened my good brother and, by implication, my family."

He moved toward me until his wizened face was so close to mine I could smell the stink of his evil breath. "You are perceptive, Margaret. More so than your insolent and foolish brother." He circled me and the tubes that connected him to the ovoid rattled overhead. "You have him to fault for this unfortunate predicament. If he had but delivered the prize I seek – a mere volume – this incident could have been avoided."

"Incident?" cried I. "The abduction of my children is not an incident. You will be hanged from The Tower if I have my way."

"Hush!" he said and wrenched my arm with such force that I screamed in pain. "You have no idea of what tortures my family has endured in the name of science, or the trials I have suffered for the betterment of our race. Do you think this display, this bastion of creation, is for my edification only?"

I stood without speaking, fearing another attack upon me or my son.

"Imagine a world without war," he continued, and the brazen gleam in his eye transferred into the gaze of the myriad of creatures surrounding us. "Imagine a world without tyrants, a world at peace. What man has dreamed of since creation, I can now achieve with the science my brother conceived – but only one has vexed my plan and he is the holder of the Cornelius Agrippa. One man cannot destroy such a dream. Can you understand that?"

"Lunacy," I said, astonished at the mad irony of his words.

Ernest retaliated with a smile. "No. We are on the verge, and my work shall be fulfilled. I will exceed my brother's achievements. The time has come to rid the world of tyranny."

"Robert will never relent," I said with defiance. I knew somewhat of the magic of the book from the tales of his voyage to the northern lands, but I was unaware of its full powers – they remain a mystery to me.

Ernest laughed and waved me away with his hand. "Oh, he will relent. Indeed, he will relent. That is why you are here – to ensure the delivery of the book."

"I will not offer myself and my children as a sacrifice to your madness," I said.

"But you will – for you see, I have your husband as well."

My breath rushed from my lungs and I would have collapsed to the floor if not for the creatures who stood by me. "You are a devil, a monster much worse than the one created by your brother," I managed to say after a few moments. "That misshapen wretch was shunned by man, and, when he sought a mate, he was betrayed by your brother. Victor Frankenstein brought his death and family misfortunes upon himself. It was he who wanted to play God – the only fault of Captain Robert Walton was his capacity for kindness, his need for friendship and brotherly love. The Frankensteins have never understood the importance of the family. You have twisted and perverted science to suit your own greed and the world will suffer under your rule."

Ernest bowed his head and closed his eyes; his subjects surrounded David and me and pulled us toward the stairs.

"They will provide for you until the appointed time. You cannot escape, and make no attempt to end your own life – you will fail."

With those words, he turned and disappeared in the haze. That was the last I saw of Ernest Frankenstein until David and I were brought before him the fateful night of June 26th. Our days and nights were counted slowly until then. It seemed months we were prisoners; the time could have been weeks or days. We never saw the passage of the hours, until that stormy night when we were released from our shackles.

Before I write of that final evening, I must regain my composure, for the scene at Wapping Docks chills my blood and stills my pen. For this, I beg your consideration and forgiveness. I will live to write another day because truth and history demand it.

September 25th, 17 –

I believe I can now relate the end of my tale and not succumb to the horrors surrounding it. If I must put down the pen, I will ask your pardon and later continue on as best I can.

The hour of destiny, the time I had feared had come to pass. David and I were taken to a home somewhere in London, we knew not where, for the carriage shades were drawn and we remained under intense scrutiny. We were not mistreated, but languished like all flowers must when plucked from their nurturing soil and arranged in the vase for display. David and I played games when we could and passed the time making up stories. But, every movement, every action, all intentions were observed by the creatures; every freedom was banished upon our imprisonment. My desire to see my husband and daughter, along with the need to protect my son, kept me alive during our dreary days in captivity.

The evening of the 26th, I knew something was afoot in the house. The warriors of Ernest's army, as my brother so aptly portrayed them, wandered the halls in increased agitation. Upon my witness, they slept but little, mostly on their feet; their energy seemed to ebb and flow like the tides. This I attributed to the source of their creation and his vitality during the day and night. As darkness fell, their obsidian eyes danced with a fierce intensity I had not witnessed since the time we were taken in Yorkshire. They became bearers of evil; I was acutely aware of their capacity for mayhem and murder. The frenzy within them built to such a pitch that their actions appeared accelerated: our supper was prepared and cleared in short order, the house was cleaned and packed, so no trace of our stay would be found. The effect was fantastical – a legion of automatons, like worker bees, attending to us and their hive.

Around ten o'clock, David and I were spirited away to an awaiting carriage. Rain had begun to fall and the wet buildings reflected the wavering lamplight that fell upon the deserted landscape. I knew not where we had been kept; the stormy gloom prevented any recognition. Lightning flashed in the distance and thunder growled in the air; however, not a living soul stirred as we were whisked into our conveyance. The ride was silent and forbidding for the creatures never spoke; this was as deathly and spectral a trip as I ever hope to take, and, of course, filled with panic. No other being should suffer such an experience, a prelude to death. Upon passing certain streets, we witnessed the flickering cast of orange flames through the shades and the smell of burning wood flowed into our coach.

The muddy wash of the Thames signaled our arrival at our destination – the embryo factory constructed by Ernest Frankenstein. Our guards ushered us through the carriage door nearest the building's entry and up the stairs. There, what a scene confronted us! My son's eyes were wide with wonder, for the full horror of the circumstance was not clear in his young mind – he saw the automatons that lined the walls and nearly filled the room to its center as gigantic toy soldiers, playthings at the service of Ernest. Indeed they were, but much more lethal. The creatures were a dozen deep around the room, all their eyes directed at the man who dominated their thoughts and to whom they displayed blind obedience. The acrid haze from our first meeting with the madman was no longer in evidence. The glass containers had been lifted toward the beams and hung, bubbling, attached to their supporting tubes and lines. But another astonishing change had occurred. In the room's center rested a huge wooden platform, over which hung eight dangling rods of glittering silver; these instruments were connected to an arch of similar glowing tentacles which flowed to the ovoid at the back of the room. Indentations were carved into the platform – room for two bodies. Serving as master over this terrible enterprise was Ernest Frankenstein.

He welcomed us, his prisoners, with a smile. A brutal air of confidence crossed his face as he said, "Our final meeting. Tonight I will realize my dream." He, attired in a black tunic decorated with regalia, stood behind his desk and his firm voice filled the room. His servants gazed upon him with humility, as worshipers before their god.

"You will not succeed," I said and then drew David close to my side. "I will not allow it."

He neither laughed nor scowled, but addressed me as the master lectures the novice. "Your brother will deliver the Agrippa to me and you will be released. For when I have the book, your fate will no longer matter, my children will be awarded their souls."

"Where is my husband?" I asked directly, without bowing to his brutality. "You promised to bring him here."

"He is below, safe, and will be released when my terms are met."

"I pity you – for what you had and what you gave away. A deep madness curses your family."

"I have no time for pity," he replied and then waved his hand. As he did so, several of his creatures surrounded us and forced us to the table. There, we stood awaiting our fate. A short time later, a brilliant flash lit the room, followed by a massive clap of thunder. In that instant, while the thunder died, the creatures stopped their movement as if frozen by the electric charge. I noted this with interest despite our precarious circumstances, for I felt perhaps we could use this momentary behavior to our advantage.

At length the storm grew in intensity and sheets of rain lashed against the glass. Ernest gazed at the containers with each thunderous roar and paced nervously behind his desk; his movements were constricted, however, by the tubes attached to his body. After much agitation, in seeming ecstasy over our plight whilst he gazed upon us with his hideous smile, Ernest settled in his chair and awaited the arrival of my brother.

Shortly thereafter, I heard the door below open and close.

How my heart swelled when Robert's steps resounded through the hall: a firmer countenance, full of defiance and grace upon certain death, I shall never witness. He clutched a slim volume, holding it before him for all to see. I was about to call his name, to seek the book's destruction, implore him to tear it up with his hands or heave it through the glass into the stormy night, when my resolve crumbled around me. I looked down upon the young head of my son who had experienced so little of life's joys and pleasures. How could I condemn him to death – so he should never grow to manhood, or enjoy the delights of fatherhood and leave his mark upon the world? For all my professed bravery, I could not allow my son and husband to die. I burst into tears and Robert, upon witnessing my behavior, held out the book and announced to Ernest, "Here is your precious volume. Take it! But first release my family."

Ernest rose like a king from his throne and without speaking gazed at my brother. A number of the creatures circled Robert and reached for the book; one of the males, a dominating beautiful man of the darkest eyes and black hair, took the Agrippa from my brother and held it in his hands. Ernest nodded and the creature opened the volume and began to leaf through its pages.

After a few minutes, Ernest spoke: "You are a wise man, Walton – you have come to your senses. The pages are unaltered; the Agrippa is in its original state. But there is one sure way to test its efficacy."

"Your promise," Robert said. "Release them now."

"I keep my word!" Ernest pointed his grotesque fingers at my brother and hellish fires blazed in his eyes. "One final test and all will be finished." As he spoke, the wind howled against the panes and it appeared all of London was illuminated by the storm's wrath.

Here my tale takes a fantastic and final twist, my dear Professor. I struggle to make sense of these scenes that race through my mind with their debilitating consequences – an assault upon my constitution – but perhaps with the telling the melancholy that swamps me will dissipate and I can return to life as it was before my family's destruction. Bear witness to these events and make of them what you will for they are the truth, and when the day comes to recount this tale you will vouch for my veracity.

The devil who held us hostage smiled, but said not a word as he released himself from the grip of his confining tentacles. He shuffled across the floor as his creatures kept their adoring eyes upon his form. He reminded me of a terrible gorgon, come from the ancient Greek myths, to wreak havoc upon mankind; he showed little struggle with the weight of his task, familiar as he was with his new incarnation, whilst the strength of his will, determination and power wouldst vanquish all obstacles.

I watched my brother as Ernest continued his strange and terrible walk toward the table. Robert's hand twitched nervously and within seconds I ascertained his planned retribution upon his enemy – my brother who had never harmed a living soul was about to take a life, of this I was certain. But any movement by Robert would seal his doom – he would be killed by the horde surrounding us, and, of course, our own lives would be ended as well. What pain, what conflict, must have filled his tortured mind!

But then a greater and more horrifying thought struck me, for it was our captor who now controlled our destinies. The male whom Ernest had called upon to read the Agrippa still stood guard at the platform; he withdrew a dagger from its sheath as his master approached. As my son stood by my side, a terrible premonition filled my head. Ernest was walking to his death in his quest for eternal life! Yes, dear Professor, the madman was to be slain and then resurrected in accordance with his diabolical plan.

Was my brother foolish enough to believe he could halt this horror?

Indeed, such was Robert's decision, for I caught the glint of silver as he withdrew the pistol from beneath his tunic.

He took aim and fired. The report echoed across the room and the smell of gunpowder filled the air.

Perhaps out of compassion, perhaps out of nervous agitation, or the judgment of fate, the ball struck Ernest above the heart rather than pierce its intended target. I know with certainty my brother did not aim at the madman's head (such was his theory for the destruction of Victor's monster) – that was his fatal mistake.

Ernest howled and clutched at his chest, the blood flowing scarlet against his dark robes. He fell to the floor in agony, yet his eyes burned with hatred until he could no longer keep them open. Certain members of his army appeared in pain as well for they clutched the exact spot on their bodies where the ball had entered their master. They swarmed around Ernest like disturbed bees and then with momentary lapses in consciousness (again mirroring Ernest) stumbled against each other, grasping, reaching, staring with their blank gaze for they had no soul, no will, no prime mover other than their creator.

As Ernest's eyes fluttered, the creatures flowed toward my brother and then receded like the tides. During one of those intervals, Robert seized the chance to rescue the Agrippa from the floundering male who stood near the platform. The book secured, my brother, brandishing the pistol, pushed through Ernest's army and ran to our side. He swept David into his arms and led us past my sentries until several bold males and females blocked our path. Fortunately, as Ernest weaved in and out of consciousness, our escape was made clear.

"Follow them," Ernest commanded. "Find the book. We must have the book!" He stared at my brother with the most foul and intense hatred I have ever witnessed; so black and threatening was his countenance that I believe a bolt from heaven struck the building as we fled down the stairs. I looked back to see the lines sparkle against the ceiling and the electricity flow, like flaming water to the platform. At that instant, the phenomenon I had observed repeated itself – the creatures' eyes sparkled fantastically and the automatons stopped their actions until the charge evaporated in the air.

I stopped at the door. "John! We must find him!"

Robert heaved open the massive entry and dragged me into the street, the rain soaking our shivering bodies. "I will go back. Take this book and run as far away from here as you can." He peered round the door and looked toward the stairs – I, too, saw the reason for his concern. A legion of creatures was descending the steps in search of us and the prized volume. Robert thrust the book into my hands and set David at my feet. My son wept to leave his arms and my brother consoled him with each new tear. "Be a good boy for your mother," he commanded, "in case I don't return. Be brave and take heart – follow your dream as I have, but be wary of those who would take you from your family. Stay close and prosper in their abiding love."

With that, the creatures appeared at the door with their dark, malevolent eyes and reached for my brother. Lightning flashed overhead and Ernest's disciples, momentarily stunned, halted their gruesome task. In this brief respite, I took my son's hand and ran across the muddy street to the shelter of a neighboring building. There, I waited and watched with increasing worry as Robert disappeared into the confines of Ernest's fortress – I doubted whether I would ever see my brother alive again and a shroud of gloom and despair fell over me.

However, out of the darkness, emerged the most fantastic sight. A hulking beast, attired in a black cloak that concealed his massive body, swept down the street. This creature radiated a purity of strength and will more than equal to those qualities displayed by Ernest and his minions. He carried a torch and, by chance, as he surveyed the surroundings, he happened to turn my way. My son drew back in horror and I likewise stood silent and shocked by the dark countenance that emerged in the flickering light. I beheld the yellow skin and black lips, and recognized immediately from Robert's description the dæmon before us. His face was hideous and grim in its determination; the twisted visage was scored with scars and wounds and ghastly in its appearance, and hid whatever generous heart he might harbor.

To my astonishment, the monster dropped the torch into the muddy street and, like a cat, clawed his way up the rough, wet stones until his massive frame was perched on the casement of a second-storey window. A terrible bolt rent the heavens, and at that moment, the creature burst through the glass and dropped with flowing cloak into the room filled with his enemies.

I know not how long the battle lasted, for time became an object with no meaning; terrible screams and great crashes split the air. Ernest's creatures filled the door and several appeared at the windows – not dead, but struggling to survive with torn limbs and shattered, bloody faces. Their agony drifted over the rain drenched and deserted street whilst with each new blast, I feared the worst for my husband and brother.

Suddenly, after one prolonged and horrible exhortation, a deathly silence filled the air and several of the creatures emerged from the building and stepped into the street, feeling their way along the stones as if they were blind. Some stumbled or collapsed as they walked.

A soft rustle issued beside me and I screamed as one of Ernest's beasts rounded the corner and fell against me. David defended us by beating against the hard flesh with his balled fists; he might as well have been pummeling rocks, so little was the effect upon the creature. But, after a few moments, the monster fell as if in sleep and settled at my feet. I looked into his cold, blank eyes and saw nothing – it was the most terrifying vision I have ever witnessed – the dark, empty stare that confirmed, in my thinking, the existence of hell.

We pushed the creature away and stood in our hiding place, awaiting any sign of our loved ones. At length, my brother emerged with a figure draped across his shoulder. I gasped and rushed in despair toward Robert for I recognized the lifeless body of my husband, John. My grief consumed me and I fell at my brother's feet, my son joining me in my outcry. I had no words for many minutes so consumed with pain was I. Robert gently placed John on the muddy street; then I saw my husband's wounds, the deep cuts that covered his body, the blood and gore that dripped from his clothing.

Robert said nothing when I screamed, "You are the one to blame for all this death – you have destroyed my family and failed me beyond measure with your broken promise! You vowed to protect my husband. It is you whom God should have taken!"

Yes, what little life was in my brother died with my curse and I saw him look toward the Thames as the rain poured upon us. My brother stepped away and I followed his movement with tear-stained eyes.

Near the bank, along the wharf, I saw a figure in white, as heavenly an angel as I have ever seen. Her form was swathed in a yellowish glow that ebbed and flowed from her body like a beacon and she carried a child. When my brother reached her, he extended his arms and drew her body close to his and whispered in her ear. She sunk to her knees and the aura faded from her form. Death swept over us as I knelt near my husband and I felt a chill arise from his torn and bleeding body. I knew the angel of death had departed from John's body and traveled to the beautiful saint who stood so forlornly on the river's edge.

I watched as the woman slowly rose to her feet and turned toward the river. In an instant with the child in her arms, she leapt into the dark waters. My brother shouted her name – Olivia – several times in agony. It would be the last time I would hear his voice.

And then, without looking my way, he too jumped into the torrent.

I ran to the river with David, but the current was dark and swiftly flowing from the rains. No bodies swirled in the waters; no cries for help rang forth – the pervading presence of death chilled me as I clung to my son. Lightning split the air far away and the heaving rumble of thunder spread over us. I held David close and then we returned to the street and prayed over my husband, that his soul be taken to heaven. I could do no more after that, except weep.

How I found my way home that early morning, I cannot say. Shock dominated my memory, but eventually I found my way through London, now washed clean of fire, ash and smoke, to Warwick Street and the kindness of neighbors. I asked an astonished man, up early for work, to organize a party and retrieve John's body, and also to look upon the Thames at the location I described. His wife informed me of Lila's safety with Mrs. Shelby, as I cried over the remains of our once beautiful home. Such were the joys at knowing both my children were safe, and such were the sorrows for my losses. My reunion with my daughter was immediate despite the hour: Lila, Mrs. Shelby and Dora – indeed all involved – dissolved into tears upon our reunion. Mrs. Shelby told me of a strange cloaked figure that had knocked upon her door and inquired of Robert's whereabouts. She had withdrawn in shock from the monstrous menacing form, but had sensed the being's preternatural powers and was certain he would find my brother despite her silence. Days later, Mrs. Shelby directed me to the public house where my brother had spent his last hours; there I paid Robert's bill and retrieved his journal and the other writings he bequeathed to my care.

That is the end of my tale, my dear Professor, for I never saw my brother again after he was swept away by the river. I have never truly known what happened when Robert returned to face Ernest or what effect Victor Frankenstein's creation had upon this tragic scene.

Oddly enough, the next morning there were reports across London, but particularly from Wapping Docks, of a foul and moldy smell emanating from discarded clothing filled with a dusty powder and stained by a blue liquid. The creatures, so diligently created by Ernest, decayed in some manner – after what I presume was his death; for with the cessation of the madman's life their sustenance evaporated. They were, after all, aside from their strength and master's brutality, as ethereal as vapor. They had no soul and no sustaining life apart from his design. The authorities, knowing my husband had died in the vicinity, sought me out for my testimony in the matter. That is why I have called upon you. You know the truth, and, I pray, can find the courage and conviction to defend my story.

My agony will not end with an inquest: I am doomed to suffer the consequences of my words, just as Robert fell victim to his dreams of adventure and fame. I do not weep for the Frankensteins, but I shed tears daily for the hateful words I spoke against my brother.

With that, I await your speedy reply and send the hope that we meet someday. There is another reason for our meeting, and that is the small book of Cornelius Agrippa that rests next to my bed. At night, I will turn to it and, after extinguishing the lamp, observe the unearthly glow that spreads across its face. I do not find it terrifying so much as astonishing, for it appears to hold the powers of the universe and is, for now, as close to God in its treasures as my mortal body could ever hope to attain. For this, I will be forever grateful to my brother Captain Robert Walton.

Yours with hope, and begging your understanding,

Mrs. Margaret Saville

LETTER FROM ROBERT WALTON, THE ORKNEY ISLANDS, TO MARGARET SAVILLE, LONDON

Hoy, February 23rd, 18 –

To Mrs. Saville, England

My dearest sister, how can I expect you to understand my silence over the years and your shock at finding me alive in a place far removed from London? I cannot request your forgiveness or understanding: I only ask that you hear my story and know that I love you and your children beyond measure.

The scenes of that terrible night so many years ago remain fresh and vivid in my mind – so much so that for what seemed an eternity I was plagued by night terrors – devils who prowled and would not let me rest wherever I lay my head. I hung by a thread over the precipice of madness, uncertain whether I would live or die, but one consuming reason assured my dominion over death. For you see, my dear Margaret, I have a son – Robert – a wonderful boy who depends on me for his sustenance and growth. He is an orphan whom I saved – the natural son of Ernest Frankenstein and Olivia Della Scalla – resurrected by the man I first called dæmon, who later became my friend. Over the years, my son has grown and prospered and is looked upon with great favor by the gentle people of this island. They know him as a handsome young man, but know nothing of his immense strength and preternatural powers bestowed by heaven above. He is fleet of foot, sturdy as the beasts of the field, his flowing blond hair and shining blue eyes add to his handsome countenance; the young women of the village admire his demeanor.

You may chastise me, perchance despise me, Margaret, for keeping my whereabouts unknown – it must be an immense shock, I presume, to find that I'm alive, for in your memory I died that terrible night. But I rescued this child, swept from his mother's arms by the awful currents, and raised him as my own. To this island I fled, to the idyllic home Victor's progeny made for his wife and adopted son, and I thought it reasonable and fitting to bring up the child among this wild and beautiful landscape and its delightful creatures. I will make my motives clear as I continue my tale.

I was ready to die the night of my battle with Ernest Frankenstein; I was prepared to give my life to save you, your children and your husband, if I could be certain that Ernest would keep his promise. Upon consideration, there was no reason for him to renege, for once he had the Agrippa in his possession his domination of the earth would have been complete. Therefore, I removed the book from its hiding place in the public house and secured it on my person. The volume was the last pawn in our deadly chess game. As you are aware, I also took my pistol, hoping to end Ernest's life before he could carry out his mad wishes.

I have, through the years, had considerable time to reflect upon the events of that summer. Today, as the snow swirls outside our window, I write at my desk, whilst my son busies himself mending a harness. In these quiet times, I am able to reason and piece together Ernest's diabolical scheme. Understand my desires and wishes, Margaret, for I have shed many tears over the death of your beloved husband and the words you spoke to me that evening. In my soul, I felt as dead as if the madman or one of his army had pierced my heart.

It is my belief that Ernest was to sacrifice himself that night in hopes of his own resurrection. The process was to be brief, with little interruption to the activity flowing through his demented brain, no more than the disruption an electric discharge caused his army. His soldier was to release the life-giving fluids and then stab him through the heart – as clearly as I can conclude – a slight reversal from the procedure developed by his own hand and Professor Waldman. Then the Agrippa would be read over his body as the fluids coursed through it. The choice of souls was up to Ernest – either good or evil – I am fairly certain of his selection.

None of these thoughts entered my head as Ernest walked to the platform; in fact, I scarcely remember my plan to kill him. It never entered my mind that his creatures might search my body and confiscate my weapon and use it upon me. I believe Ernest let down his guard only because he was so fixated on the Agrippa. My hand shook as I fired the shot – my first attempt (and last, I vow) at killing another man – and the ball struck the bloody and painful blow that led to his demise. I aimed for the heart rather than the head, for I could not force myself to end a man's life in such a cowardly way. I was uncertain from the beginning whether I should succeed – of course, I failed, grabbed the book from his slave and then directed our escape.

When I left you and returned to the structure, I searched for your husband, but in the confusion, John was nowhere to be found. The creatures kept about me, constantly searching for the book which I had placed in your care. I ascended the stairs to find Ernest on the platform, his wound staunched with a bloody cloth, the tubes and life-sustaining elixirs hooked to his body. He hissed, pointed to me and I was surrounded by his followers.

"Leave me alone, or you will never recover the book," said I, and the creatures retreated. Ernest drifted in and out of consciousness and with each flutter of his eyes, his army lost its bearings.

Finding some strength, Ernest glared at me and said, "My blood flows freely and I am dying." The soldier with the dagger moved toward him and placed it over his heart. "Plunge it swiftly and then release the life force," he commanded. "I would rather be immortal without a soul than die in such agony."

I started toward the madman, but halted when a thunderous and terrible shock resounded behind me. I turned, petrified of my fate, to find my friend, the monster named Frankenstein, had crashed through a window and stood but an arm's length away. Bits of glass clung to his dark cloak and the fires of revenge burned in his eyes.

Ernest was stunned by the apparition standing before him, but waved the dagger away from his body and shouted, "Kill the fiend!"

Ernest's followers fell upon Victor's creation with horrendous force, clutching and stabbing at the gigantic being with all their might. I heard the horrific rip of his garments followed by the rending of flesh and bone; I fought against them, but they pushed me away with their great strength as my friend was swamped in a sea of the marauders. Ernest lay strapped to the platform whilst he barked out his foul commands in his death throes. The massive hand of the creature burst forth from the assault and clutched at Ernest.

I was certain my friend would die in the attack, when with gargantuan effort, he burst forth from the pile and struck the hapless Ernest. It was his supreme final effort, for as he struggled with his adversary, I witnessed the piteous sight of his torn and bloody legs; the wounds were too much for even his miraculous restorative powers. With his last reserves of strength, he reached for the glittering tools that hung suspended from the ceiling. His bloody hand clutched the silver rod, positioned above Ernest's head, whilst the creatures continued to rip at his tortured body. "Die, Frankenstein," he said. "I avenge the deaths of my son and wife at Belrive." He then plunged the instrument through the madman's forehead into his brain. Ernest screamed, shook and then collapsed with a great exhalation as the dark hand of Death claimed his victim. A strange silence fell over the room and the creatures relented in their attack. By degrees, they drifted away, as if they were rudderless ships, their black eyes empty and devoid of life. Several crumpled near me and others groped blindly against the walls.

Ernest lay lifeless, eyes open in shock, his head pinioned to the wood by the bloody spear. As his army drifted away, I bent over the creature known as Frankenstein. His limbs had been torn asunder; he bled from his throat and mouth. His final moments upon the earth had arrived and I was powerless to save him. His sentence was pronounced: I could only grieve.

"I am dying, my friend," he said, his breath gurgling in his throat. "Take care of my wife and child. At least, my spirit will sleep in peace with my father."

My friend struggled against death's eternal powers, and tears flooded my eyes as quickly as the night's rain. I held his hand and tried to staunch the flow of blood from his neck. "I believed you died on Hoy," I said, sobbing over his form. "Ernest told me of your death . . . ."

"I jumped from the cliff near my home, and they did not follow . . . ."

"Please live . . . Frankenstein," I pleaded.

"The wounds are too great for my rejuvenation; but I take solace that I have a soul," he said with intense courage and struggle. "At least my father gave me that." He grimaced in pain and then said, "I had to end Ernest's life or he would have ended mine – Ernest proved his capacity for revenge on my island. I knew I must find you– I followed his army . . . and your scent." A smile creased his dark lips and after those words, he sputtered and I believed he had breathed his last; but, after a moment, he drew a final breath and said, "My journey is over. Farewell, my friend, and fear not the bitter sting. I shall keep watch over you." With that he closed his eyes and died as I caressed his face. The irradiation of his spirit fled from his body and I wept without shame.

Through my torment, I wandered through Ernest's laboratory, smashing what containers I could whilst his despicable minions fell to the floor, limbs broken or bleeding from the battle, their eyes devoid of sight. I kicked at their foul bodies; I confess, I was happy to see them dead. Several of them wandered near me and collapsed before my eyes, and a foul, rancid smell wafted from them in their death throes.

At length, my rage brought me to the first floor where a similar sight awaited me. My anger was tempered, however, by the torn and bloody figure that lay crumpled in the corner. There, I found your husband, John. Fighting the revulsion and shame that filled my throat, I lifted his limp form over my shoulder and carried him into the night. I knew not whether you had remained – I hoped you had fled with David for your safety – instead I found you rushing toward me. My senses were numbed beyond all reason and I could not feel my feet as I walked. Then came your words – as final as the last spade of earth tossed upon the grave. Yet, dear sister, you were correct in your curse: I hold no

193

grudge, for it was I who deserted the family to slake my thirst for exploration and adventure. It was I who followed blind ambition to act as God with Ernest and Maximilian. My shame, my failure to preserve our family, drove me to this tortured landscape as much as my desire to raise the child I had rescued. I was the unfortunate being that set the terrible forces in motion.

Little remains of my recollection from that time on – flashes, those small scenes reserved for those who have discarded tormented memories. I recall placing John's body in the street and then awakening far down the muddy bank of the Thames clutching the child I now call my son. I crawled out of the wash and found my footing despite the dismal rain. We found shelter that night in the doorway of an abandoned building; I clutched his small body to mine and prayed that we would not be taken by death. I wandered with him for several days through the East End, begging for food and clothing, yet his constitution did not waiver. When I would look into his eyes, they would sparkle with a strength and life I had never witnessed from any human being, and thus I knew the power of the soul that rested within. Here was a child imbued with the greatest evil and then with an even greater good extracted from the heavens – I prayed he might embody all the physical characteristics of his father, yet remain free from the madness that destroyed his soul. His beautiful mother lives on in him, as well – a woman so sweet, so like the angels, too fragile to accept the news of her beloved husband's death. So, I made it my life's work and penitence to make this child a home where he could develop his amazing powers for good – perhaps the start of a new race for mankind – one so strong and great that he might eschew evil and madness in all its forms and thus restore our faith in the beneficence of science.

After several months of nomadic existence, I engaged myself to a trading vessel bound for the northern lands. I smuggled the child on board in a bag; the deception was soon discovered; however, the crew was good enough to love the boy as I did and shortly thereafter he found the attention of as many loving fathers as he could have wished. Thus, I found my way to Hoy.

We arrived upon the island on a wild and windy day in the fall of that year when the waves broke heavily upon the shore and the hills rested their peaks in the sheltering clouds. The villagers knew the child upon sight and welcomed him with open arms. I told them of the unfortunate deaths of the man and woman they had come to know through good works and kindnesses; and, the inhabitants, in gratitude for the past, vowed to bestow what future fortunes they could upon the child. They likewise told me of the ship carrying strange beings who sought the creature out the day of my visit upon the privateer; he had escaped death by securing his wife and the boy in a place of safety and then carried out his deception at the cliff.

I walked through the heath, leading the child, where I found the stone structure still resting upon the valley crest. The kind people had attended the land whilst the owners were absent – the grateful cats and dogs crowded around me and I opened the door to a scene of domestic bliss like the one I witnessed on my previous visit to the island. The creature who called himself Frankenstein had promised to look over me and I felt his warm presence upon entering. Here, I have remained as Robert grows into young manhood and here I have vowed to live out my days.

I have told my son of how he came to be and of his mother and father, being frugal with the details. The scar upon his chest from his mortal wound appears now to be a mere scratch. In effect, he has had three providers: Ernest, his natural father; the creature who adopted him; and me. I thank God that I have been taught true humility as a result of my friendship with Victor Frankenstein, and I want the same for my son. I want him to think of his natural mother and father with love and blot out the curse of revenge. It was Victor's failures with his unfortunate science – and my thirst for revenge upon his death – that led me to the tragic promise I could not fulfill and, thus, turned your life to shambles. You lost your husband, your home, and through my own neglect, your brother.

I pray you will forgive me, dear Margaret, for my trials and journeys have cast misfortune upon you. You were the victim and I was the perpetrator.

I know not if we will ever meet again; I plan no journeys to London. If you, in your heart, wish to visit my sanctuary, know that you are welcome on our island home. Robert, my son, will love you as I do, of that I am certain.

I must end my letter, for the light grows faint and it is time to shelter the animals against the brutal winter winds. As I write, I recall Victor's words as he talked with me aboard my vessel those years ago, those I was fortunate enough to transcribe into my journal. He spoke of the relationship with his father, and the irresistible hold his work had secured upon his imagination: *I then thought that my father would be unjust if he ascribed my neglect to vice, or faultiness on my part: but I am now convinced that he was justified in conceiving that I should not be altogether free from blame. A human being in perfection ought always to preserve a calm and peaceful mind, and never allow a passion or a transitory desire to disturb his tranquility. I do not think that the pursuit of knowledge is an exception to this rule.*

If the study to which you apply yourself has a tendency to weaken your affections, and to destroy your taste for those simple pleasures in which no alloy can possibly mix, then that study is certainly unlawful, that is to say, not befitting the human mind. If this rule were always observed; if no man allowed any pursuit whatsoever to interfere with the tranquility of his domestic affections, Greece had not been enslaved; Cæsar would have spared his country; America would have been discovered more gradually; and the empires of Mexico and Peru had not been destroyed.

And, with those words, I leave you, dear Margaret, for they resonate in my ears. I will neither enslave my son to science nor destroy the small empire I have built here. I pray that your life and the lives of your children have been of late as tranquil as mine, despite the tragedies of my vengeance and quest for knowledge. Heaven shower its blessings upon you.

With fondest affection, your loving brother

R. Walton

AUTHOR'S AFTERWORD

Robert Walton's letter to his sister was the last document recovered from the antiquities dealer. A few other pieces were in the trunk: ephemera, newspaper clippings and other notes of no consequence to the tale told by the sea captain. The truth of the story cannot be confirmed, for no public record exists of a Mrs. Margaret Saville in that time. One fact the author can confirm, however, were discolorations upon the final letter – the ink smeared and the paper crinkled in spots as if stained by tears.

SOME THOUGHTS UPON THE NOVEL

I knew very little of *Frankenstein*, the book by Mary Shelley, until later in life. I picked up a copy at my local Barnes & Noble for eight dollars and proceeded to read it over several days. The book had always been on my list of required "classics;" however, Frankenstein, the monster, was at the bottom of my list of the unholy triumvirate: Dracula, The Wolfman and the unnamed dæmon. Dracula was always first on my list. He was intensely more interesting because of his sophisticated, yet horrifying, persona and creepy sexual subtext. The book by Bram Stoker can rightly be deemed a classic as well. I also enjoyed the terror inspired by the dual personality of the werewolf and, in the iconic 1941 movie, Lon Chaney Jr.'s ravishing change on screen from ordinary Larry Talbot to murderous beast. Frankenstein's monster, however, held no such interest for me. For the most part, I viewed him as a putz with little to recommend him in the horror category except his malleable, frightening face and super-human strength. Thus, I was never in a rush to read Shelley's seminal work of fiction, which was first published anonymously in 1818 to great success. I had escaped my high school and college careers without having to read this often required work.

What revelations blossomed when I read the book. Who knew the monster could speak so eloquently (and by extension, write?) – his talents overwhelmed this humble author. Like many, my acquaintance with Victor Frankenstein's creation came from the 1931 classic movie and the various adaptations following, including Mel Brook's raucous 1974 comedy *Young Frankenstein*. James Whale's movie, although establishing sympathy for the monster, played by Boris Karloff, often portrayed the creature as a bumbling, incoherent ogre of death. Despite the prevalent one-note tone, many scenes are memorable, including the creature's encounter with the blind man in the peasant hut and the child who falls to the monster's ill-fated attempt at compassion. Wonderful filmmaking, but somehow far removed from Shelley's novel. The closest movie adaptation to the novel is *Mary Shelley's Frankenstein*, starring Kenneth Branagh and Robert DeNiro, an adaptation from 1994. Even this film takes liberties with the original story, but DeNiro's monster is articulate and sympathetic, and Branagh exudes much of Victor's controlled madness.

As with many of my ideas for novels, this one took me by surprise. I rarely set out to write about a certain topic – rather they choose me. I had no idea when I picked up *Frankenstein* that I would write what I termed a "sequel." What author would be inspired to do so? Apparently, more than one. *Frankenstein's Monster*, a novel by Susan Heyboer O'Keefe, was published in October 2010 a few weeks before I finished the revisions on my own work. Perhaps, as in my case, the original screamed at Ms. O'Keefe to finish the story completed nearly 200 years ago by Shelley. Oddly enough, Karen Karbiener, in her introduction to the volume produced by B&N, defined just that point. She wrote, *There is something unsettling about the way the story ends – a lack of closure that points to a sequel that was never written (at least by Mary herself). We are left wondering . . . .* And Ms. Karbiener concluded, *It's difficult to imagine that a creature as sociable as the monster would leave society forever, or that a being who values its existence so highly would exterminate itself.*

During my reading, the thoughts articulated by Ms. Karbiener never crossed my mind. It was only upon finishing the novel, before I read the introduction, that it struck me a sequel might be possible. This is not odd behavior for me – I usually read the foreword or introduction after I finish a book, in order to enrich my understanding of the themes and characters – the scholarly viewpoint so to speak. Why read about plot points and characters before you even start the book? At least, that's my feeling. I want to be the explorer, to discover the excitement of the work, or lack thereof – not be swayed by a scholar's introduction.

Ms. Karbiener's notes confirmed what I was thinking as Victor's creature escaped across the ice at the close of *Frankenstein*.

As a note on the writing: I have tried as much as possible to retain the 19th Century voice while plotting from a 21st Century frame of mind. Let's face it, parts of *Frankenstein* are tedious to today's readers – not that I condone a less than thorough reading of Shelley's work, but contemporary writers must work with the tastes of today's readers. I made no attempt to copy Mary Shelley's style, nor could I duplicate her voice, try as I might. I have done the best I could with the tale of Captain Robert Walton, the most contemporary, I believe, of the three voices in *Frankenstein*. I attempted to write my book in the spirit of the original in terms of length and tone. Whether I succeeded in that task is entirely up to the reader.

Some original text from *Frankenstein* has been appropriated for my novel. I have quoted the material or made it clear that the particular passage came from Shelley's work. At other points, I have used bit and pieces of phrases to retain the sense of character and voice. This technique I used sparingly and only when called for.

I expect novels like Ms. O'Keefe's and mine might generate some literary discussion – at least I hope they do. There will be those who say, such a work is unnecessary, much as the ill-fated scene-for-scene remake of *Psycho*. Art can be labeled sacrosanct – joining the pantheon of the untouchable and undisturbed. *Frankenstein* may be such art. Others may say, my book is not ingenious enough – or that it is too contemporary. Indeed, it is a book of its time, but I have tried to meld the myths and themes of the original work with my own vision. It is an *entertainment* – just as the original idea for Shelley's novel grew out of the ghostly tales told during a dreary summer on the shores of Lake Geneva.

I would like to thank my beta readers: Scott Colella, Robert Pinsky, Veronika Levine and Michael Grenier. In great appreciation, I thank Karen Kendall, Heather Graham, Kathleen Pickering, Traci E. Hall and Melissa Alvarez, all members of the wonderful and vivacious Florida Romance Writers, for their valuable insights and editorial support. Without this company of readers and writers this book would not have been published. I would also like to thank the authors and poets of The Writers'

Rcom of Boston, where I cut my writing teeth more years ago than I care to remember.

This book is dedicated to James E. Gunn, my extraordinary fiction professor at the University of Kansas, who stoked the fire so long ago.

Author photo by Suzanne Lunsford

Michael Meeske writes across genres, including romance, mystery, suspense, horror and gothic fiction, a genre that blends horror and romance, and has its roots in some of the earliest novels ever written. *Frankenstein's Dæmon* is his first novel offered through Usher Books.

From 2008 to 2010, he served as Vice President of Florida Romance Writers (FRW). He has been a member of FRW and the Romance Writers of America since 2002. He also was an active member of the Writers' Room of Boston, a non-profit working space for novelists, poets and playwrights.

Michael's writing credits include the co-authorship of *His Weekend Proposal*, a tender category romance published in August 2009 by The Wild Rose Press under the pen name of Alexa Grayson; *Zombieville*, a short story included in a 2011 anthology by FRW writers, available at Amazon.com, and *Tears*, a short-story published in the Fall 2000 issue of *Space & Time*, a magazine of fantasy and science fiction. Usher Books will publish additional works by Michael in 2012.

Some of his influences are Edgar Allan Poe, H.P. Lovecraft, Shirley Jackson, Oscar Wilde, Daphne du Maurier, Richard Matheson, Sir Arthur Conan Doyle and any work by the exquisite Brontë sisters. You can contact Michael at michaelmeeske@live.com.

www.ingramcontent.com/pod-product-compliance
Lightning Source LLC
Chambersburg PA
CBHW070014260626
47159CB00005B/1803